THE CHRYSANTHEMUM CHAIN

James Melville

D0204592

FAWCETT CREST • NEW YORK

First published in Great Britain by Martin Secker & Warburg Ltd.

A Fawcett Crest Book
Published by Ballantine Books
Copyright © 1982 by James Melville

Library of Congress Catalog Card Number: 82-5546

ISBN 0-449-20822-2

This edition published by arrangement with St. Martin's Press, Inc.

Manufactured in the United States of America

First Ballantine Books Edition: April 1986

"We watch in growing fascination as the police and diplomats work, separately and together, to unravel the puzzle. The large cast of Japanese and British characters, the diplomatic and police politics, the Japanese underworld and changing way of life in Japan, the interplay of Japanese and British cultures, all are brilliantly done and often quite funny. . . .it's more than a satisfying mystery. It's also very Japanese, very British, very elegant."

Publishers Weekly

"A Japanese police procedural [written] with the fascinating observation that an intelligent, sympathetic outsider can bring to another culture . . . An excellent series in the mold of Gideon and Maigret . . . Melville weaves in the subtleties of Japanese manners and the stylized protocol of diplomatic life with delicious irony."

Washington Post Book World

"The plot is as neatly crafted as a Zen garden, and the lovingly detailed pictures of Japanese life add a lingering flavor to the mystery."

London Tribune

"Impeccably written and carefully organized, with the Japanese background drawn in with a calligrapher's pen."

(London) Times Literary Supplement

Fawcett Crest Titles
by James Melville:

THE WAGES OF ZEN

A SORT OF SAMURAI

For my sons, with love

AUTHOR'S NOTE

There is a British Consulate General in Osaka; and the headquarters of the Hyogo Prefectural Police is in Kobe. It is perhaps necessary therefore to emphasise that this book is a work of fiction and that none of the characters in it is based upon or intended to resemble in any way an actual British or Japanese official, past or present.

WEEK ONE

Saturday

THE MUGGY HEAT HUNG LIKE A PALL OVER WESTERN JApan that second Saturday in July, and there wasn't even the consolation of a bit of blue sky. Andrew Walker felt distinctly sorry for himself as he wiped his hand on his shirt before making another note. Then he reflected that it must be even worse for the candidates. The finals of the annual contest arranged in Osaka by the Federation of English-Speaking Societies of Western Japan were in full swing, with only one contestant left to speak before the lunch break. This was a Miss Fusako Yamaguchi of Nara Women's College, who now made her way to the flower-bedecked platform and took her place at the lectern under a huge white streamer which announced that this was the eighteenth contest of its kind and that it enjoyed the patronage and sponsorship of no less a publication than the *Kobe Shimbun*, which might be thought of as the *Yorkshire Post* —or at least the *Liverpool Echo*—of Japan.

Miss Yamaguchi was wearing a powder-blue suit which made her look a little like a very new bride in her going-away outfit. Her legs were rather bandy but shapely all the same, and she stood there bravely for the next seven minutes attacking the vice of complacency in tones of great conviction

3

and in English which was serviceable if not stylish. Perhaps an Honourable Mention, Walker thought to himself. Probably not a prize. He glanced round at his two fellow judges, sitting in different parts of the auditorium and both scribbling busily as Miss Yamaguchi came to her peroration, concluded her remarks and bowed in acknowledgement of the applause from the fifty or so young people who constituted the audience. This was no more than polite, except in the case of three girls who evidently constituted her claque from Nara and who courageously staged a mini-ovation. Walker had met the other judges for the first time on his arrival that morning. One was a fundamentalist missionary, a Canadian woman with a peaky white face dressed in a flowered smock with a drooping hemline, and the other an apparently amiable but bewildered young Englishman with a huge black beard whom Ken Takamura had introduced as a newly arrived freelance language teacher.

Takamura was there on duty, in his capacity as a senior staff reporter on the *Kobe Shimbun* with special responsibilities for foreign news, and was acting as master of ceremonies. He now announced the lunch break, then made his way towards Walker as the audience dispersed. ''Ken'' is a very ordinary Japanese male first name, as indeed is ''Dan'', but it has a disarming effect on Westerners. This, combined with the fact that Takamura had lived for several years in Washington as a foreign correspondent, made it seem quite natural for Walker to be on first-name terms with him. In fact, Takamura was one of his easiest and most relaxed Japanese acquaintances.

''You look like a man who could use a beer,'' he now said cheerily. Walker unfolded his long body and retrieved his jacket from the back of his chair. ''Eight down, six to go. Ken, I must have been insane to take this on. I suppose there *may* be other countries where students of English submit themselves to public humiliation for a chance of a prize of a few textbooks, a certificate to hang on the wall and a silver cup with red and white ribbons attached. But why the Press should encourage them I can't imagine. How about the other learned judges?''

4

Takamura winked. "All fixed. They're being entertained by the organising committee. I explained that you being British Vice-Consul, you had to check in during the lunch hour. I didn't say you were checking in to a restaurant with me. A man can take just so much. C'mon, Andy, let's get the hell out of here." Walker's spirits rose, and he followed Takamura with alacrity. Ten minutes later they were in the Rainbow Grill by Yodoyabashi Station drinking beer. "You weren't so dumb, Andy," observed Takamura as he refilled his glass from the bottle between them. "There are speech contests and speech contests, and I have in my pocket the paper's warm expression of thanks to you. It takes the form of a gift envelope with red and white cord around it, your name in classy calligraphy on the back and a number of nice new banknotes inside. Now that wouldn't come your way if the contest was organised by a league of housewives or a junior high school. They'd expect you to do it for fun. I hope you won't feel obliged to turn our little gift over to your Queen."

Their steaks arrived, and Takamura attacked his with relish as Walker asked the waiter for mustard. "We have exceedingly strict rules relating to the acceptance of gifts by British officials, I'll have you know. But there's a splendid bit about local circumstances and not giving offence. I'd hate to give offence to the *Kobe Shimbun*," said Walker after his own first mouthful. "Tell you what. Wasn't it Harry Truman who used to say that if you can eat it, drink it or smoke it in a day you can keep it? Well, I won't say anything to the Queen if you'll give me a ring soon to fix a date for an evening out on me." Takamura cocked a bright black eye and smiled. "You've got a deal," he said.

Although it was necessarily hurried, the rest of the meal passed very pleasantly, and the two men made their way back for the afternoon session well fortified. It was just as well: the atmosphere in the auditorium was even heavier in the dead, humid heat of the afternoon, and even the many electric fans seemed to spin listlessly, stirring up the stale air to little effect. Walker envied Takamura the brisk, cheerful vigour with which he handled the afternoon's proceedings. The last finalist was a spotty boy in an old-fashioned military-style black student uniform buttoned up to the neck who harangued the wilting audience with seven minutes' worth on atmospheric pollution, and the judges withdrew for their consultations at a little after three-thirty.

Fortunately their deliberations were brief. The Canadian missionary felt that their decisions should be based on the moral quality of the candidates' thinking, but as chairman of the judges Walker was able to shoot her down reasonably easily with the support of his bearded compatriot, who seemed to be in a mild state of shock at the end of his first experience of this nature. They eventually agreed without much fuss on the names of the three prize winners, adopted Walker's suggestion of an Honourable Mention for Miss Yamaguchi, and filed back into the hall for the closing ceremony. Walker was fairly familiar with the sort of flannel which was required for a few minutes while the appropriate names were ink-brushed on to the certificates, and was able to string together enough clichés to fill in the time.

It also fell to him to hand over the prizes. As he murmured his congratulations and the *Kobe Shimbun* photographer popped his flash gun, he found himself wondering what other fledgling diplomats were doing at that moment in odd corners of the globe. A basically indolent man, Walker was efficient in the office mainly in order to enjoy the sensation of a clear desk and nothing to do. An introvert, he often stared solemnly at himself in the bathroom mirror as he shaved, trying to imagine how his thin face and jug ears would look in twenty years' time. What and where would he be, this functional man in his middle age? Would he be a correct, protocol-conscious Head of Chancery somewhere in a well-cut suit and flashing glasses, laying papers meticulously one by one before a vague, bumbling Ambassador? Or a geographical desk man in the office in London, with much power and little authority? Or perhaps a clever, cynical alcoholic jetting from conference to conference, whispering advice to a self-important politician?

He would have denied being particularly ambitious, but had an unthinking confidence in the development of his career. He took it for granted that he would join the ranks of the élite in due course, perhaps as a Grade 2 Ambassador in his fifties. He would sometimes try the phrase "Sir Andrew Walker" out on himself for size, as it were. Would there be a Lady Walker? He always visualised himself with an elderly wife at the end of his career; never with a young one in the near future. Fond as he was of brooding, Walker cultivated an affable manner with his fellows, and a rather stately courtesy towards the women he met which endeared him to some of the older ones but tended to be counter-productive with his contemporaries. He would have been both surprised and hurt to know how many of his male colleagues disliked him for what one of the other junior attachés studying Japanese with him in Tokyo had called his modestly arrogant technique of backing into the limelight.

The last item on the proceedings was the proposal of a vote of thanks to the judges by the first prize-winner, another personable young woman who had done very well with her set piece and now passed with flying colours the supreme test of speaking extempore in English. She did, it is true, thank Walker for his "suggestive remarks" at the end, but he had heard this particular turn of phrase before and hardly noticed it until he realised that the bearded Englishman at his side had gone crimson and was blowing his nose with excessive violence.

It was all over by four-fifteen, and Walker made his good-byes and strolled along the canal side before turning into Midosuji Boulevard towards the Consulate General building where he had left his car. It really was most disagreeable weather, even though he was not as a rule much troubled by heat. His tall and stringy body seemed not to accumulate fat however much he ate and drank, and during the early part of his first summer in Japan he had much enjoyed the solid warmth which had come as a welcome contrast to the chill drizzle of March and early April. But then the sky had begun to stay grey and soupy all day; people became edgy and listless, and sought relief in the airconditioning of the department stores. June and July were wretched months, and there was even a trace of pleasure in the anxious expectation of the first typhoon. At least the day or two of murderous winds,

7

walls of rain, floods, landslides and destruction would be followed by high clear blue skies, washed and purged of the ugly hot menace of the dog days.

The office block which housed the British Consulate General was only two or three blocks along, and Walker soon arrived and unlocked his modest Cortina, rolling down both front windows to admit some air. The gift envelope which Takamura had given him before they parted was burning a hole in his pocket, and he opened it before he started the engine. Twenty-five thousand yen. Not bad. Even in Japan's overheated economy it was pretty good recompense for what had after all been an undemanding use of a free day, and it would buy Takamura and himself a decent dinner and an hour in a bar afterwards.

He eased the car into the traffic stream and headed for home, the airstream through the open front windows giving an illusion of pleasant freshness to the late afternoon. He switched on the car radio halfway through a news bulletin, and turned the knob till he found a recital of classical *koto* music. The cascade of bright points of sound was cool and untroubled, and Walker was quite regretful when he arrived at the small block of anonymous ''luxury'' flats where he lived near Ashiyagawa Station on the Hankyu line. He had just retrieved the evening paper from his mail-box in the small entry hall when Mrs Mori came toiling through the glass doors, a huge shopping bag suspended from each small hand. Her broad smooth forehead glistened damply, but she managed a dazzling smile for the tall young foreigner.

Walker had his finger hooked through the collar loop of the jacket slung over his shoulder, and he now hung it over the end of the stair rail and reached out for the bags. ''Please . . .'' he murmured, and Mrs Mori struggled feebly, protesting with voluble and elaborate courtesies before relinquishing her burden. Walker's Japanese was easy and correct, especially in the small change of social encounters, and he brushed off Mrs Mori's flustered hesitations elegantly. When she had finally conceded defeat with another brilliant smile, Walker led the way up to the Moris' front door opposite his own on the second floor, deposited the bags there

8

and turned to wait for Mrs Mori. She seemed to float up the stairs, carrying his jacket like a sacramental offering, her light cotton summer kimono falling away from her slender arms.

"You are always so kind, Waruka-san," she said, bowing slightly as she offered him the jacket. In spite of the heat there was nothing but an elusive fragrance about her, and Walker was uncomfortably aware that he was in urgent need of a shower. Mrs Mori was in her mid-thirties, certainly a good seven or eight years older than himself. She always comported herself as the most scrupulously correct bourgeoise, yet Walker was conscious whenever they encountered each other of a gentle and wholly pleasurable tension in himself. He enjoyed particularly the rare occasions, as now, when she looked him in the eyes. Though she held it for only a fraction of a second, her gaze had an almost hypnotic quality of hungry intensity, and Walker to his fury found himself beginning to blush. Hurriedly he took the proffered jacket, and found his bunch of keys in a flurry of hasty excuses as Mrs Mori bowed again before turning to her own front door.

It was not easy to shake off the awareness of Mrs Mori's powerful femininity, but by the time he had showered and changed into fresh clothes in front of the airconditioner turned on full blast in his bedroom he was in excellent spirits. Going out into his living-room and closing the bedroom door carefully behind him to keep it cool in there, he switched on the lights and looked around, suddenly determined to do something about his surroundings. Other people who lived alone seemed to be able to impress some trace of their personalities on their belongings, but his flat was as impersonal as an hotel. It wasn't that the furniture provided by the Property Services Agency of the Department of the Environment was shoddy: just that its careful utilitarian neutrality rendered it more or less invisible. Would a really good piece of modern pottery help? he wondered. Or some avant-garde calligraphy? Antiques would be hopeless in such a functional eggbox of a room.

Walker's musings were interrupted by the ringing of the telephone. He went over and picked up the receiver, which was warm and sticky to his touch in the humid air. It was with some surprise that he recognised Takamura's voice. "Hello, Ken—you certainly didn't waste any time taking up my offer," he said in response to Takamura's greeting, which sounded oddly strained. Walker grew steadily more bewildered as the conversation proceeded. "Yeah. Well, not exactly, Andy," said Takamura. "What I called to ask you—do you know David Murrow?" "Of course I do. Everybody in the Kansai knows him." "Is he a friend of yours?" "Well, yes, in a way I suppose." "Is he a very close friend?" Takamura pressed further, and at this point Walker drew the line. "Now look, Ken, what is all this? If you're implying what I think you may be implying. . ."

There was a lengthy silence at the other end of the line and Walker let it drag on, his mind racing. At last Takamura said, "Murrow has just been found murdered in the garden at his home. Stabbed. I want a statement for the paper, Andy. Sorry, but Murrow's British and you're Vice-Consul." Walker was stunned, but not yet totally bereft of the powers of thought. After a moment he said, "Ken, you know as well as I do that I can't give you a statement. Of course I'm horrified. Anybody would be. But we haven't been informed officially yet, and if any statement is to be made from our side it'll be by the Consul General or someone on behalf of the Embassy in Tokyo, not me."

Takamura was not easily put off. "Okay, off the record then, Andy. What do you make of it? Murder's not very common in Japan and hell, I don't believe more than a handful of Westerners have been murdered here in peacetime since the nineteenth century. Plenty of rough-housing among seamen in the bars on the waterfront, but that's different. My information is that Murrow was stabbed repeatedly, but there's no obvious motive. The police found more than thirty thousand yen on him, and he still had his Rolex and other stuff."

"Burglary? Anything gone from the house? Who found him?" The questions tumbled from Walker until he collected his thoughts. "Ken, I'm sorry I can't give you an official reaction. But I'd really appreciate it if you could fill me in on anything that comes your way. I'll do my best to be helpful to you later."

Takamura was philosophical. "Okay. I see your problem. I don't know much myself yet. I know the guy at prefectural police headquarters who's handling it at this stage. I'll see what I can get out of him, but it won't be tonight, that's for sure. His super wasn't too pleased when he heard the ambulance men had talked to us. He'll want to agree a line with his own boss before opening his mouth. Keep in touch."

The line went dead as Takamura rang off. Walker thought for a moment, then pressed the receiver rest and let it spring up again to give him a dialling tone. Of the five or six British diplomats assigned to the Osaka-Kobe area at any time, two or three are usually qualified interpreters; but Walker remembered that Taylor the Commercial Consul and Osterley the Information Officer were away for the weekend. Joe Endsleigh was not a Japanese speaker, and would soon be needing help.

Superintendent Tetsuo Otani was not best pleased when the telephone rang in the quiet old house at the end of the road where it petered out into the footpaths on the lower slopes of Mount Rokko. The Commander of the Hyogo Prefectural Police was in the tiny but perfect garden at the side of the house wearing nothing but a light cotton yukata and wooden geta sandals, messing about with his miniature trees. As dusk approached a welcome light breeze from the Inland Sea stirred the air, and he felt reasonably cool for the first time that day.

Most of the little trees in their fine old ceramic bowls were older than he was, and he could remember coming clattering home from high school as a boy in the late thirties to find his father pottering with the same secateurs he now held in his own hand, snipping away at infinitesimal irregularities as the big old wireless set crackled Government statements about economic development in Manchukuo and Formosa. As a full Professor at Osaka University in those days, Otani senior was not only an eminent person but also a civil servant, torn by a painful conflict of loyalties: at once dedicated to the service of his Emperor, and a scientist of high intellectual integrity opposed to any form of thought control.

As the telephone rang again Otani put the secateurs down regretfully and stepped out of his geta up to the wooden platform. Normally his wife would have answered it immediately, but Hanae was still out shopping, and he had had the house to himself since getting home at lunchtime. The pine tree had caught his eye first, then the perfect little maple had seemed to invite a few minor attentions, and one way and another the afternoon seemed to have sunk most pleasantly without trace.

He picked up the receiver, and identified himself. "I am disturbing you," said a familiar voice in the conventional phrase. "You are indeed, Kimura-kun," Otani replied in an indulgent manner. He found it difficult to muster even mock anger towards Jiro Kimura, even though he was constantly and crustily sarcastic about his subordinate's habits of dress and speech, and his ultra-modern life-style. Kimura was an inspector and head of the section with special responsibility for matters affecting foreigners. "What is it?"

"Your car has been sent to your house, sir," said Kimura with what was for him most unusual formality. "I thought it possible that you may wish to acquaint yourself personally with the details of a case which has just been notified to me. A foreign resident, an Englishman called Murrow, has been murdered. There are some features of the matter which I think you should know about."

It was rare indeed for Kimura to ask for support from above. Quite the contrary; during their years together Otani had often enough had cause to tick him off for taking too much upon himself, but never too little. Although Kimura was getting on for forty, Ontani thought of him as a bright young man; a wartime baby who had no recollection of the hateful old-style police with their Dangerous Thoughts specialists and casual brutality which had so distressed upright old Professor Otani. Cosmopolitan Kimura with his fluent English and French, his familiarity with Europe and his casual dismissal of tradition was asking for help from old stick-in-the-mud? Well, well.

"I'll get dressed," Otani said briefly. "Have you told Tomita where to go?"

"Yes. I'm at Murrow's house now. It's in central Kobe, in the old part between Sannomiya and the hills. Your driver has instructions. Thank you. I apologise for the intrusion." Otani put the telephone down thoughtfully, and went upstairs to dress. After a moment's hesitation he took his light summer uniform out of the big cupboard and regretfully put on a shirt and tie. Murder, and a foreigner at that, called for uniform,

He was making his way down the polished wooden stairs again when he heard Hanae enter the porch and call, "I'm home!" "Welcome back!" he said cheerily in the time-honoured reply, and was touched to see her face fall as she came into view and she took in his appearance. "Are you going out?" she said, and he reached out and tweaked her nose gently.

"What a question," said Otani. "What does it look like? I'm sorry, Ha-chan. Something's cropped up that has worried Kimura-kun. I shall have to go and see what it's all about. I'll try not to be long. Promise. Buy anything nice?"

Long years of marriage to a policeman had inured Hanae Otani to sudden disturbances of domestic routine. It had been a lot worse when their daughter Akiko was little and Father still alive and unreconciled to his son's choice of profession. Then her Tetsuo had been away often enough for days on end with only the most perfunctory messages about his whereabouts and when he might possibly return. She smiled rather sadly. "Nothing special. I was very extravagant and bought you a piece of Matsuzaka steak. Perhaps you'll have it tomorrow." She hovered in the little entrance hall as her husband sat on the wooden step and tied his shoelaces, then went out of the door, along the short path to the outer gate, and looked out. "There's your car coming," she said to Otani as he emerged from the house.

As the black and white Toyota Police Special went past and turned at the end of the road Otani stood and smiled at Hanae, his normally grim face illuminated by tenderness. "I would have loved a steak tonight. Thank you. I'm sure it'll taste even better tomorrow. I'll ring you to let you know when to expect me."

They bowed to each other in a gesture which years of familiarity had done nothing to rob of sincerity, and Otani stepped out into the roadway as the car pulled up and Tomita jumped out and opened the rear door. "Go and return!" Hanae said cheerfully enough. "Good evening, Tomita-san."

"Good evening, Madam," said Tomita, saluting. Then, greatly daring, "I will bring the Commander home as soon as possible." He saluted again and took his place behind the wheel.

Otani sat back as the car moved on. His uniform cap was on his lap, and he ran a finger over the gold-braided peak as he spoke. "I believe you know where to go, Tomita." The driver caught Otani's eye in the driving mirror. "Yes, sir."

"How is it that you happened to be on duty?" Tomita was his personal driver, and they tended to have the same day off. Tomita stiffened in his seat. "A little overtime, sir. I noticed a problem with the timing earlier today. I worked on it this afternoon and was about to go off when the message came to the garage. Sato should be driving you tonight but I don't like the way he treats the gearbox."

Otani grunted non-committally, privately relieved that he was to be spared the Grand Prix technique of Constable Sato. Tomita drove gently down the winding roads of the residential area as far as the junction with the main Osaka-Kobe Number Two road, turned right and put on speed. There was a fair amount of traffic so early in the evening, but they made good time and in little more than fifteen minutes from leaving the house were at the Sannomiya concourse, alive with winking lights and bustling shoppers. Tomita cursed briefly in a muffled voice as he had to brake suddenly to avoid an elderly lady who stopped half-way across the road and began to rummage in her shopping bag, and Otani leaned forward to see what was going on. "Think yourself lucky, Tomita," he said mildly. "There are far more people down in the underground shopping centre than there are up here. Do you know exactly where the house is?" Tomita hated to admit ignorance about anything and had more than once delivered his chief to a destination by what Otani suspected was an extremely circuitous

14

route and with more assistance from the gods than from adequate prior briefing.

This time he seemed confident, and, after a few complex but apparently justifiable right turns through the elaborate one-way system of central Kobe, brought the car triumphantly to a halt behind another police car in a narrow, ill-lit street. It was now completely dark, and the contrast with the neon signs and bustle of Sannomiya was striking and abrupt. Otani emerged from the car and put on his hat, looking around him as he adjusted his belt and freed his backside from the clammy embrace of his drill trousers.

It was obviously a very respectable district; a far cry from the hurly-burly of sailors' bars with names like "Hawaii", "Lucky" and "Sweetheart" and the short-time "love hotels" a block or two away. Here were solid wooden houses not unlike his own, each discreet behind its high fence, beside each gate the wooden or illuminated glass sign with the name of the householder painted on it in Chinese characters. Otani noticed briefly that the nearest one read "Matsumoto", while almost immediately opposite on the other side of the narrow lane lived the Wakabayashis.

The scene of the crime was evidently the next one along on the left, since a uniformed constable stood at the open gate. As Otani approached he looked for the name-plate, and the word MARO in the squared phonetic lettering reserved for foreign words jumped out of the darkness at him. Maro. Yes, that was the name Kimura had mentioned. He returned the constable's salute and went through the gate. The little garden was flooded with light from the open front door, and Otani took appreciative note of the beautifully chosen stones which formed the cobbles of the short path, and the admirable design of the stone lantern on a moss-covered hillock. He reminded himself to mention it to Hanae, who kept putting off getting one for their own garden. It would look charming with a light powdering of snow on top.

Inspector Kimura was waiting inside. As the two men exchanged greetings, Otani scuffed off his shoes and ascended the single polished wooden step up into the house. It was simply beautiful. The tatami matting of the small entrance

15

hall was fragrant with newness, and on a set of tiny irregular shelves let into the back wall was a single ornament, an incense burner of chaste simplicity which looked extremely expensive. It was rather like looking through the wrong end of a telescope at the entrance to one of the most exclusive traditional restaurants in Kyoto.

"Perhaps you would come this way," said Kimura. Otani looked him up and down, from the thick black hair above the intelligent, sardonic eyes and mobile face to the elegant silk socks on his feet. "Lead the way, Kimura-kun." The small room to which Kimura took him was devoid of all furniture except for two flat brocade cushions on the floor-mats. In the *tokonoma* alcove a modest flower arrangement stood in a simple bowl on a slab of black lacquered wood, and on one plain brown rough-plastered wall hung a boldly brushed calligraphic scroll. A Japanese boy of about nineteen was sitting cross-legged on one of the cushions, but scrambled hurriedly to his feet as the two men entered, and bowed.

He was good-looking in a hefty, athletic way, and was taller than either Otani or Kimura. He was dressed in a pair of cotton trousers and a plain white short-sleeved shirt. His feet were bare. "This is Hirata, Sei-ichi. He is a student, and lives here in the house. He reported finding the body of the foreigner Murrow in the garden on returning from an English oratorical contest held in Osaka today." Otani nodded to the boy, who was evidently keeping himself under rigid control with a good deal of difficulty. His pleasant, open face was set in a mask of impassivity, and his fists were tightly clenched. "You may sit down again, Hirata-san," Otani said. Hirata bowed again, then crossed to the built-in cupboard beside the alcove and brought out another cushion which he placed immediately in front of the alcove as a place of honour for Otani. Then he waited till the two police officers had taken their seats before resuming his own.

"If I may, sir, I will go over what Hirata-san has told me. I should first explain that the death was reported at five-twenty this afternoon." As Kimura spoke, Otani glanced at his watch. Ten to eight. "Hirata-san ran along to the police box at the corner of the block and told the patrol constable
16

that he had arrived home just after five and called out to Mr Murrow in the usual way. There was no reply, so he went to see if Mr Murrow was sleeping. Then he saw him in the garden, in a heap." Hirata was still sitting immobile but with tension in every visible muscle. He had yet to utter a word in Otani's hearing.

"All this he reported to the patrolman, who came back here with Hirata san to satisfy himself that Mr Murrow was indeed dead. Then the patrolman telephoned the duty officer at headquarters, who ordered an ambulance and very correctly alerted me. I was not on duty, and it took me a little time to get here." Kimura coloured very slightly, and Otani concluded that he had been spending the afternoon in some kind of dalliance in his smart new Western-style flat. "By the time I arrived, the duty officer had authorised the removal of the body after photographs."

"Why the hurry?" Otani inquired, though he was not particularly surprised. Motive for murder is usually so obvious in Japan that forensic scientists have little say in the ordering of events immediately after a crime has been discovered.

"Well, the weather is hardly suitable . . ." "Of course. I understand," Otani cut in, still watching the boy's face.

"The examining doctor's provisional oral report is that Mr Murrow died from multiple stab wounds at about noon. At that time Hirata-san had already been out of the house for several hours. He says he has been in the company of friends all day who will confirm this." Kimura stopped, obviously wanting a lead from Otani, who now addressed himself direct to Hirata.

"You say you live here," he said gently. "What is your registered permanent address?"

At last the boy raided his eyes and looked straight at Otani. "I am from Takamatsu in Shikoku Island," he said in a pleasant but unsteady voice with something of a baritone singer's quality in it. "I am a student in the economics department at Shindai-Kobe National University."

"What is your position in this house? You lodge here?"

Hirata nodded. "Yes, sir. Mr Murrow is—was . . ." he faltered, then began again. "Mr Murrow was a lecturer at a

17

private university. He taught English, and also gave private lessons. I came to him for conversation practice and last year he offered me a room here free in exchange for helping him with house-work, and with correspondence in Japanese.''

"Could he speak Japanese?" Kimura interjected.

Hirata spoke a little more easily now, though his misery seemed if anything even more profound. "Yes. He spoke it quite well and could read a little. But he found it impossible to deal with official papers without help.''

"This is a beautiful house," Otani remarked. "It must take a lot of effort to live so simply.''

The boy managed the ghost of a smile. "Yes, it does. Mr Murrow had a passion for pure Japanese style. Some people used to say that he was more Japanese than the Japanese. The house belongs to the university and I think it was in poor condition when they let Mr Murrow use it four or five years ago. He spent a lot of money on it. A few months ago they sent photographers from a magazine in Tokyo to do a feature on how to live in the authentic Japanese manner.''

"Have you a copy of the article?" said Otani.

"Yes, sir. Upstairs.''

"Please fetch it.''

Kimura made to follow as Hirata left the room, but Otani put a hand on his arm to restrain him. They heard his footsteps on the stairs. "Is he clear?" Otani asked quietly.

"Yes, I'm sure of it. But I think we should take him in overnight. I want to have the house searched. Then I shall have to notify the British authorities through the consular liaison office,'' said Kimura. Otani nodded as the boy came back, a glossy magazine in his hand. He handed it to Otani, who riffled through the pages. It was not difficult to find the article. There were several photographs of the house, of the room in which they were sitting, of a classic four-and-a-half-mat tea room with a blond foreigner in full formal Japanese dress performing the tea ceremony, a shot of a bathroom with a wooden tub, and one of the traditional kitchen. Then one which Otani scrutinised with some amazement. This showed the foreigner, evidently Murrow, in the garden pointing out a goldfish pond to a young Japanese. Murrow was in ki-

18

mono, the Japanese was dressed in a black student uniform. It was Hirata, and Murrow towered over him. Even allowing for the fact that he was wearing high wooden geta on his feet, he was quite outlandishly tall. Otani looked again at Hirata's substantial, rugger-player's frame. "How tall was he, in heaven's name?" he asked.

"Two metres, almost exactly," said the boy. "People always used to stare at him in the street. His fair hair was striking, but it was his height that people joked about. He sometimes used to call himself the Kobe Tower." In the midst of his sudden animation Hirata seemed to become ashamed of the tone of his response, and relapsed again into impassive silence.

Otani let it drag on for a few minutes, then spoke again in the same gentle, courteous way. "I realise that you are shocked and upset. I should like to assure you that your account of your own movements today is satisfactory. Nevertheless, I think that we must seal this house tonight, and I shall therefore ask you to spend the night in accommodation at police headquarters. Please do not be alarmed. You are not under arrest and I will ensure that you are made comfortable, but we must clearly ask you many more questions." Hirata bowed his acknowledgement and acceptance. "Inspector Kimura will now arrange for you to be escorted there. Please do so, Inspector. Then join me here again." Otani himself bowed slightly and left the room, then stared unseeingly at the calligraphy on the wall. A nice boy. Not unlike a younger version of Akiko's husband. Pity Hanae and he had never had a son. He sighed, not really all that sorry.

The phone rang for what seemed like minutes on end, and Walker was on the point of ringing off when he heard a click and then Heather's very English voice saying "Hello?" in her peculiarly timid way. It was due, he knew, to her terror at the prospect of having to try to speak Japanese. "Heather? Andrew Walker here. I'm sorry to bother you, but is Joe home please? It's rather important."

Heather's voice went at once into happily high gear. "Andrew, how very nice. We've only this second come in. We had such a splendid day out. That funny old Mr Wadakura with the spats took us to a pottery and there was a marvellous man there and, do you know, he's been designated as a Living National Treasure by the government. He said that before he was an Intangible Cultural Asset. Isn't it a scream? I told Joe he didn't look as if he'd ever been very tangible to me . . ."

Walker cut in. "I'm really terribly sorry to interrupt, but could I speak to Joe please? It really is rather urgent."

"Oh all right, you boring thing. If you'd rather talk to Joe than hear about cultural assets, I shall have a drink. Why don't you come and have one too? Here's Joe."

Endsleigh came on the line at last, and Walker unconsciously tightened his grip on the receiver. Though the Consul General was an amiable and civilised man he rather scared Walker, who found it difficult to respond to the standing invitation to call him "Joe" and therefore usually called him nothing at all to his face.

Joseph L'Estrange Endsleigh, CMG, OBE, Her Britannic Majesty's Consul General at Osaka, was an impressive figure who would almost certainly move on to an Ambassadorship next time. At fifty-one he was the right age: he was mellow and polished in his manner, and beautifully tailored. Walker had often reflected on the career set out in the Diplomatic List: the "good war" as a very young man, followed by the ex-serviceman's award to Cambridge; then the steady climb up the Foreign Office ladder from a Third Secretaryship in Madrid to his present eminence by way of Montevideo, Kuala Lumpur and two or three useful spells in London. Walker remembered the exact terms of the entry about his domestic life: "m. Heather Anne Turnbull, 1952, one s. 1954, one d. 1957." She was certainly an attractive woman even now and must have been a stunner in her day, but why on earth had Endsleigh married such a featherbrained creature as Heather?

"Andrew? What can I do for you? No, dear, not just now. No, not you, Andrew, I was talking to Heather. Anything up?"

"I'm afraid so. I think you'll probably be getting a message
20

from the Gaimusho Liaison Office in Osaka soon. I've heard that David Murrow, the teacher at the Nishinomiya Gakuin College—he's been murdered. But it's Saturday so the Foreign Office protocol may go wrong, and I wondered if you'd like me to talk to the police and find out whether it's true." Walker paused, and could almost see Endsleigh's ponderously handsome face settling into thoughtfulness.

"Thank you, Andrew, but I think not. If the poor fellow has been murdered there's precious little we can do about it except wait to be informed of the fact through the proper channels. How did you hear about it?" Walker explained and there was another pause. "I suppose he was registered with us? The old hands are often forgetful. I think, Andrew, that if you aren't otherwise engaged it would be a help if you would go down to the office and see if we have a resident's card for him. We shall need to get a message off to a next of kin as soon as we hear anything authoritative. Then, if you could come here, I should be very grateful for your help when The Inspector Calls. I dare say Heather could scramble some eggs or something."

Walker was at the Consulate General before eight. He had often enough been required to go there out of hours as Duty Officer to carry out routine security checks. They kept very little classified material, and there were no security officers like those who manned the Embassy in Tokyo round the clock. Even so, he never cared much for the business of memorising the current combination for the main safe-room lock, or wandering through dimly-lit rooms searching his colleague's desk-drawers to see if they had left any classified files lying about. His present task was different, and he felt brisk and almost chirpy as he unlocked the consular records file cabinet and flipped through the card index of registered British subjects. It never ceased to surprise him that there were so many; nearly four hundred resident in the consular district, the overwhelming majority in the Kobe-Osaka-Kyoto triangle.

The news of Murrow's murder was unquestionably shocking, but Walker's personal emotions had not been touched, and he found himself reflecting on Takamura's questions. It

21

was quite true murder *was* rare in Japan and tended to be a speciality of gang-land, as in the Chicago of the thirties. Come to think of it, Takamura would have fitted pretty well into that kind of environment himself: he would probably love to see himself as a hard-bitten newsman with a green eye-shade and elastic round his shirt-sleeves shouting, "Hold the front page!" Japanese are great rôle-players.

Liddenham, Ludlow, Manning, Melville, Meredith, Murrow . . . Murrow. The CG had been right. Murrow had last renewed his registration three years before. People get casual in an affluent, open society. They wouldn't forget to register in Teheran or Budapest. Walker did some mental arithmetic as he studied the slightly dog-eared card. Murrow was thirty-four. Father deceased. Next of kin Mrs Dorothy Murrow, mother, address near Worcester. Poor Mrs Murrow. Lousy job for the bobby who would have to go and tell her that her son was dead, foul play not only suspected but quite certain. Walker put the card in his pocket, and closed and locked the cabinet. Then he left the building and drove to the Consul General's residence in a select suburb of Kóbe, seven or eight miles away.

Endsleigh must have heard the slamming of the door, because he was ready and waiting at his front door as Walker approached it. He was soberly dressed in a dark suit in spite of the sultry heat. "Well, you were right, Andrew," he said. "Ambassador Tsunematsu telephoned me himself about a quarter of an hour ago. Wanted to know whether we could formally identify the body. I told him I'd go down to police headquarters and on to the mortuary with you. You knew Murrow pretty well, didn't you?"

"Yes, I did. You met him as well, of course."

"Mmm. Great tall chap. Unlikely to forget him. He was at the QBP last month. Well, better get on. Disagreeable business. Mind driving the office car? I don't like to make Iwai-san turn out again tonight. He's had a long day."

He handed over the keys and the two men walked round to the garage at the side of the house. Endsleigh attended to the doors, closing them after Walker had reversed the glossy black Austin Princess out into the driveway. Before getting

22

in beside Walker, he walked round and removed the black plastic cover from the furled consular Union Jack on its stubby chromium staff on the front wing, and freed the little flag. "Better go in full canonicals, I suppose. Down towards Kobe harbour, please, Andrew. It's near the New Port Hotel, I believe."

They set off down the hill, the lights of Kobe far below merging into the velvety blackness of the Inland Sea beyond. Endsleigh settled back in his seat. "Well, my dear Andrew, what do you make of it? What would a chap like Murrow do to get himself killed, do you suppose? You went to his house once or twice, didn't you?"

"Once," said Walker. "It was quite an experience. I met him first soon after I arrived here, at that cocktail party you gave for the Minister of State from the Department of Trade."

"What a paralysing bore that man was," said Endsleigh reminiscently. "But then most politicians are. Sorry, go on."

"We got talking and discovered we'd both been at Durham, and agreed that there are a lot of bogus teachers of English around. He said there used to be a lot more; what he called the dharma bums and hippies who used to drift here by way of Afghanistan, Nepal and Thailand. He was very amusing on the subject of the way so many Japanese think it's much more important to be able to say they're studying with a genuine Brit than to make any progress in actually learning the language. Murrow himself was one of the other kind, of course. He was properly qualified, had his solid lectureship at a reputable college which got him his work permit, and was really well dug in to the educational system here. People like him can pick and choose what extra teaching or correcting work they want. They get plenty of approaches, and it's lucrative."

Walker broke off as he waited his chance to edge into the still fairly steady stream of traffic on the main road. The turn having been safely negotiated, he took up the thread. "Anyway, I met him more or less by accident a few times after that, and enjoyed talking to him. I heard about his reputation for living in a very old-fashioned Japanese style, and I must admit I fished for an invitation to visit the famous house he was supposed to have

23

reconstructed so carefully. Well, he invited me to dinner and I went. One evening last January.''

"Queer, I believe. Was that your impression?" Endsleigh asked.

"Yes. He didn't make much of a secret of it. When I went there I met a kind of living-in house-boy. It was pretty obvious. Bernard, he was called.''

"Bernard? What an extraordinary name for a Japanese. I presume he was Japanese?''

"Yes, a student. A pleasant sort of person. He spoke excellent English, and told me that Murrow made all his conversation students take an English first name. They hate using their Japanese given names so. Murrow had a theory that using English names would break the ice. It seemed to work with Bernard.''

"Bernard. Good Lord.'' Endsleigh rolled the name round his tongue a few times as Walker continued.

"He apparently chose it in honour of Bernard Leach, the potter. Leach is venerated here, of course. Murrow said it was quite a sober choice—it seems that some of his students get rather carried away. He told he that one demure little girl said she wanted to be known as Scarlett. Then I think he said he had a Bendix Hashimoto and a Spike Suzuki. Anyway, I had a marvellous dinner there, and I really was very impressed with the house. It's had an enormous amount of loving care lavished on it, as well as quite a bit of money.''

They were approaching the city centre. "I'll turn here,'' said Walker. "I know where the perfectural police office is. I can come at it from the side more easily. Well, that was my one and only visit to David Murrow. It was a pleasant evening. I remembered being startled when the phone rang—it seemed so out of place in that house. But of course he had a Western-style study. He showed it to me. Curious . . . I remember that he was very annoyed by the phone call for some reason. But he glossed it over.'' He pulled up outside a monumental building which looked something like a Victorian family tomb but on a bigger scale. "Here we are. Hyogo Prefectural Police. I'm sorry to have talked so much. Especially as I haven't a clue why anyone should want to kill him. I've

24

been trying to think of a reason ever since Takamura asked me.''

They got out of the car and Walker followed Endsleigh up the short flight of steps to the main entrance. A middle-aged constable sat at a plain deal table with a cheap school exercise book and a telephone in front of him, in the middle of a lofty and distinctly dusty lobby innocent of any other furniture. There was, however, a large varnished notice board on one wall which looked to Walker like a tally of the various sections and departments with the names of their heads painted in white Chinese characters on it. The constable sprang to his feet as the two tall Englishmen entered. Walker identified himself and announced Endsleigh, who had strolled over to the notice board and was examining it with every appearance of keen interest.

The policeman sat down again and made a long and complex entry in his exercise book before picking up the telephone and in turn announcing the identity of the visitors to the person at the other end. It was now shortly before nine-thirty, and Walker became conscious of feeling extremely tired. It seemed incredible that so much had happened in the past four hours; not to mention the fact that he had missed his supper. He was just about to allow himself to feel indignant at being kept waiting when he heard a light footstep on the stone stairway at the side of the lobby and looked up to see a dapper Japanese descending towards them.

He was slight but compact in build, and was wearing impeccably pressed pale blue lightweight trousers and a cotton golfing shirt which fitted him snugly, showing off a well-muscled chest. On his feet were canvas shoes with rope soles, and he had a jaunty air with a touch of insolence in it. He looked like a model in an advertisement for Martini, and Walker was not at all sure that he liked him.

''Gentlemen, I'm very sorry to keep you waiting,'' he said in excellent English, making for Endsleigh with hand outstretched. ''Mr Consul General? My name is Jiro Kimura. We have met, sir. At the Governor's reception for the Consular Corps.''

Endsleigh touched the proffered hand briefly. ''Mr Kimu-

25

ra," he agreed slightly frostily. "This is Mr Walker, one of my Vice-Consuls. Mr Walker will interpret for me as necessary." Kimura swung round to Walker and gripped his hand warmly, addressing him in Japanese which Walker decided was unnecessarily colloquial and complex, but which fortunately he could understand. He had not met Kimura before but had heard all about him from colleagues. So this was the inspector who headed the pretentiously titled Foreign Affairs Section and who rather fancied himself, both as a linguist and as a Lothario with a particular taste for American and European secretaries.

"Would you prefer me to use English, Mr Walker?" Kimura concluded with a flourish of lifemanship after introducing himself, apologising for inconveniencing the two of them and commiserating with Walker on the difficulties of learning Japanese. Walker was half inclined to take up the implied challenge and insist on sticking to Japanese, but something in Endsleigh's face dissuaded him. "I really don't think the Consul General needs my services in speaking with you, Inspector," he said mildly in English. "Perhaps you'd be kind enough to explain how we can help."

The flicker of challenge passed, and Kimura ushered them up the stairs, explaining that the Commander was waiting to receive them in his office. "Are you acquainted with Superintendent Otani, sir?" he asked Endsleigh. Endsleigh shook his head, being a little out of breath after managing to mount the stairs at the same cracking pace as Kimura. "If I may say so, you'll find him a very courteous gentleman. He is honoured to receive you here. He does not speak English," added Kimura. He led them through a pair of swing doors into a wide corridor with walls painted a dismal kind of industrial custard, and evidently a great many years before. The floor was covered with brown linoleum, with a narrow runner of frayed coconut matting down the middle. Along the walls hung a series of photographs in heavy frames, from which glowered grim-faced officials in uniform.

Endsleigh paused to study one. "One of the Commander's predecessors, no doubt?" he asked. "Yes indeed, sir. That is Baron Fujita. He was related to the Imperial Family." Kimura grinned with a directness which made Walker feel more kindly towards him. "People used to take the police rather more seriously in those days than they do now. I don't regret the change. Here we are." He indicated a pair of massive varnished double doors. From the upper frame there protruded a flat wooden sign with a name painted on it. "Otani Tetsuo," said Walker as he deciphered it. Fortunately it was one of the less weird proper names. "Right!" said Kimura, sounding a little surprised. He knocked at the door and opened it immediately, gesturing Endsleigh and Walker to precede him into the room.

It was furnished rather as Walker imagined the lobby of a respectable but modest hotel in Edwardian London must have been. There were potted palms, lacy antimacassars on the dusty green plush of the armchairs, and a painting in the Western style on one wall depicting if not the original Stag at Bay, at any rate an animal looking defensive in a rural setting. It all looked quaint and old-maidish, and not at all what Walker expected of a senior police official's room. The severely utilitarian filing cabinets, the In and Out trays and the modern telephones on the big desk, and the big electric fan with bright plastic blades turning lazily in one corner, struck a note of positive incongruity.

Commander Otani bowed stiffly as they all entered and Kimura closed the door behind them.

Otani was in a state of uncharacteristic indecisiveness and, to give himself time to feel his way, received the two British diplomats in a manner which might have been thought slightly excessive for royalty itself. During most of his career the occupation of policemen had been rated very low indeed in the public estimation, a kind of contempt having replaced in the Japanese mind the dread and terror of the apparatus of totalitarianism which had gripped the country for more than a decade. Like most of his contemporaries, Otani had therefore always been very attentive to his image, and conducted his public relations with a formality somewhat unusual even in Japan.

Profuse and elaborate expressions of regret, the organising

27

of a supply of green tea and a good deal of discussion about the most appropriate chair for the Consul General gave him a chance to size the visitors up. Over the years in a cosmopolitan seaport like Kobe, Otani had learned to accept that foreigners in general and Westerners in particular do not necessarily have to be treated like men from Mars, but like most Japanese he still found them objects of lively curiosity. Quite apart from that, and even in an area with a large resident foreign population and a brisk international tourist traffic, foreigners called for special handling.

To be faced with the necessity to deal with British diplomats in a case involving the murder of a well-known member of their national community put Otani in an acutely embarrassing position. His men were tough and seasoned in handling drunken merchant seamen, and he knew that Kimura and his opposite number Noguchi in the drugs section had often enough to summon consular officials of various nationalities to negotiate the release of their troublesome charges from the arms of the law.

This was a different pot of broth entirely. No wonder Kimura had come running to him. He was only just beginning to envisage the bureaucratic entanglements they were in for with the prefectural governor's office, the Foreign Ministry and heaven knew who else. There would be a good deal of pressure to actually solve the murder, too. Otani enjoyed reading *krimi* or detective stories, but often reflected that the celebrated investigators of Western fiction available in translation on every bookstall in Japan would be likely to have to find alternative employment in his own country.

True, the Hyogo force over which he presided had a crime investigation section; but the pattern of crime they looked into was remarkably settled. Most murders were done by women, who killed their husbands, mothers-in-law, children and very often themselves, usually out of despair and frustration when the quietly submissive and rigid self-control in which they were schooled from childhood finally broke. But they never seemed to plan their crimes, and seldom attempted even the sketchiest concealment of them.

Then, all big cities, and a good many smaller ones including some in Otani's own parish, had their underworlds of gangsterism. The highly organised protection rackets and territorial quarrels arising from them quite often led to killings which could only really be thought of as executions. One had to be fatalistic about internecine slaughter in the gangs. It was hardly worth intervening. Even though "Ninja" Noguchi could almost always tell Otani why a particular gangster had been killed, he rarely knew who had been the executioner. They were collective crimes with, in a sense, symbolic victims. As a good if unconscious Confucian, Otani set no great store by individual rights, and lost no sleep over the death of a young thug in a teeming but tightly controlled slum area of Amagasaki, the gangster ghetto of nearby Osaka, or in the waterfront areas of his own Kobe territory.

His face revealed nothing as he welcomed his visitors with a sinking feeling that he would have to accept personal accountability for an investigation which would have to produce a conclusion acceptable to the dignified Englishman with the young assistant now in his office as well as to his own masters.

It seemed that the thin young man with the big ears could speak Japanese, and that Kimura was going to let him do the interpreting. This was proper, and Otani found himself becoming quite impressed by his performance. What an odd language English seemed to be. A quite long and complicated statement by himself would be rendered into a brief sentence or two; and conversely, the Consul General's peremptory grunts were translated into perfectly civilised Japanese courtesies, which of course took much longer.

After apologising for the failure of vigilance on the part of his men which had led to this unfortunate incident and pressing his visitors to have another cup of tea, Otani felt he ought to begin to come to the point. He therefore confirmed that there could be little doubt that Murrow had been murdered, but that the question of motive presented a puzzle, since nothing seemed to be missing from the house, and the dead man had a considerable sum of money and other valuables on him. The young man passed this on to the Consul General with a brevity which suggested that he had deprived the statement of any trace of decent verbal ornament, and the older man replied with equal lack of ceremony. Then, although they had talked for barely half an hour, the Vice-Consul all at once implied that they ought to be on their way so as to get the business of identification over and done with. The haste with which foreigners proceeded never ceased to surprise Otani, who nevertheless stood up and took his cap from its peg on the wall.

Kimura opened the door and led the way out and down the stairs again, with Otani bringing up the rear. When they were outside the building Otani looked down at the black official car outside, with its little flag drooping sadly at the front. The absence of a driver startled him, and he barked sharp instruction to the duty constable to find the Consul General's chauffeur at once. It took a little time for Otani to realise that the younger Englishman was trying to get it across to him that he, the Englishman, would be driving the consular car. Odd though this was in itself, Otani was even more bewildered when the Consul General settled himself in the front passenger seat instead of occupying the back as was proper. This lack of respect for due forms and seemliness was not encouraging.

At least Tomita knew his job, and saluted smartly as Otani grimly clambered into the back of his own car and beckoned Kimura to follow him. The little cavalcade set off for the Municipal Hospital. Although it was still only about ten-fifteen, the normally busy city streets were already quiet and almost empty. Neon signs winked unnoticed, and the only traffic seemed to consist of cruising taxis and late trams.

"I wish you'd keep a change of clothes at the office, Kimura-san," Otani burst our crossly. "You look like a damned tennis player. I can't imagine what those two *gaijin* thought of the sort of organisation I run." Kimura had regained a good deal of his habitual bounce, but realised that his superior needed tactful handling. He usually addressed Otani as "Chief", using a slang expression common on television which he knew amused Otani more than it exasperated him as a rule. Not a very good idea tonight, though.

"I'm sorry," he said quite politely. "I realise it's not very

30

suitable dress for a mortuary. But I *was* off duty, and didn't realise we'd be in for all this.''

Otani grunted, mollified. "Never mind. You'd better come in anyway. That young fellow speaks Japanese quite well. He hasn't been here long, has he?''

"He was posted to Osaka last year. Before that he was attached to their Embassy in Tokyo for a couple of years specially to study the language full-time. They don't do badly, really.''

Otani's mouth twitched slightly at the note of condescension in Kimura's voice. "What does he do here?''

"I think he's a kind of general dogsbody. They have more senior people on the visa and shipping and commercial sides. He seems to act as a general assistant to the Consul General. He lives very quietly; behaves himself.''

"More than some I could name," said Otani, now in a better humour. "We're nearly there. We'll get this over, and ask the Consul General to notify the family. They'll have to organise a funeral very soon. We can't keep a dead foreigner in the mortuary for ever. Then I'm going home. Not a lot you or I can do before Monday. The CID must go through that house and garden with a fine-tooth comb. Not that I expect them to find a knife with any interesting initials on it.''

"I'll talk to the Hirata boy tomorrow," said Kimura as they stopped outside the hospital and Tomita shot out to open the door.

"Yes, of course. I'd forgotten him for the moment. Then you might as well let him go back to the house once it has been thoroughly searched. He'll have to get it ready for the condolence ceremonies, I suppose.''

They got out of the car and stood at the hospital gates waiting for Endsleigh and Walker. Their car was not far behind, and within a minute or two all four men walked through the glass doors into the brightly-lit reception area of the hospital. Late though it was, Otani had made sure that they would be expected and properly received.

On the way Walker had ventured to offer Endsleigh a small bet that the Medical Superintendent would be there to greet them and offer yet more tea and conversation; and in spite of their general sombreness of mood they found it hard at first to keep straight faces when events developed exactly as Walker had predicted they would. The Director of the hospital was a Professor Hirabayashi, an elderly gentleman in a spotless white coat worn over a formal suit complete with waistcoat and watch-chain. He wore rimless glasses which perched unevenly on his nose, and when he spoke he revealed a number of false teeth made of a silvery metallic substance.

The introductions over, it was with no little difficulty that Walker fended off the Professor's pressing invitation to the distinguished visitors to take some refreshment in his office and intimated that in view of the lateness of the hour the Consul General would be grateful if the formalities could be completed as expeditiously as possible. He was not helped in his task when Kimura caught his eye and winked at him very slowly and deliberately.

Eventually he made his point, and the Professor bowed stiffly and with resignation and led the way. Endsleigh followed, then Walker, and Otani came next with Kimura bringing up the rear. Nurses on night duty, crisp in white uniforms, stockings and white shoes, stood curiously in doorways. They lowered their heads decorously as the entourage swept importantly past, sneaking sideways looks at the two tall foreigners. They all knew perfectly well what was afoot, and the atmosphere was highly charged.

The mortuary was at the back of the building and separated from it by a short covered hallway. Professor Hirabayashi rapped with his knuckles on the frosted glass pane of the door and an attendant opened it from inside. It was delightfully cool in there after the muggy heat outside, but Walker knew that his involuntary shudder had little to do with temperature. This was his first real experience of proximity to a human cadaver, but the scene which met his eyes might have been from any one of dozens of films. There was the white-coated male attendant; there was the still figure under the concealing sheet with the cold clinical white tiles beyond and the large sink in the corner. There too were the tiled floor and the all too obviously functional drain. He could hardly find the scene visually unexpected: its disconcerting quality arose from the fact that it was all real, and that he had a role himself in this particular dramatic cliché.

He was curiously moved when Endsleigh turned to him and said quietly, "Have you ever had to do this before, Andrew?" and could only shake his head head dumbly. Endsleigh continued gently as the Director, the two police officers and the mortuary attendant stood by in attentive silence, making an odd little tableau like an old-fashioned Royal Academy problem picture. "I'm sorry, but in our business it had to happen to you sooner or later. You knew Murrow much better than I. So I'm afraid I shall have to ask you to go through with it. It'll only take a moment."

He nodded to the attendant, and the man drew down the sheet. Walker forced himself to look at David Murrow's dead face. The features were set in an expression of surprise, the blond hair lank and dull. It was not so bad as he had feared, even though he wished the staring eyes had been closed, and he felt no physical reaction. This was a relief, as he had been quite convinced he would be sick. He heard Otani asking in formal terms whether he identified the body as that of David Murrow, a British national resident in Japan; and listened to his own voice replying with an equally formal affirmative.

Then it was all over, but he was obscurely grateful to realise that Endsleigh had unobtrusively taken his arm as they left the mortuary and walked back through the hospital. He was able to get through the formalities of departure well enough, and to interpret into Japanese Endsleigh's undertaking to provide instructions on behalf of the British authorities for the disposal of the body as soon as possible. Otani saluted as they drove off, while Professor Hirabayashi bowed in disapproval of the perfunctoriness of it all, and Kimura made a curious little gesture of farewell, almost as if he were seeing a friend off on a train.

Endsleigh remained silent for a few minutes, until they had turned out of the road in which the hospital stood. Then he said, "You did very well, Andrew. Stop the car, please." Surprised, Walker did as he was told. Endsleigh got out,

33

walked round to the driver's side, opened the door and said, "Move over. I'm taking you home. You'll stay with us tonight." Walker protested vaguely as he slid across to the passenger side, "No, really, I'll go back to Ashiya . . ." It was not until Endsleigh had started the car moving again that he realised that he was shaking like a leaf, and he felt the wetness of tears on his face.

Endsleigh drove with careful deliberation and in silence, and by the time they arrived back at the big house on the hillside above Nishinomiya Walker was more or less himself again, but was glad enough of company. Heather had not yet gone to bed, and was drifting about with apparent aimlessness in a long batik gown in bold blues and yellows which she could scarcely have chosen personally. "What a pretty, er . . . dress?" said Walker uncertainly, not even convincing himself.

"It's a lounger, darling, and it's *hideous*," she cried cheerfully. "That awful Hilda Wentworth who's drunk all the time brought it back for me from Singapore. Still, it fits where it touches, and I use it to frighten Joe. Sandwiches? That would be the thing, I expect?" Endsleigh had already had a hurried whispered conference with her, and there was a good deal more purpose in her actions than at first appeared. Within minutes Endsleigh and Walker were dealing with a plate of chicken and ham sandwiches, and a stiffish whisky was loosening Walker's taut nerves. Heather then disappeared, murmuring vaguely about sheets, and left the two of them in the big comfortable living-room.

"Must get a signal off before we call it a day," said Endsleigh, drawing a silver propelling pencil and a note-pad towards him.

"I've got the registration card in my pocket," Walker remembered aloud through a mouthful of sandwich, and went to fetch it from his jacket which was now draped over the back of a chair. Endsleigh studied it, and scribbled for a while.

"Get the Embassy on the phone, there's a good chap," he said as he crossed out parts of what he had written and substituted other wording. "Tell them I want to send an immediate in cipher. Nuisance, but they'll just have to get Sparks and the code clerk back from the pub. The duty officer will have to ring me back here anyway to get authentication from me. Let's see, it's just on midnight, so it's about three in the afternoon in London. Quite convenient really.''

Walker raised the night security officer at the Embassy without too much trouble, and left the message. Less than ten minutes later the telephone rang, and Endsleigh raised an eyebrow as he heaved himself up to answer it. ''By George, what's come over them? Trying to make the Guinness Book of Records?'' He wandered out into the hall clutching his piece of paper and Walker overheard the first few words. ''Hello? Yes, Endsleigh here. Who's that? Richard? How are you, my dear fellow? And Veronica? Splendid. Now, look here, Richard, I know this is a bore for you, but . . .'' Walker let the voice recede into the background of his consciousness, and took another sandwich, though he didn't really need it. He was half-asleep when Endsleigh came back and gave him the paper to read.

''There you are, Andrew. They'll fill in the serial number and so forth and send us the flimsy for the file. Immediately, category A.'' Walker read the text set out in Endsleigh's bold hand—

DAVID PHILIP MURROW BRITISH SUBJECT RESIDENT KOBE FOUND DEAD 1700 APPROX SATURDAY 12 JULY LOCAL TIME CAUSE OF DEATH MULTIPLE STAB WOUNDS PLEASE REQUEST POLICE TO NOTIFY NEXT OF KIN MOTHER MRS DOROTHY MURROW RECTORY COTTAGE NEW LANE HANDCOTT WORCESTER SEEK URGENTEST INSTRUCTIONS FUNERAL OR REPATRIATION OF RE- MAINS AND ASSURE HER JAPANESE AUTHORITIES UN- DERTAKING FULLEST INVESTIGATION ENDSLEIGH OSAKA

''That should cover it,'' said Endsleigh. ''With any luck we'll have a reply before the end of tomorrow. I hope so, anyway. Well, time for bed. Heather's gone up. Another drink?''

"No, thank you. That was marvellous, but I think if I had another I wouldn't make it up the stairs."

Walker watched as Endsleigh moved round the room switching off lights, then followed him up the stairs. He had been in the house many times, but it felt very odd to be going to bed there. "In here," said Endsleigh, leading the way into one of the guest rooms. "You'd be surprised how many eminent heads have rested on that pillow, and how many weighty bottoms have sat on the loo." The room was spacious and comfortable in an English country house way, very different from Walker's bare little shoe-box of a bedroom in the flat at Ashiya. The door to the adjacent bathroom was ajar, and the bed was turned down. On one wall was a watercolour of Salisbury Cathedral, the muted colours seeming to reflect the pale green of the deep carpet. "You'll find a toothbrush and shaving gear and so on in there. Want some pyjamas?"

Walker shook his head. "No thank you. I never wear them. This is really very kind of you."

"Not at all," said Endsleigh briskly. "It's not as if you can claim subsistence. Right. See you in the morning. Get up when you feel like it. I doubt if there'll be anything for either of us to do until pretty late in the day." He hovered in the doorway a moment longer and seemed about to speak again, then extended one thumb upwards in a gesture of support and was gone. Walker was just in time to prevent himself from saying goodnight to a closed door.

He wandered about the room for a while after taking his third shower of the day and getting ready for bed. It would clearly be quite impossible to sleep, and he wondered which of the books in the small shelf on top of the tallboy he would try to interest himself in. There was an odd selection. Wavell's anthology of poetry was next door to a tattered paperback of *Fanny Hill*; there was a privately printed history of the foreign settlements in Kobe presented by the author, two Barbara Cartlands and an out-of-date *Nagel's Guide to Japan*. At least it made a change from the Gideon Bible and directory of services you got in hotel rooms.

Walker put on the bedside lamp and turned off the overhead lights, then padded over to the windows, enjoying the feel of the carpet against his bare toes. It would be unlikely that anyone would see his bony nudity or care much if they did. He opened the heavy lined curtains, dodging the stream of cold air which issued from the airconditioner at thigh height almost as though it had been aimed at him, and looked out the window. After a moment he crossed and switched off the bedside lamp, then went back to enjoy the view fully. The house was at an elevation of only a hundred feet, but from the window he could see the lights of Kobe seemingly far below and to his right, and then a stretch of blackness which was the Inland Sea, with lights at what must be the tip of Awaji Island in the far distance. Away to the left was Osaka.

Walker turned off the airconditioner and opened a window. He was quite suddenly overcome by black waves of exhaustion. *Fanny Hill* would have to wait. He slid into the cool sheets and was asleep within minutes.

A few yards away Endsleigh was standing in silk pyjamas of a distinguished mulberry hue unseeingly contemplating the same view, when Heather slipped her arms round him from behind. ''Bedtime for Joe,'' she said.

Sunday

J IRO KIMURA SAT AT HIS DESK IN THE FOREIGN AFFAIRS
Section looking across at Sei-ichi Hirata. "Tell me again how
you first met Mr Murrow," he said in a calm, almost casual
manner.

The young man sitting opposite had lost some of his impassivity, but still held himself under tight control. "I have
already told you twice," he replied with a touch of exasperation.

Kimura nodded. "And I have assured you more than once
that the medical evidence suggests very strongly that you are
not under personal suspicion. Nevertheless, you are in a position to help us, and this will mean going over the same
ground as often as necessary."

Hirata shrugged and crossed his brawny arms in his first
relaxed posture. "Mr Murrow came to address the English-
speaking Society at my university. We invite foreigners about
once a month. It was soon after the beginning of the last academic year, in late April or May last year. I was a freshman,
and could hardly speak English at all. After the lecture some
of us went to a coffee bar with Mr Murrow and I found that
he gave free conversation lessons to some students in return

for a few hours' housework. He said I could go to his house to meet him if I wanted."

"And then?" Kimura leant back and lit a cigarette with an elegant gas lighter.

"I joined in, worked in the house and garden for a while each week, and had a few lessons. Then in the autumn I was talking about changing my lodgings, and he asked if I would like to live at the house and help him in various ways."

"Why do you suppose he did that?"

Hirata shrugged again. "There had been someone else before me, on the same basis. The other student graduated and moved away. Mr Murrow needed help with official papers and so on."

Kimura studied the boy thoughtfully, wondering how to put his next question. Hirata's manner was consonant with a degree of shock at finding his employer's body and an entirely natural and human distress at what had occurred. He had answered forthrightly when questioned about his status in the household. "Who were his friends?" he asked after a while.

Hirata looked at him straight in the eye, totally unembarrassed. "Mr Murrow was not interested in women," he said. "He was kind and helpful to his girl students, but all his friends were men."

"*Gaijin* as well as Japanese?"

The boy nodded. "Yes. He had many *gaijin* friends. People who live in Japan. Businessmen, journalists. And many foreign friends who come here occasionally on business or holiday. And Japanese too, of course."

It was time to home in. "Did these people come to stay at the house?"

Hirata was now perceptibly more relaxed. "Hardly ever," he said. "Mr Murrow used to go out for meals with them, and sometimes sightseeing. But he was usually busy, and talked to his friends a lot by telephone."

"How much did he pay you?" Kimura asked, hardening his manner a little.

"Nothing. Except that I lived in the house free and had all

39

my food free. I have a small allowance from my parents in Takamatsu.''

Kimura stubbed out his cigarette to cover his own hesitation, speaking as he did so. ''Did you sleep with him?''

Again this surprising lack of embarrassment. ''Sometimes. Not very often. Mr Murrow was not much interested in sex.''

As a devout heterosexual, Kimura found himself unexpectedly shocked by the boy's admission. ''I see,'' he said. ''Well, what do you propose to do now?''

Hirata unfolded his arms and sat up straight in the wooden chair. ''I am under much obligation to Mr Murrow,'' he said formally. ''Someone must make arrangements for the condolence visits and the funeral ceremonies. I think I and his other students must do this; unless there are other instructions.''

Kimura had to admit to himself that he hadn't thought of this. ''Yes, let me see . . .'' he said meaninglessly. It was mid-morning, and prefectural police headquarters was usually quiet at this time on a Sunday. Hardly any of the administrative staff were there, and the duty officer and his team were at the other end of the rambling old building. He gazed absently at the reeded glass partition as somebody went by, a uniformed constable, bareheaded. ''It's a little complicated,'' he said at last. ''We shall have to wait for funeral instructions from the British Consulate General. They are in touch with Mr Murrow's family.''

Hirata set his jaw obdurately. ''There must still be some arrangements for condolence visits,'' he insisted. ''And I must take care of them. I am responsible for the household.'' Kimura nodded. It was indeed an iron requirement, anchored deeply in Japanese custom. Better let the boy do what he could. He made up his mind quickly. ''Very well. You may go back to the house now, and make contact with undertakers to prepare the place for the callers. The incense money will cover that expense, and if necessary I will explain to the British authorities. It is quite probable that one of their officials will visit the house. As for you, you must report to this office personally every day." Kimura gestured in dismissal, and said formally, "I apologise for having detained you."

Hirata stood and bowed. "Not at all," he said. "The Inspector may wish to know that I have met a British consul or vice-consul at Mr Murrow's house."

Kimura controlled his reaction with some difficulty. "Indeed? Who? And when?" "Some month ago. It was a Mr Walker. He came to dinner." Kimura reflected, then pressed an intercom button on his desk. When the duty constable answered, he gave instructions for Hirata to be escorted from the building. While he was waiting for the escort to arrive, Kimura stood up and looked at the burly young man. Extraordinary to think of him in bed with the gangling blond foreigner.

"Just a formality, Hirata-san," he said, using his name deliberately for the sake of courtesy. "Did you kill Mr Murrow?"

The blood rushed up the boy's neck and cheeks. "Of course not," he said.

"Do you know who might have done?" Hirata shook his head decisively. "Or why?"

The question hung a little longer in the air than the others, before the boy shook his head again. "I cannot think of any reason," he said as there was a discreet rap on the door.

Kimura went to open it. "There will be more questions, I regret to say. It is unpleasant for you, I know." Hirata had reverted to rigid impassivity, and he inclined his head in the most formal of acknowledgements as he left the room.

As soon as he was alone again, Kimura went over to a steel cupboard in the corner of his office, a much smaller room and more obviously functional than Otani's. Fishing a bunch of keys from his trouser pocket, he unlocked the cupboard and opened its two doors. Inside were a number of shelves containing a clutter of folders, reference books, including Japanese-English and Japanese-French dictionaries, some startling German pornographic magazines which Ninja Noguchi had presented to him as a memento of a drug raid on one of the more expensive brothels in Kobe, and a miscellany of other bric-a-brac.

One deep shelf in the middle had been cleared of all other material and now contained a number of plastic bags full of assorted documents, and beside them a little nest of six plastic drawers, each about four inches by three and perhaps ten inches deep. Kimura lifted the whole thing out of the cupboard and put it on his desk, then sat down, opened one drawer and began to riffle through the cards. They were neatly categorised by dividers, with the Japanese phonetic *hiragana* syllables printed on them in sequence. Kimura noticed that Murrow had for his own convenience written the equivalent in Roman script on each one, so the tags at the top of the dividers read A, I, U, E, O, then KA, KI, KU, KE, KO, SA, SHI, SU, SE, SO and so on.

He was about to start on the actual cards when the door was opened and Otani walked in. Kimura was almost too dumbfounded to react, and it was by instinctive reflex that he shot to his feet to greet his superior. Otani was himself in more casual dress than Kimura recalled ever seeing him wear before, in that he had on a pair of neat grey slacks, suede shoes and a crisp plain white short-sleeved open-necked shirt. "Good morning, Kimura-kun," said Otani amiably. "They told me I'd find you here. Don't look so dazed, man—I *have* been in this office before, you know." He sat down and gestured to Kimura to follow suit. "Though I suppose it was rather a long time ago," he added slightly defensively.

Kimura recovered his presence of mind. "I'm very glad to see you, Chief," he said, judging that Otani's attire argued a reasonably approachable state of mind and that his habitual slangy mode of address would do.

"I thought I would look in," Otani said. "It was a late night last night. I'd planned to keep out of things till tomorrow, but I've already had Ambassador Tsunematsu on the telephone at home. He seems to be in an unnecessarily fidgety state over this Murrow business for some reason." He glanced at the nest of drawers on Kimura's desk. "What have you got there?"

"Name cards," said Kimura. "Taken from Murrow's study. It seems he kept the visiting cards of all his acquaintances."

'Not unusual,'' said Otani off-handedly. ''You can get those boxes of index drawers in any stationery shop. My clerk keeps one for me, if it comes to that. Still, it will be interesting to see what sort of people he knew. How many cards?''

''It's quite full,'' said Kimura. ''Perhaps five hundred in each drawer. Six drawers, so getting on for three thousand, I'd say.''

''How much did you get out of our young friend, what was his name, Hiroyama?'' Otani asked.

''Hirata, sir. It was strange really. He was quite forthcoming, openly admitted having a homosexual relationship with the dead man, and seems to have been genuinely fond of him. Anyway, he's very concerned about getting the house laid out for the formal visits, so I've let him go back there, and told him to report every day . . . Ah, Chief?''

''That sounds reasonable. What's on your mind?'' asked Otani, leaning back and patting his own chest. Kimura hesitated a little.

''There's a problem,'' he said after a pause. ''I had some trouble persuading the criminal investigation people to let me take Murrow's papers and these cards into my custody. They're not too happy about my being involved in the actual investigation. But I tried to explain that the murder of a foreigner puts the whole thing on my desk. I think you'll be getting a complaint from Sakamoto tomorrow.''

Otani sighed inwardly, visualising Inspector Sakamoto standing ramrod-straight before his desk, woodenly insisting on his section's rights. Sakamoto was a bureaucrat's bureaucrat, and the senior colleague he liked least. It was essential that Kimura should be kept on the case, whatever childish squabbling resulted. He thought fast. ''Well, even if I wanted to keep out of this affair I don't think our local Foreign Ministry man would let me. So we'll make a virtue of necessity. I'll take charge of the case myself. I'll need to use Sakamoto's people and you and yours, it seems to me.'' Kimura noted with satisfaction the intention to use Sakamoto's staff but apparently not old Wooden-Face personally.

''Thank you, Chief. Glad to serve under your command,'' he said cheerfully, and Otani stared at him for a second or two with the blank poker face which was his best means of disconcerting the younger man.

"I'll let you know any time you're *not* under my command, my dear Inspector," he said then. "That will probably be when I get rid of you at last. I hear they need gigolos in that new bar in Tokyo for lonely women." Kimura became uncomfortably aware that from where Otani sat he could probably see into the cupboard and might very well have a view of the cover of one of Noguchi's trophies. He busied himself ostentatiously with the first few cards in the open drawer, tilting them forward as he read aloud.

"Akita Shusaburo, Professor of English—sounds respectable. Azuma Masao, Section Head, Sumitomo Holdings—I know him. A tedious man. Most people would use the Higashi reading. Pure snobbery to pronounce it Azuma . . ."

"Wait a moment." Otani fished his glasses from the breast pocket of his shirt and put them on. "There's something on the back of those cards. I can see writing. Would it be English?"

Kimura plucked the two cards out of the drawer and turned them over. "Interesting, he seems to have noted down when and how he met these people." He smiled suddenly. "Sense of humour, too."

Otani drummed on the desktop with some impatience. "What do they say, Kimura-kun?"

Kimura peered at the cramped, fastidious handwriting and translated as he read. "I'm sorry . . . it's not easy to make out. He's put the romanised spelling on the front of each card, of course, so the first part is simply a translation of the rest of the information. Professor of English, name of the university, address and so forth. Then he says something like 'Met him 11.76 at Shakespeare conference, Hiroshima. Earnest, effusive man. Typical English scholar, can't speak English . . . bad breath'. Now Azuma. 'Met him early 74 soon after arrival. Possibility conversation work. Neat hands'. . . ."

Kimura broke off as Otani gave a snort of mingled amusement and derision. "Neat hands? Bad breath? Well, it's one way to remember people, I suppose."

44

Kimura was still studying the card. "There's more, added later . . . dated 2.77, that's Showa fifty-two."

"I may not know English, but I do understand their dates, Inspector," said Otani testily. "No need to put them into Showa numbers."

Kimura nodded an absent-minded apology as he stared at the card. "I wonder what he means . . . 'Useful now, promoted with much VBM contact. Possibilities'. VBM, VBM . . ." He pondered all the English phrases that might fit, on the analogy of VIP. Very Busy Man? Very Big Man? "I'm sorry. I can't make head or tail of that," he confessed.

"You'd better put your staff to work tomorrow," said Otani, intrigued by the mysterious scribblings. "Photocopy the lot, and make translations of all these notes." He glanced at his old-style wristwatch, which unlike Kimura's smart electronic model had a face and hands and never went wrong. "I must be on my way soon. My wife and I are going to meet my daughter and her husband for lunch. Give me one of those drawers to glance through."

Kimura pulled the remaining five open, and looked up abruptly. "Ah, I should have thought of that," he said. "The last one is all *gaijin*. It's divided up according to the English alphabet. You know the way people who come here on business usually have Japanese-style name-cards printed for them." A thought struck him. "Business Man . . ." he murmured in English. "Very . . . Very . . . of course, Visiting. Visiting Business Man. VBM." He beamed in triumph at Otani as he explained his theory.

Otani nodded in mild approval. "If you say so. Perhaps you have some small talent as a detective after all."

He reached across and pulled out the open drawer nearest him, put it down conveniently and began to glance through the cards at random, noting with distaste the ugly Roman script above each name. The Chinese characters were so much more seemly than the spidery angular line that passed for writing in the West. "They look an ordinary enough collection of people to me," he said. "He seems to have quite a few Tokyo and Nagoya business acquaintances . . . Well, now, that's odd. Why should he know a film producer?" He

45

went on fingering his way through the cards with mounting interest. "And here's that fellow who's always on the television . . . I always told Hanae I thought he was queer . . . *Ara!*" He looked at Kimura as he removed a card from the drawer before him. "Just tell me what he wrote on the back."

Kimura took the card and studied it for almost a minute before he spoke. When he did, his voice too betrayed his excitement. "It's very strange," he began slowly.

"I know that," Otani cut in. "Just tell me what it says." He glanced round the room. The partitions did not reach the ceiling. "And keep your voice down."

Kimura began again. "Vice-Minister of . . ."

Otani raised a hand. "Just when and how they met, and personal comments. We know *who* he is."

Kimura started for the third time. "The first entry is dated 1976. They met at a reception in Tokyo. He doesn't say exactly what the occasion was. Then he goes on . . . 'Highly intelligent, frustrated. Instant rapport. Query respectable'—that's underlined—'respectable married man'. Then another note, 2.77—'Not frustrated now!'—with an exclamation mark. Then there's a jumble of letters and numbers, with just the odd word here and there. I'm sorry, I can't make sense of it."

The two men stared at each other in silence in the hot and stuffy room. "You can't handle it all yourself," said Otani at length. "Have you a translator you can trust?" Kimura nodded. "Get him called in today. Do the photocopying between you, and weed out the run-of-the-mill names. Give those to another translator to handle. No hurry for them. I want a list of any more like this eminent gentleman, with as much translation as you can manage, on my desk first thing in the morning. No, not on my desk. Locked up in your cupboard. And tell your clerk that if *one name* leaks out he's said good bye to his job and his pension. Yours too, I'm afraid. And if you have any more trouble with the Investigation Section, tell them you have my full authority to call on their resources. That goes for Sakamoto-san too."

He stood up and went over to the open cupboard. "What's this other stuff?" he said.

Kimura coloured and said, "Oh, just rubbish Ninja found in a brothel . . ."

Otani cut in, "No, I don't mean your bedside reading. The plastic bags."

Kimura collected himself. "Sorry," he said. "That's the personal papers, bank book and so on that Sakamoto's people sealed. I haven't looked at them yet."

Otani stalked out of the room without another word. As he made his way towards the entrance through the quiet Sunday corridors his mind was racing, and he barely acknowledged the respectful salutes of the few policemen and staff he met. At the top of the steps he stood for a moment in the humid midday heat. It was positively hard work to breathe. He went back inside and the duty constable hauled himself to his feet again and stood to attention.

"Inspector Kimura will be working late today," he said. "Send out for a packed lunch for him. And some beer. He likes Kirin. Have it charged to my account." He wheeled round and went out again to find a taxi. Hanae would be sure to ask him if he'd thought about some food for Kimura.

Walker was sitting with Endsleigh in the garden at the Consul General's house going through the newspapers. Between the old-fashioned bamboo chairs was a low table on which stood their drinks. Endsleigh had a tall glass of gin and tonic, Walker beer in a pewter tankard bearing the facsimile signatures of the members of the Montevideo Badminton and Darts Club, 1952. Heather could be heard singing "Oh What a Beautiful Morning" with a good deal of rubato and many repeats as she moved about the kitchen. It was fresher up on the hillside than down at sea-level, and there was even a hint of movement in the air.

Endsleigh rustled the pages of the English-language *Mainichi Daily News*. "Nothing here," he said. "Just the usual agency stuff and that dreadful woman's gossip column. Listen to this: 'Debonair Ambassador Olveira and his dark-eyed Senhora were host to many well-known Tokyo-ites at their glittering National Day reception Thursday. Attractive Mrs Dean Freeman—Betsy to her friends—flew in just in time to show off her newest gown by Hong Kong's talented Christopher Wong.' It makes one's heart bleed for the language.'' He dropped the paper to the grass and took a long pull at his drink. ''Betsy to her friends indeed. I wonder if the long-suffering Mr Dean Freeman has any idea how many friends Betsy has. Not for nothing is her driver known as Leporello.''

The allusion was lost on Walker, who looked up from his own paper, the Japanese-language *Asahi Shimbun*. ''There wouldn't be time for it to be in the *Mainichi*,'' he said mildly. ''What you've got there is the Tokyo Saturday edition reprinted down here word for word.'' The English-language paper was delivered to the house daily, and Walter had strolled down the hill to the station to pick up the Japanese dailies. ''It's in all these. I picked up the *Asahi*, the *Yomiuri* and the *Kobe Shimbun* itself. The *Yomiuri* and the *Asahi* seem to have exactly the same wording, as far as I can judge. 'Death of Respected English Resident' is the headline on all three, then there's a statement from Hyogo Prefectural Police Headquarters saying that Murrow was found dead yesterday afternoon and that energetic enquiries are being pursued. I was just looking at Takamura's bit in the Kobe paper. It's the same as the others except that he mentions us.'' Endsleigh looked at him over his glass, and cocked an eyebrow enquiringly. ''It says a representative of the British Consulate General declined to comment. They've all got hold of a photo of Murrow somehow.'' Walker passed over the folded paper, pointing out a small, oval and quite unrecognisable photograph of a face which could conceivably have been that of David Murrow. As Endsleigh took it, he went on.

''I wonder if we shouldn't put out a Press release anyway?'' he asked tentatively.

Endsleigh looked surprised. ''What are we supposed to say to them, Andrew? That we think it's frightfully bad form for our nationals to be done in? My goodness, in most of the posts I've served in it happened practically all the time.''

Walker patiently, in his best didactic manner, tried to explain the unique nature of the crime along the lines expounded by Takamura in the original telephone call the

48

previous day. He broke off in confusion when he saw Endsleigh's mouth working and realised that he was trying not to laugh.

"I'm sorry, Andrew. I'm really not making light of it. It's a wretched business and I'm afraid you're going to be in the thick of it for a while yet. Even if you hadn't been in it at the beginning like this I should have asked you to handle it. But there really isn't any point in our rushing into print at this stage, if at all. Perhaps when the local sleuths find out why and by whom Murrow was sent to his reward we may want to comment. But not yet, not yet."

Walker buried his nose in the beer tankard feeling deflated. He had wanted to go back to his flat after breakfast but had been pressed by Heather to stay for lunch. Much more of this beer and he'd have to go back to the Endsleighs' spare bedroom to sleep the afternoon away. It was quiet in the garden; at least in the sense that there was no sound of traffic. The crickets were in noisy form, and Heather was scarcely unobtrusive. Nevertheless, there were worse ways of passing a Sunday morning than this. His reverie was interrupted by the sound of the telephone bell. Both men looked towards the sound, which stopped after a couple of rings as Heather picked up the receiver. A moment later she appeared at the open back door. "Up you get, drunken sots both," she called. "It's the Embassy. John Wilkinson. I thought they were on leave, but he said they've been back for simply *months*. Poor Adrian's got mumps. Doesn't that make you impotent or something?"

"I'll go," said Endsleigh. As he reached the door he called back to Walker. "Explain to this person that we have been discussing matters of State and that we have barely touched our drinks. Furthermore," as he disappeared inside, "that we're on the point of starvation." Heather came out and winked hugely at Walker. "I've had two in the kitchen. Mean, isn't it? Anyway, lunch is ready. You're only getting a whopping great salad in any case. It's much too hot to cook." She bent down to pick up the paper from the grass, causing Walker to avert his eyes in some haste from the generous breasts revealed by the loose neckline of her light sum-

49

mer dress. The sight prompted a sudden inclination on his part to go for a swim at the Kobe Club after lunch. He might meet Nicole from the French Consulate there.

Endsleigh came out of the house with a piece of paper in his hand and gave it to Walker, who read the reply to the previous night's telegram. It seemed odd to see it in the same handwriting.

IMMEDIATE FOR CONSUL GENERAL OSAKA VIA TOKYO YOUR 01436 MESSAGE DELIVERED TO MRS MURROW WHO AUTHORISES CREMATION IN JAPAN AND BURIAL OF ASHES WITH CHRISTIAN RITES PLEASE PROCEED WITH ARRANGEMENTS BUT DEFER FUNERAL UNTIL AFTER TUESDAY FIFTEENTH WHEN SURVIVING SON JAMES MURROW WILL ARRIVE OSAKA FLIGHT DETAILS FOLLOW

"I didn't bother to add the signature," said Endsleigh. "I don't *really* think they got the Secretary of State out of bed to put his cross on it. Busy day for you tomorrow, Andrew. What about lunch?"

They all went into the light, airy kitchen and sat round the big table there. "Right, no shop here please, my darlings," said Heather briskly.

"We wouldn't think of it," Endsleigh replied. "And don't call him darling. I've just been expounding a view widely current in Tokyo about the promiscuous habits of a lady who moves in what the paper calls glamorous diplomatic circles. Don't want people to mix the two of you up." He uncorked a bottle of Alsace wine from the refrigerator and filled Heather's glass, then his own after Walker declined with a gesture at the tankard he had brought in with him.

It was a pleasant meal, and now that he could begin to plan what he would have to do next, Walker felt much happier. He had an old-maidish passion for organising his time, and had been thoroughly unsettled by the events of the last twenty-four hours. He still wished he could join in the banter which seemed such a feature of life in the Consul General's residence, and felt as immature and slow-witted as he had at

50

breakfast. Over a mouthful of potato salad he looked at his superior, admiring his ability to switch off completely from official concerns and to relax into a persona which was as completely natural to him as the dignity he brought to his official duties, yet somehow separate and obviously invulnerably private.

When lunch was over and he again attempted to take his leave, no obstacle was put in his way. It was just after two-thirty when he expressed his gratefulness to Heather yet again and she put a stop to further repetitions by planting a perceptibly wine-flavoured kiss on his lips and then pushed him away. "It was lovely to have you, Andrew. Now off you go and enjoy yourself, and leave us geriatrics to dodder about." Endsleigh walked him to his car, and Walker turned back to wave as he went out of the gate.

"See you in the morning, Andrew," Endsleigh said through the open window of the car as Walker started the engine. "I'm leaving everything up to you. Come to me if you really need, not otherwise. Mmmm?" He stood back as Walker nodded and let in the clutch, and waited till the car had disappeared round the corner before returning to the house.

It meant an extra twenty-five minutes' drive, but Walker felt it was well worth having been home and changed into shorts, sandals and a sports shirt before going to the Kobe Club. He paused to look at the notice board before going through to the open-air pool. Thank goodness it would be a week or two before the main body of teenage children would arrive from their English boarding schools for the summer holidays, but plans were obviously afoot. A Fancy Dress Competition would take place at the end of the month. Categories were Most Original, Most Comical, Best Historical Couple and so forth. Before that, smaller children were invited to enter their pets for the Cutest Puppy Contest. A departing Dutch family wished to dispose of two airconditioners and a deep-freeze, while the Committee pointed out that booklets of bar vouchers were temporarily unavailable. Cash would be accepted exceptionally until further notice.

Walker changed into his swimming shorts and went out to

the pool. Small European children splashed about with rubber toys from home watched by mothers in printed cotton frocks, pudgy arms reddened by the sun, feet in sensible sandals, talking quietly of home leave, the servant problem and the way the drinks had run out at the Queen's Birthday Party the previous month. Walker had ambivalent feelings about his role in local society. He accepted the demands of his official status and put in an appearance at the club bar from time to time. Though not very gregarious he was basically amiable, and managed a reasonably good-humoured response to the usual barrage of not altogether friendly wisecracks about his study of the Japanese language and his interest in exploring temples and festivals off the beaten track. He grinned tolerantly when the young married men with spreading waistlines nudged him with envious knowingness and offered to bet that he knew every bar, hostess and Turkish bath in town.

Even Nicole tended to make fun of him, in a nice way. He peered round the poolside area. There were only two or three bikini-clad bodies which might have belonged to her, but none did. Just as well, perhaps. The last time they had met had not been a great success, and a cooling-off period might be a good idea. In fact, there was nobody there that he really knew, and after a few lengths of the pool and nods and waves to a number of casual acquaintances he showered and dressed again and went back to his flat, arriving soon after five.

Now that he was completely alone again, he found it difficult to suppress the mental images of the previous evening, and the trace of chlorine left in his hair from the swimming-pool water reminded him of the disinfectant smell of the hospital and the mortuary. He leafed through a three-week old airmail edition of The *Times*, its flimsy paper creased and dispirited after much handling. He was the last on the circulation list in the office, and it was hardly worth bothering by the time his turn came.

Murrow's staring dead eyes came to him again as he watched the television news. The election campaign seemed to be following predictable lines. He switched off the set and went to potter in his kitchen, ending by cooking himself some

52

instant noodles, remembering as he did so the exact words put to him by the police superintendent in the neat summer uniform. The evening wore on, and he almost decided to dial Nicole's number in case she was perhaps at a loose end too; then in exasperation settled down to write a duty letter to his mother. A new attempt on Nicole had better wait till he was in a more decisive mood.

Walker finally fell asleep in front of the television again, rousing himself barely enough to undress and go to bed. The atmosphere was so heavy that a storm must surely be building up. He left the airconditioner on all night.

Monday

By the time Walker arrived at the Consulate
General at nine a further telegram had already been received
in Tokyo and telephoned through, giving the promised details about the flight to be taken by the dead man's brother.
Someone had been sensible in advising him to travel by way
of Hong Kong to Osaka rather than over the Pole to Tokyo.
The few hours' flying time saved on the Polar route would
have been more than eaten up by the transfer from Tokyo,
not to mention the ever-present possibility of trouble at the
controversial new airport there. James Murrow was due to
arrive at ten-thirty in the morning on the following day, and
there was a good deal to be done before he did.

The first thing was obviously to make contact with Bernard if he was at the house, and to set up the funeral arrangements. Walker looked up the number and dialled it, not
greatly optimistic about the prospect of a reply. In fact Bernard answered almost at once, sounding quite self-pos-
sessed. He explained that he had been expecting Walker's call
and that he had already put matters in hand. It was noticeable
that after Walker had identified himself Bernard at once began to speak English, and this Walker found oddly irritating.
Moreover, his assurance that Walker would be welcome to

go to the house at any time sounded at once a shade proprie-
torial and almost sociable. It was with some stiffness that he
told Bernard to expect him in about half an hour, and put the
receiver down.

At this time of the day the interurban train was very much
quicker and more comfortable than going by car. Nevertheless, it was more like an hour later that Walker made his way
from the station and stopped short as he rounded the corner
of the street in which Murrow's house stood. When Bernard
had said that arrangements were in hand Walker had visualised something in the nature of telephone calls. In fact, work
had already begun on the "dressing" of the house.

The exterior fence, which was of plain wood some seven
feet high, was already half covered with cotton drapes in
broad vertical bands of black and white, and two young men
who looked like students were helping an old workman with
the next stretch. Women of the neighbourhood stood about
watching and talking quietly. Many were in summer kimonos, and the whole street had taken on an almost medieval
aspect, in spite of the cars parked here and there.

Walker approached the open front door, consciously ignoring the curious glances of the women and of the three men
at work outside, and found Bernard draping the tiny entrance
hall with plain white material which looked like silk but was
more probably nylon. Walker's momentary irritation with the
young Japanese had long since passed, and as Bernard sank
to his knees and bowed low in greeting he himself bowed and
tried clumsily to express his condolences. Bernard received
them with silent dignity, then rose and said, "Won't you
please come this way, Mr Walker?"

Taking off his shoes, Walker stepped up into the house and
followed Bernard to the principal room, where a large photograph of Murrow, its frame draped with black silk, had been
set up on a makeshift altar in the alcove. It felt strange to be
sitting there under the likeness of the dead man's eye discussing the arrangements for the funeral. Bernard had so obviously taken charge that at first there seemed little for Walker
to say beyond explaining about the arrival of the brother the
following day. It then emerged that the transformation of the

55

house was solely in preparation for the reception of the visitors who would call to express formal regrets.

"I didn't know Mr Murrow very well," said Walker. "But I feel that he would have wished for the traditional Japanese forms to be observed. May I say how very grateful we are to you for the arrangements you are making here, Hirata-san?"

"It is my duty," said Bernard simply. After an awkward pause, Walker told him about the wish of Murrow's mother that her son should be cremated and that his ashes should be given a Christian burial. The funeral service would therefore have to be conducted by the English chaplain, and the final rites would take place at the foreigners' cemetery.

Bernard's composure seemed almost too perfect. He sat calmly on his cushion, the stillness seeming odd in a beefy young man in blue jeans and an open shirt. The only times the merest shadow crossed his smooth face were at the mention of Murrow's mother or brother, and he nodded agreement to everything Walker said. Only once did he take the initiative, on hearing that the dead man's brother was due to arrive at ten-thirty in the morning. He asked his first name. "James," said Walker.

"I hope that it will not be inconvenient for Mr James Murrow to receive the condolence visitors here from three in the afternoon of the same day," said Bernard in a manner which admitted no dissent. "You will please bring him at two-thirty. It is customary for gentlemen in European dress to wear a black arm-band."

"I know," Walker replied rather sharply. "I have been to funerals in Japan before."

Bernard nodded stiffly. "I have asked my friends to take charge of the table outside the front door. They will receive the name-cards and incense money, and distribute the return gifts as the visitors leave. I have ordered mourning handkerchiefs in suitable boxes from the undertaker. I hope that I have not acted wrongly."

"Of course not," said Walker hastily, glad to be reminded of the obligations of the representatives of the deceased. An awkward silence fell, and Walker racked his brains for something else to say, conscious of beads of sweat

56

trickling down his arms in the stuffy, oppressive heat of the room. Bernard eased his departure. "Thank you for your call, Mr Walker. My friends and I will now be clear about what we should do. I believe you said that the funeral would be on Wednesday? Then on Thursday I think that Mr Murrow from England will wish to go through his brother's possessions to settle his affairs. I believe he will find everything in order."

It was Walker's turn to nod. "I'm sure he will," he said, getting to his feet. "I must leave you now, Hirata-san. I'll see you at two-thirty tomorrow."

Hanae was putting the bedding away in the big cupboard when Otani came upstairs from the bathroom in his underpants. "Will you wear your uniform today?" she asked as he hovered indecisively.

He made up his mind suddenly. "No. I think not. I may have to go to see Ambassador Tsunematsu in Osaka. He's very touchy about police uniforms." Hanae pulled a face as she handed him a plain white shirt and stood with the trousers of an ordinary "salary-man" suit over her arms waiting while he buttoned it up. "You can't really blame him," Otani went on. "Men of his age have no particular reason to welcome visits from the police."

Hanae indulged in a mild explosion. "I think you're much too patient with people like that," she said. "I could understand it with Father when he was alive, but Tsunematsu-san isn't very much older than you are. He's been glad enough of your help before this." She paused, curious. Otani had come back very late on Saturday night, and had been uncommunicative about his abrupt decision to look in at the office the previous day, telling her he would join them all at the restaurant for lunch. In the old days when he had been active as an investigating officer he often used to discuss cases with her, but it happened much more rarely now. "I thought Kimura-san did all your work with the Foreign Ministry staff now," she said in an exploratory way.

Otani looked at her with pretended grimness, and finding it hard to keep a straight face turned to the open door of the hanging cupboard to choose a tie. He had six, and they were all virtually identical anyway. "Madam," he said in his best formal official manner, "you are most unconvincing when you attempt to mislead the authorities. What you really want to know is why I went to my office yesterday, and why Kimura wanted my help on Saturday."

"Yes," said Hanae in a small voice.

He looked at her. "I haven't time to tell you now, Ha-chan. And it doesn't make sense anyway. We'll have that expensive steak tonight and I'll try to explain then. You know that if a foreigner is killed things become complicated anyway. When it's murder it becomes more complicated still. I've had to take charge of this case myself. Now, no gossiping to Aki-chan on the phone. Or to the ladies in your cookery class at the YWCA." He had no idea what the initials stood for, and would have teased Hanae unmercifully if he had. It would have been a perfect comeback for her occasional remarks about his precious Rotary Club.

Hanae bridled. "I *never* gossip about your work," she protested.

"I know that. That's why I talk to you about it when you ask. Wait just a little, *ne*?" She nodded, content, and preceded him down the stairs to fetch his lacquered lunch box from the kitchen. Otani looked at it in her hands as he put on his shoes in the outer entrance. "What have you given me today?" he enquired.

"Nothing special. Wait and see at lunchtime." Hanae handed it to him and they exchanged the formal farewells being said in millions of households throughout Japan at about that time of the morning: "I'm going and returning!" with the invariable answer, "Go and welcome back!"

Kimura was waiting for Otani in the Commander's big office, a large envelope under his arm. He too was wearing a nondescript dark suit and tie with a white shirt, which had the effect of diminishing his personality, though the eyes were as lively and questing as ever.

"I gave you a busy day yesterday," Otani said, a more perfunctory apology in his voice.

"Busy, but interesting," said Kimura chirpily. "And

thank you for the beer, Chief.'' He offered Otani the envelope. "I don't like to let this out of my sight," he remarked, "and I don't think you will. There are over eighty names on the list. Some of the foreigners may not be of interest . . . I checked all the cards and picked out all those with coded notes on the back. There are a much higher percentage among the foreigners than the Japanese.''

Otani took the envelope to his desk, sat down and slit it open with a paper-knife fashioned like a miniature samurai sword. Inside were almost a dozen foolscap-sized sheets of photocopy paper, neatly clipped together. Otani spread them out on the sheet of glass before him. When he had been appointed to his command the Governor of Hyogo Prefecture had presented him with a handsome leather blotter, which now reposed in a cupboard against the extremely improbable eventuality of the Governor's taking it into his head to pay a call. It was ridiculously small for a man who liked to spread himself.

Kimura positioned himself at Otani's elbow and went on talking. "There were a couple of hundred cards for *gaijin*," he said. "More than half were VBM—Visiting Business Men. I'm sure I was right about that, by the way. Some of them evidently come to Japan quite frequently. Most of the rest were residents. A few teachers, officials, the American doctor and so on, but mainly business people again. Tokyo, Yokohama, the usual addresses.''

"You can tell me about the foreigners later," said Otani. "Let me look through these Japanese." He studied the sheets in silence for a while, then sat back and took off his glasses, polishing them to an unnecessarily glittering perfection to give himself time to think. "Are you sure you can trust your translator?" he said at last. "He hasn't seen these," said Kimura. "I did the weeding myself, and put him to work on the others. Those are my own translations of the English notes. Where I've been able to make anything of them, that is.''

Otani picked up a second sheet and shook his head slowly as he studied the photocopied face and reverse of each of the eight or so cards reproduced on it, with the Japanese version of the notes in Kimura's neat calligraphy beside each one.

Then he turned to a photocopy of a group of foreigners' cards. These, though the same size as the others were printed on both sides, the name and description in English on the reverse.

"Murrow filed those with the English side to the front," said Kimura helpfully, "and squeezed his notes into the spaces on the Japanese side. As I say, there were a lot of these with the coded type of notes. Look at this one, for example." He extended a slim finger to the middle of the sheet. Only the odd word was in Japanese, and Otani gazed at the entry without comprehension. The name was that of a German business representative, apparently resident in Yokohama, the notes pure gibberish:

> 71 through G. 72-4, 6,7 (2) then HL
> 73 — AK or ST
> 50 — 75 punctual

"What do you make of it?" Otani asked.

"Nothing much yet," Kimura admitted. "Except that it doesn't seem like much of a code to me. I'm no cryptographer, but I'd say it was very amateurish; more like a kind of shorthand probably."

Otani reflected. "We could get help from the Security Service, but . . ." He was interrupted by the buzzer on his telephone, and picked up the receiver. After listening for a moment, he put his hand over the mouthpiece and raised his eyes to heaven. "Sakamoto," he said to Kimura. "Would you like to stay while I see him?" Kimura grinned and shook his head. "In ten minutes," said Otani crisply, and put the phone down.

"No thank you, Chief. I seem to annoy Sakamoto-san just by being in the same room."

Otani grunted indulgently. "I know the feeling," he said. "Very well, Kimura-san. Take these papers away and see what you can do with them. And keep the cards in your personal custody. If we can do without the security people so much the better. I have a feeling they may already be in on the edge of this one, and I don't like it a bit."

After Kimura left the room Otani sat brooding. The fact

that Ambassador Tsunematsu had taken the unusual step of telephoning him at home, and on a Sunday, was indicative of a sensitivity which might or might not be justified in the circumstances of the murder of a foreigner of solid professional status and modest local personal fame. Even so, there had been something about his insistence on being kept informed about the progress of the investigation which nagged at Otani, especially in the light of what the file of name-cards had revealed about the extent of Murrow's circle of acquaintances. He decided to telephone Tsunematsu in the afternoon, when there might be more to go on. In the meantime, there was Inspector Sakamoto to be sorted out. Otani braced himself, and picked up the phone to tell his clerk to send him in.

Walker made his way to Sannomiya Station and took the Hanshin electric train back to Osaka, walking the mile or so through the business district from the terminus to the Consulate General and arriving there just before lunchtime. As he entered the bank building which housed the offices he noticed that the tattered posters which detailed numerous complaints by the Japanese bank staff against their British employers were now almost unreadable. This reminded him that he was running short of ready cash, and he made a small diversion into the banking hall, scribbled a cheque and passed it to the meticulously courteous teller, cool and immaculate in his white shirt with an incongruous red arm-band proclaiming that he was in bitter dispute with the management. Behind him in dim recesses of the banking hall pink young English under-managers worked quietly in their little alcoves. Walker almost asked the teller how the go slow was proceeding, but decided against and made his way out of the building again to find a quick lunch before what promised to be a heavy afternoon's telephoning.

When he did get back to his own room shortly after one, he found a little heap of neatly labelled cuttings on his desk, and went to thank little Miss Tsuchida in the Information Section. She blinked with pleasure through her large and unsuitable glasses at him, gratified at having anticipated a probable request for the cuttings, and returned happily to her earnest scrutiny of a two-month-old edition of the *Illustrated London News*.

There was nothing new in the cuttings, just more of them; and Walker pushed them to one side. The first thing he ought to do was to let the police know about Mrs Murrow's instructions over the funeral. After wondering momentarily whether Endsleigh had really meant it when he had delegated responsibility to him, he took the bull by the horns and asked the switchboard operator to connect him with the Commander's office at prefectural police headquarters, feeling rather dashing as he did so.

As he waited to be put through, Walker ran through in his mind some of the appropriate formal courtesies which he would need if the Commander proved to be there and willing to speak. He was more than a little relieved when the operator said, "Mr Walker? The Commander is not available just now. Inspector Kimura is on the line." Kimura was affability itself, thanking Walker fervently for the message and assuring him that it would be conveyed to Otani right away. He added that the British representatives could be assured that the investigation was proceeding with all speed, and that he, Kimura, would personally advise the hospital authorities that the, er, late Mr Murrow's, ah, remains were to be handed over to the undertaker who generally dealt with the English church. Did Mr Walker know who that was? He did? That was just great.

Walker rang off in a slightly bemused state, which persisted during much of his next conversation, which was with the Chaplain to the Missions to Seamen. The Reverend Hilary Allsop was not known as Ballsup among the expatriate community for nothing, and it took some time for Walker to get it across to him that Murrow was not only dead but in urgent need of a funeral. When eventually he grasped the point, the padre became quite enthusiastic, pointing out that he could probably get the Bishop of Kobe to officiate. This would almost certainly please the old gentleman, who had, Mr Allsop thought, never had the chance to bury an Englishman before.

Walker took a firm line and repeated the details of the ultimate agreed arrangement several times, emphasising that the Consul General would be present and that the Consulate General would make all necessary contact with the undertaker. All Mr Allsop had to do was to arrange for the Church to be opened on Wednesday afternoon, take the service and preside over the interment of the ashes at the cemetery afterwards.

Even though he had to do it in Japanese, negotiating with the undertaker was simplicity itself after dealing with the chaplain, and Walker decided he had everything pretty well buttoned up by the time he left the office at the end of the afternoon. At least James Murrow should have no cause for complaint about the efficiency of the Consulate General when he arrived the next day. As he got up from his desk and wiped his hands, sweaty from the telephone, Walker looked down at the blurred newspaper photographs of Murrow in the cuttings on his desk, comparing them in his mind's eye with the portrait swathed in black silk he had seen at the house earlier, and the living David Murrow as he remembered him. He wondered idly whether brother James would be tall and blond too.

"I had a difficult conversation with Tsunematsu in the end," said Otani, standing in the bathroom doorway. Hanae had given him his own bath and he was now lounging at ease in a fresh cotton yukata, watching Hanae take hers after him. Her hair protected by a small towel, she had first tipped several bowls of warm water over her body and soaped herself thoroughly before rinsing off in the same way and finally stepping into the clean hot water in the deep square bath itself. She now sat immersed up to her chin, knees drawn up to her still shapely breasts. Although Otani greatly enjoyed Hanae's ministrations nearly every evening, he rarely returned the compliment by offering to wash her. As Hanae herself pointed out with ill-concealed satisfaction, it almost always led to one thing.

"Hardly surprising," she now said. She had listened enthralled to Otani's account of the Murrow menage and the article in the Tokyo magazine devoted to gracious living; of the equivocal status of the Hirata boy in the household and of the discovery of the collection of name-cards. Though Otani had mentioned no names and she had not pressed him to, her eyes grew wide when he told her that the list included several politicians, including two of very high rank, a number of senior officials and prominent film and television personalities. He said nothing about the annotations on the backs of the cards. Time enough for that if and when Kimura managed to decipher them.

"I formed a strong impression that the Ambassador was trying to pump me to see how much I knew about the foreigner's circle of friends," Otani continued after a pause. "Needless to say, I didn't mention the cards, but said I would quite expect that as a fairly well-known foreign resident he would have got to know a lot of people here in the Kansai. But Tsunematsu kept hinting that there should be as little publicity as possible, and altogether sounded more uneasy than he should have been under the circumstances. Much the same as when he rang me here yesterday, but more pressing."

"There must be some scandal and he doesn't want it to come out," said Hanae firmly, standing up in a small cascade of water like a naiad and pulling out the bath-plug.

"Well, that's beginning to become fairly obvious," Otani said, handing her another tiny hand-towel with which Hanae dabbed her plump but comely body more or less dry before slipping into a similar yukata and uncovering her hair. "What interests me is whether there might be a connection with the murder. Anyway, I shall let Kimura do most of the puzzling about that. We had a message from the British this afternoon. They had a cable from London. It seems that a brother will come tomorrow to represent the family. Funeral Wednesday. He had no father living. His mother is staying in England."

"Poor woman," said Hanae as she went to the kitchen to serve their evening meal. "It must be dreadful for her."

Tuesday

A QUICK GLANCE AT THE ARRIVALS BOARD ESTABLISHED that the Cathay Pacific Flight from Hong Kong via Taipeh was expected to be twenty minutes late. Walker usually filled in waiting time at the airport quite happily, browsing through the magazines at the bookstall or sitting over a beer watching the world go by. It promised to be a complicated sort of day, though, and he fidgeted restively until a whirring, clattering sound came from the indicator board and the little matt black rectangles rearranged themselves to announce that the flight mentioned in the second telegram from London was on the ground.

As Walker approached the Customs area he took his diplomatic identity card from his pocket and handed it to the security man on duty at the staff doorway. The guard was a wizened, almost elderly man with a face like a walnut, and he studied the card with care and every appearance of deep suspicion, sucking in air through his teeth as he did so. At last he handed it back to Walker, saluted and waved him through officiously. The first passengers were already at immigration on the mezzanine floor at the back of the hall, and Walker posted himself where he could see them come through. Experience had made him confident that he could spot a lone British male among a planeload of travellers of mixed nationalities, but the recollection of David Murrow's height and colouring proved a hindrance rather than a help.

The man Walker eventually approached after a good deal of hesitation was not tall and blond. He was plump, untidy and prematurely balding, looking at least forty, and was wearing a cheap-looking suit which must have been in a thoroughly crumpled state even at the beginning of the long flight from London. It now looked quite deplorable, and the bags under its wearer's eyes contributed to an effect at once pathetic and repulsive. Nevertheless, the man admitted to being James Murrow, and pointed out a plastic suitcase on the baggage carousel as his. Walker offered to deal with it, and for this purpose took Murrow's dog-eared passport with the case over to the Customs bench. On the way he flipped through it with a practised hand, curious to see the entries for age and occupation.

James Murrow was just over twenty-eight, and described himself unhelpfully as "salesman". He had travelled widely, but only in Europe so far as Walker could tell from a quick glance. The Customs officer was more impressed than the security guard had at first been by Walker's diplomatic pass, and he took Murrow's passport at once, produced a little ivory seal, pressed it on a tiny red inkpad the size of a thumbnail and added an elegant oval endorsement to the immigration stamp. He didn't ask for the case to be opened, which was something of a pity as Walker would have liked a look inside.

Walker went back to Murrow, who was standing apathetically in the middle of the hall, his round, rather dirty face swivelling from side to side as he took in the unfamiliarity of his surroundings. Walker explained that he had a small spare bedroom at his flat and Murrow accepted the offer of hospitality with a reasonable grace as they made their way out to Walker's car. His speaking voice was odd, in that he had clearly been well educated, but had a coarseness and awkwardness of expression which seemed to belie the fact.

In any case, the two men spoke little during the half-hour drive to Walker's flat. Walker tried to express the shock he had felt personally on learning of the manner of David Murrow's death and his belief that the Japanese police would pull out all the stops to clear up the affair. Most of the rest of their perfunctory conversation consisted of the usual clichés about the flight and the oppressive weather, and Walker's few attempts to orient Murrow to his physical surroundings fell flat.

They arrived at the flat shortly before noon, and as Walker lugged the tawdry plastic suitcase up the stairs he found himself hoping that it contained a clean shirt. He was relieved when Murrow appeared after a good half hour in the bathroom looking quite presentable in a dark grey suit, reasonably white shirt and black tie. He had shaved and apparently washed his hair, which was plastered thinly to his pink scalp. Though spruced up to this extent, Murrow was still vague and rather stupid in his reactions. Walker had personal experience of jet lag, and bustled about, ensconcing Murrow in an armchair and providing him with beer. It was something of a relief that Murrow merely sipped at it: it would hard enough for him to stay awake in the afternoon anyway.

"I'm truly sorry you have to go through the business of condolence visits so soon after your flight," Walker said after a while. "But at least all you have to do is sit there and bow slightly as each person passes. The drill is that people come to the house and sign a visitors' book, leaving their cards and gifts at the entrance. The gifts are always sums of money in special envelopes. It's called 'incense money' and in fact goes towards the funeral expenses: a kind of rough and ready social insurance really. Then people file through a sort of improvised shrine where there's a photograph of the . . ." Walker fumbled for the right word, but couldn't find it and continued clumsily, ". . . of the person, and the relatives are there and a priest chanting Buddhist scripture, only there won't be one today because of course David wasn't a Buddhist, and they put a pinch of incense in the burner and bow, and pray for a minute, and then go away."

Murrow gaped at him in silence. "But it may take a couple of hours for everyone to file through," Walker added with a false heartiness which made him wince as he heard his own words, "so you'll be able to sit quietly for that long, and the great thing is that you don't have to say anything. There are

67

some conventional phrases for these occasions, but of course you aren't expected to know them. I'll be beside you and I'll do the talking on your behalf."

Murrow rubbed a pudgy hand over his face before speaking. Then the harsh, unmusical voice broke the silence, his vulgarity jarring on Walker. "Look, mate, you're doing your job and I appreciate your trouble. But I can do without the background notes. It's all a big fat mess as far as I'm concerned. I haven't seen Dave since I was a kid. He never gave a bugger about us, and now I have to chase half-way round the world and sit and *bow* at a lot of creepy Nips because he's been done in."

"I'm sorry," said Walker huffily. "I was only trying to be helpful."

Murrow waved a hand in a vaguely conciliatory way. "Yeah. Yeah. Don't mind me. You just tell me what to do and I'll do it. I'll be a bit more grateful after a night's sleep."

Otani agreed again that it seemed likely that they could expect a welcome thunderstorm within a few days and that this would clear the air a little; but that real relief would not come till after the first typhoon which might not be before late August. Nevertheless, Ambassador Tsunematsu pointed out, here on the coast they did at least have the evening breeze from the Inland Sea to look forward to every day. He had been at the Mayor of Kyoto's reception for the Consular Corps recently and had found the experience distinctly trying. That, Otani surmised, would be because of the surrounding hills. Eventually he was able to ring off, and after doing so he immediately buzzed his clerk to bring some green tea. Most people drank it cold in the summer, but Otani found the cooling effect greater when he took it hot.

When the tea arrived, Otani asked his clerk to see if Kimura was in his office and could join him, then took his cup over to the corner and positioned himself near the electric fan as he sipped. Kimura came into the room before he had finished and nodded sympathetically. "Good morning, Chief," he said. "I really think it's getting hotter."

"Not you too, Kimura-kun," Otani said in exasperation.

"I've just spent at least fifteen minutes discussing the weather with Tsunematsu. That was after I talked him out of going to the foreigner's funeral tomorrow. I told him that it would be a funny way of avoiding publicity for the Foreign Office to be formally represented at the funeral of a private individual. He seemed quite surprised. Well, any news?"

Kimura sniffed and caressed his upper lip. Otani looked at him carefully. "Is that supposed to be a *moustache*?" he demanded.

Kimura had the grace to look confused. "Well, I had thought of growing one," he admitted. "But it's only been a few days . . ." He put his hands firmly behind his back and avoided Otani's eye. "I'm making some headway with Murrow's notes," he said. "The numbers are mostly dates, I think. Most of them are seventy-something, which suggests frequency of meetings. There are others that don't fit, but I'm beginning to have an idea about them. Otherwise . . . let me see. Young Hirata reported in as instructed. The condolence visits at the house are to start at three this afternoon. The brother is arriving this morning, of course. I was wondering if we ought to have someone there to keep on eye on things?"

Otani pondered. "I wonder. I had thought of going along to the cemetery tomorrow myself, more out of curiosity than anything, but I obviously couldn't visit the house. On the other hand, it would be interesting to see who turns up."

"A job for Ninja Noguchi?" suggested Kimura offhandedly.

Otani nodded and walked back to his desk to put his cup down. "Good idea, if he's available. Are you two on speaking terms at the moment?"

Kimura smiled. "Ninja and I get along much better than you might think, Chief. Shall I talk to him?"

"Do. Fill him in generally, but keep quiet about the people on your list. Just ask him to keep a look-out for anyone who doesn't seem to fit. And if he can get sight of the cards people leave at the entrance, it might be useful. Tricky, though."

As it turned out, Murrow comported himself very well at his dead brother's house. Walker had to stop him entering

69

with his shoes on, and he peered in an irreverent way at the photograph, making a curious growling noise in his throat. Then he settled down quietly enough in the place allotted to him in the reception room. In deference to Murrow's unfamiliarity with Japanese ways, Bernard had arranged a back and arm rest for him to make sitting on the floor less uncomfortable.

Bernard himself was pale and dignified in full Japanese dress, the crest of his family on the back and sleeves of his black silk *haori*, the long striped divided skirt of the *hakama* below falling in crisp folds as he knelt and bowed low in formal greeting. He addressed Walker in Japanese and Walker took the hint. James Murrow never guessed that the impressive young Japanese in the traditional clothes and setting of his race spoke English rather more elegantly than he did himself.

On the dot of three the ceremonies began, and the drowsy heaviness of the summer heat became almost insupportable as the long afternoon wore on. Bernard acted as master of ceremonies while other young men in neat suits, obviously fellow-students, received the visitors at a trestle table outside the porch. Bernard posted himself at the entrance to the main room, which had been draped with white cloth to create a kind of corridor through which the visitors passed in single file. Each bowed low to Murrow and Walker; then took a pinch of incense from a bowl, dropped it into the burner and bowed again to the photograph, before going out by way of the garden. Now and then Walker exchanged a few murmured phrases with a visitor, but in general the silence remained unbroken as the heavy smell of incense became more and more cloying.

The visitors were mostly male, but there were a few women among them. The Japanese women without exception wore the kimono, but most of the men were in dark suits. There were a number of Westerners, the Endsleighs among the earlier arrivals. Heather looked charming in her black silk and tiny hat, an expression of solemnity giving her naturally cheerful face the look of small girl reciting a poem. It was the Europeans who spoke to James Murrow, muttering awkward clichés of sympathy. Whenever this happened Murrow lost a little of his listlessness and even shook hands with some. He soon evolved a formula: "Howdjado? Very kind."

It took nearly three hours, and dusk was beginning to gather when the last visitor had gone and Bernard approached Walker with a large bundle wrapped in a white cloth, explaining that it was the incense money and visiting cards. As they left the house the young men had already shed their jackets and begun to strip the cloth coverings from the outer fence, and Walker marvelled to himself at the rapidity of the transition from the traditional formality of the afternoon to the matter-of-fact and unsentimental business of clearing up.

"Yes, of course he can come in as he is. He always does," said Otani into the telephone. He was impatient to get home but had waited about for word from Inspector Noguchi, nominally head of the Drugs Section but in practise Otani's link with the whole spectrum of organised crime throughout the prefecture. The trouble with Noguchi was that he was possessed of such remarkable personal skills that he had to do most of the work himself.

Otani looked at him appreciatively as he shambled into the room. The original *ninja* had been professional assassins and spies employed by the old feudal lords, and evolved a whole repertory of clandestine techniques and a range of disguises so effective that they led to a popular belief that *ninja* could make themselves literally invisible. Noguchi merited his nickname. He was a tough, barrel-chested man in his fifties, and his stocky body was dressed in the clothes of a day-labourer, down to the rubber-soled sock leggings with the separate compartment for the big toe and the faded blue knitted belly-band which protruded from the top of his breeches. His dirty singlet was dark with sweat, and Otani instinctively moved upwind as he rose to greet him. "I take it you didn't offer your own condolences," he said.

Noguchi scratched the grey bristles on his bullet head and arranged his battered features in what passed for a smile. "Wouldn't have been much chance of hanging around if I'd gone in," he said. "Decided to do a bit of work on some-

71

body's fence instead. Be pleased when they get back and find it freshly creosoted. Name of Wakabayashi, according to the sign on the gate.''

"Well,'' Otani asked. "Did anything strike you?'' Noguchi raised a hand and ticked off the fingers one by one.

"Whatever that *gaijin* was up to, he had some funny friends. One of old Yamamoto's boys was there, a heavy from Yokohama that I happened to recognise, and young Suzuki from Nagoya. Those for sure. There were others that had a look about them. A few *gaijin*, all straights as far as I know, and the rest the usual neighbours and so on. A good many professors. Kimura said the guy was a college teacher. Natural they'd send people. Well, I'll be off. Unless you want anything else?''

"Not at the moment. Thank you, Ninja. Keep this to yourself please, except for Kimura.'' Noguchi inclined his head almost imperceptibly and was gone almost before Otani had finished speaking. Otani went back to the desk and picked up the telephone to tell them to send Tomita round with his car. Unusually, he lit a cigarette as he left the room, even though he tried to do without them in the car as a rule. He had been told about the contents of the plastic bags in Kimura's cupboard, and had rather a lot to think about.

Walker had no hesitation in giving them both a drink when they finally arrived back in the flat at Ashiya and settled down to go through the envelopes of incense money. Murrow seemed to pay only perfunctory attention as the pile of banknotes grew, but Walker's interest mounted as he began to assess the likely final amount. He had heard that this kind of gift on the death of a prominent person could amount to the equivalent of many hundreds of pounds, and this proved it. Eventually he looked up at Murrow. "Nearly a million yen,'' he almost whispered. "Getting on for two thousand pounds!''

A slow smile spread over Murrow's coarse features. "That,'' he said with satisfaction, "is a useful bit of bread. What was it you said this morning? Handouts from the neighbours to pay for the funeral? Should be a good bit to spare, right?'' Walker picked up a stack of empty gift envelopes and

72

riffled through them, the opulent paper fatly soft in his hands. He shuffled them and looked unseeingly at the beautiful calligraphy on them, mostly done in the old way with the brush, but a good many with a black felt-tipped pen.

"Yes," he said thoughtfully. "Yes. I should think there's at least three or four times what will be needed here. And of course we don't know how much David was worth anyway." Murrow picked up one of the envelopes in fat fingers and turned it over curiously. "What's it say?" he demanded.

Walker leaned over to look at it. Then, becoming unpleasantly conscious of the stale, sweaty smell of his companion, he took the fold of paper from him and studied the writing. "Well, this particular one is fairly typical," he said. "It says, 'Condolences', and then gives the name of the person. He's called Something Nakamura—I can't read the first name—and he's a professor at David's college. Like a visiting card, almost. Then down here is the amount of the gift, written in Chinese numerals. Two thousand five hundred yen. About a fiver. Quite correct and appropriate for a man in his position and relationship to David."

"Good old Nakamura," said Murrow. The more Walker saw of this unprepossessing creature, the less he liked him. Since he had grown up there had been a couple of deaths involving his own modestly cultivated, minor professional family circle; and he was conditioned to put a premium on quiet dignity in such circumstances. Murrow's tetchy irreverence and crude personal behaviour—he had twice audibly farted during the ceremonies at the house without apparent embarrassment—seemed very shocking to him. Nevertheless, Walker pulled himself together. "Will you check this money over with me, please?" he asked. "Then I'll lock it away here and put it in the safe at the office tomorrow."

They sorted out the notes into piles by denomination. It was all paper money, the smallest unit being five hundred yen, and the job was soon done. They agreed the total of 943,000 yen, and Walker sealed the notes in a large manila envelope which he locked in his official Government briefcase. The briefcase itself he locked in his desk. "That will

73

have to do for tonight," he said to Murrow. "I expect you're hungry."

"Bit peckish, since you mention it," said Murrow in a friendly enough way. The two men left the flat and Walker led the way to a small Western-style restaurant nearby. Here Murrow's appetite burgeoned and he made a hearty dinner. He even asked Walker a few questions about himself, but Walker felt heavy and listlessly depressed and made little effort to respond. He was just moodily finishing the last mouthful of breaded pork cutlet when Murrow's harsh voice broke the silence which had fallen.

"That money, and whatever Dave turns out to have left. Can I get it to England?"

Walker had at the back of his mind realised that this would have to be gone into, but had not had the time to look up the rules. "Well, of course there'll be a good many formalities with the Bank of Japan, but I'm sure we'll be able to arrange everything satisfactorily. What we don't know yet is whether David made a will."

This seemed to amuse Murrow, who grinned as he poured himself another glass of beer. "That's not very likely. Blokes his age with no family don't make wills. You might just as well expect me to make a will." He surveyed Walker over his glass. "I know what I meant to ask you," he said. "How did all that lot know when to come? This afternoon, I mean."

Walker didn't like to seem ill-informed, but had to think for awhile. "Well, so far as the neighbours and the university people were concerned, the word soon got round. That chap in the Japanese dress will have phoned the university."

"Dave's poofy pal, you mean?"

Walker nodded frostily. "And I told the Consul General and had messages passed to the foreigners who would have been likely to know David. I don't know about the others. David's death was mentioned in the papers, of course, and I expect people rang the house. That would be normal. Quite often there's a special announcement put in the local paper. That might have been done." He was floundering, and knew it. He also had a small suspicion that Murrow knew it too.

They finished their meal and returned to the flat, and

Walker nervously checked that the desk, his briefcase and the envelope containing the incense money were all undisturbed. It was still only nine in the evening, but Walker was not surprised that Murrow took himself off to bed at once. Part of his boorishness might well have been due to simple exhaustion after the long flight from England. Then there were the personal and emotional pressures to which he had been subjected so soon after his arrival in Japan, no matter what he had thought of his brother. All the same, it was good to be free of his company for the first time in many hours. Walker poured a rather larger whisky than he usually permitted himself, and reflected on the events of the day as he drank it. He went to bed himself before ten o'clock.

Wednesday

WALKER FOUND THE ACTUAL FUNERAL SOMETHING OF an anticlimax. He had spent the morning at the office catching up with routine work and setting afoot enquiries into the procedure for remitting the proceeds of David Murrow's estate to England, leaving James to his own devices at the flat until he went to pick him up in time for the service. Only a handful of people turned up at the dreary little brick-built Anglican church used by the British community and a few American episcopalians, and the colourless monotone in which Mr Allsop hurried through the service matched his moon-pale face. The Endsleighs were there, and after the concluding prayers took the padre with them in their official car to the cemetery. It was taken for granted that Walker was James Murrow's keeper, and the two of them made for Walker's car without speaking.

The pressure of development over the years has led to saturation point in building between Kobe and Osaka, and the two cities form a single sprawl along the narrow stretch of relatively flat land near the coast. On the other side of Kobe towards Akashi and the next sizeable town of Himeji there is still even now a hint of the old Kobe of treaty-port days, with a few big old houses still occupied by the representatives of the venerable trading companies estab lished in the nineteenth century. It was to Futatabi on the western outskirts of the city that the original cemetery for foreigners and a few Japanese Christians had been transferred and to which David Murrow's unobtrusive cortège made its way.

The hearse had gone ahead to the strictly functional little city crematorium, and by the time the little group of mourners had ranged themselves around the small hole indicated by the Japanese custodian they had only a few minutes to wait before the big black vehicle, more like a cross between a delivery van and a small motor caravan than the hearses of England, turned in at the gates below. The sun had broken through for the first time in days, and though it was blisteringly hot on the hillside above the built-up area, there was less humidity in the air. The crickets were very loud and the grass round the graves smelt sweet.

They all watched as the undertaker's man in his formal morning suit approached, holding a neat little whitewood casket in his outstretched arms. The Reverend Hilary Allsop, whose surplice was billowing in the slight breeze in the approved manner and who was leafing interestedly through his prayer book as though reading it for the first time, suddenly looked up. With an affable smile he pointed the prayer book at Walker, who waved a cautionary hand at the casket bearer and directed his attention to Murrow.

As he took delivery of his brother's ashes, Murrow at first reacted as though he had been stung, and looked around a little wildly. "I think you're supposed to kneel down and put it in the grave," Walker muttered to him out of the side of his mouth, realising that no guidance seemed likely to be forthcoming from any other quarter. A little mat had been laid at the side of the shallow hole dug to receive the casket, and Murrow knelt clumsily, then gingerly laid his burden down.

As the chaplain intoned the final prayers and the benediction, Walker looked around surreptitiously at his companions. James Murrow had his eyes wide open and stared blankly in front of him, dark patches of sweat showing on

77

his back and sides. Bernard, in European dress, looked cool and unflustered in spite of the heat. His shirt was crisp and immaculately white, his enigmatic face immobile as he kept his eyes fixed on the parson. Heather Endsleigh's nose was twitching, but her eyes were closed; and one gloved hand rested on her husband's forearm. The Consul General was beautifully turned out as always, but from time to time dabbed his forehead with a large and snowy handkerchief. Walker himself felt hot, sticky and curiously ill at ease.

They were of course by no mean the only people in the cemetery. Nevertheless, it was not until the interment of the ashes was complete and the temporary wooden marker in place that Walker realised, in the middle of a reminder to Murrow that his instructions for a permanent headstone would be needed, that three Japanese had remained fairly near the party of mourners throughout. Two of them, Walker was fairly sure, had been among the visitors of the previous day. They were middle-aged and dressed in correct but indefinably flashy suits, unlike the baggy and old-fashioned clothes of the professors who had come from the university to pay their respects, or the humdrum attire of the officials and other middle-class people who had predominated throughout the afternoon.

These two wore sunglasses, too; and stood loosely, feet slightly apart, hands hanging at their sides as though not properly attached to their bodies. The third man was some distance away and was quietly watching the other two. Though he was not in uniform, Walker thought he looked uncommonly like Police Superintendent Otani. Whether he was or was not, he was certainly not disposed to catch Walker's eye.

The Endsleighs had offered to take Murrow back with them for the evening, and as soon as he decently could, Walker handed him over to them, volunteering to take the padre back into town. He gave Murrow a key to the flat, and agreed with him that they would go through his late brother's papers and possessions the next day.

Otani felt a little remorseful at having excluded Inspector Sakamoto from his council of war, but had always preferred to think aloud in the company of Kimura and Noguchi. Sakamoto the stiff-necked would have been bound to draw attention to some obscure regulation and insist on its punctilious observance. He had, needless to say, sternly acknowledged his Chief's undoubted right to take personal charge of the investigation into the murder of David Murrow and had stalked off in a huff in which, with luck, he would remain for some days.

"You didn't see the body, of course, Ninja. The wounds might have given a lead," said Kimura. They were all sitting in Otani's office at the end of the afternoon.

"Had a look at the pictures," Noguchi grunted, sipping his tea with surprising delicacy. He was dressed slightly more conventionally than on the previous day, in a shabby cotton jacket, open shirt and drill trousers with sandals. He looked like a deck-chair attendant. "Knife job. Knew what he was doing."

Otani stirred. "Would you say it was a professional?" he asked.

"Fairly safe bet," said Noguchi. "No trademark that I could see in the pictures, but that lad had done it before, take it from me." He had never been known to address Otani as "sir" or in the honorific third person, but tended to put questions to him in a manner which for him constituted courtesy, and Otani knew and appreciated it. "I understood you to say that you saw a couple of mobsters at the cemetery? Together?" he now asked.

Otani nodded. "Together. And they were talking to each other. I'm sure the Hirata boy noticed them. He didn't look at all happy to see them."

Noguchi put his cup down. "Were you able to see them arrive or go?"

"I saw them go. They split up. One drove off in a blue Mazda with an Osaka registration. I have the number for you, Ninja. The other stopped a taxi. I went by taxi myself, of course, but I expect they knew me."

Kimura stretched his legs and contemplated the gleaming toe-caps of his shoes. "I have something to report, Chief," he said carefully. "The Governor's chief secretary was on the phone this afternoon while you were out. He wanted to speak to you, but asked for me when he was told you weren't available.'' Otani raised an eyebrow, but said nothing, waiting for Kimura to continue.

"He spent a good deal of time coming to the point, but eventually what it amounted to was that the Governor had been told of an interest in this case in Tokyo. Then he said something about the election campaign. Expected it to be uneventful.'' Kimura looked up. "Well, I'm not so clever as you at sorting out the nods and winks that the politicians go in for, but I got a distinct impression that we were being warned off.''

Released from immediate duties after dropping the padre at his house, Walker drove to a little tea-room of the kind which abound in Kobe and ordered iced tea with lemon and a cake from the solitary waitress, who was all gentle femininity to the hem of her overall dress. Thereunder she was all hearty girlishness, with sturdy muscular legs descending to ankle socks and white tennis shoes. After contemplating the salmon-coloured sugary object the girl brought him for a moment, he consulted his diary and crossed the small room to the pink pay telephone, inserted a ten-yen piece and dialled the *Kobe Shimbun* office. Miraculously, Takamura was there.

"Ken, I wonder if I could have some advice from you? And I have some things to tell you—not for the record, I'm afraid. Could we meet please?''

Takamura sounded amused, but his reply was amiable. "Sure, Andy. Glad to see you. My contact at police headquarters says this Murrow business has caused a lot of hustle, but the brass there are playing it like a poker hand.''

They agreed to meet in the lobby of the Kobe Oriental Hotel at seven, which gave Walker time to go back to the flat for a leisurely shower and change of clothes. When he arrived there he glanced in the mailbox in the gloomy little lobby, as was his invariable habit. There were two letters for him. One was the usual monthly member's circular from the Kobe Club, the other a bulky letter which appeared to have been delivered by hand. It was addressed to him correctly and precisely, but though Roman script had been used, the handwriting was, to Walker's eyes, obviously Japanese.

Something about the weight and bulk of the letter made him hesitate to open it. The diplomatic staff in Japan had not yet had to contend with letter or parcel bombs, but had received all the warnings and guidance notes sent out to British missions by the Foreign Office in London. Walker gingerly turned the envelope over, then relaxed as he read the sender's name and address on the back. He remembered that Sei-ichi Hirata was Bernard's real name, and the address was that of Murrow's house.

Reassured, Walker opened the envelope when he had mounted the stairs and was in his flat. It contained two keys wrapped in tissue paper, and a letter on a single sheet. It was in English:

Kobe, 16 July

Dear Mr Walker

Please forgive this impoliteness by writing to you. I have finished all matters concerning the yesterday's arrangements. The bills will be given to your office. The big key is the main door key and the other one is for Mr Murrow's study.

I have taken my books and clothes and have made the house clean, but I have taken nothing which is not mine. I will go to my home in Shikoku to rest after these terrible days.

Please give my respects to Mr James Murrow and take care of yourself in this hot weather.

Yours truly
Sei-ichi Hirata (Bernard)

PS I will see you at the ceremony this afternoon but it will be inconvenient to disturb you then.

Walker found it curiously moving, and flung himself into an armchair to muse about Bernard for a while, rather glad

81

that he wouldn't be there the next day during the business of going through the dead man's belongings. During his stay in Japan Walker had met a good many Bernards: Japanese who were in some ways the counterparts of himself, fascinated by Western ways just as he was himself intrigued by things Japanese.

Every resident foreigner or foreign institution attracted a network of Japanese adherents, ranging from realists and opportunists with a lively awareness of the advantages to be secured from association with *gaijin*, all the way to the pathetic hangers-on who from some accident of heredity or experience were unable or unwilling to be assimilated into a conventional social framework. These found reassurance in the company of strangers to whom their own neuroses and eccentricities might perhaps seem less abnormal.

In the former category were some of the vast army of language students, for whom contact with native speakers was an obvious and commonsense advantage. Some cynical Old Japan Hands among the expatriates borrowed the expression "rice Christians" from the China missionaries to describe all Japanese who sought out Westerners for any reason; but Walker saw no occasion to criticise the motives of earnest students of English, given that proficiency in the language was becoming more and more essential in a surprising variety of occupations in modern Japan.

The motive might be at root economic, but was none the worse for that. Even the bar girls who worked the places favoured by the merchant seamen who put in at Kobe and Yokohama were not wholly mercenary. Success in their profession depended on extracting the money from the sailors' pockets. Nevertheless, many of them learned a good deal more English than the few crude endearments and obscenities that sufficed for most conversations, and were genuinely interested in and curious about the background from which their customers came. In affluent Japan there are plenty of ways to make a living, and the kind of people who throng diplomatic parties have no need of material charity. Benefits of other kinds are a different matter, and people's motives are rarely unmixed.

Bernard had, it would seem, enjoyed a very comfortable and privileged niche as Murrow's Man Friday. It had no doubt worked out very well for both of them. Even the most fluent Japanese speaker among foreigners needs the help of a translator with the written language, especially with the business of form-filling and the routines of officialdom. Bernard had probably also advised Murrow in his endless quest for authenticity and Japanese tradition, perhaps smiling a little to himself in the consciousness of the essential vanity of the enterprise.

In return he had been housed in comfort, instead of sharing cramped and probably sordid quarters with other students. He had no doubt eaten well and sensibly, instead of living on rice and insipid curry sauce. Above all, through daily association with Murrow he had acquired an excellent command of English which would always serve him well, and that elevated status in the eyes of his fellows which comes from being selected as *deshi* or disciple by a person of academic standing. Walker felt sorry for Bernard in the stress which the sudden upheaval in his life had thrown upon him, but reflected that he had not done too badly. And thus reflecting, he roused himself to get ready to meet Takamura.

In the small downstairs room they used for general purposes, Otani switched impatiently from channel to channel in an attempt to find a television programme that would hold his interest, while Hanae looked on a shade apprehensively. She had looked forward to another installment of the account begun a couple of days earlier, but Otani had come home with a face like the thunder which was rumbling in the evening sky far away somewhere. There was nothing to be done when he was in that sort of mood, except busy herself with supper.

Not that he was ever discourteous or overbearing with her; she knew he had tried very hard to make conversation as they ate their chilled *harusame* noodles and the chicken salad she had made to resemble a flower garden. Whenever she had tried to steer the talk round to his own day his face had closed up, though. He mentioned the funeral briefly, and there was a flash of his more usual sardonic humour when he described the extraordinary garb of the English priest. He had looked, he said, a bit like a miniature Mount Fuji in winter.

Then he had plonked himself down in front of the television. With so many channels to choose from he usually found something; but only the sumo wrestling held him for more than a few minutes.

Walker arrived early at the Oriental, but Takamura was already there, brisk in the airconditioning, looking about him like a questing bird. An extroverted Japanese is not a great rarity, but a sensitive and intelligent extrovert Japanese is a pearl beyond price. Walker found himself conceiving a continually higher regard for Takamura, who now led him firmly downstairs to the basement bar. He talked non-stop about the weather, the international news and the forth coming elections until they were ensconced in a corner of the cool, dimly lit room with drinks before them.

"Rule Number One, Mister Vice-Consul," he said then. "If you want to have a private talk, have it in a public place. I could take you to a bar neither of us had ever been in before and within a few minutes everyone in town would know that the British wanted a quiet word with the Press. I could take you to Osaka and the same thing would happen. Or Kyoto. Maybe we could get away with it in Tokyo, but not west of Nagoya. We're both too conspicuous. So we come here. The barman knows us both, but he doesn't care. This is the accepted casual meeting-place, and it doesn't mean a thing for us to have a drink here." He took a deep gulp from his glass after this stagey speech, and looked reflectively at Walker. "So, what's new?"

Now that the moment had come, Walker found it almost impossible to speak. It was not as if he knew Takamura well. Again, in principle Walker disliked and distrusted the trade of journalism. Yet he had a strong instinctive feeling of security in Takamura's presence. Eventually he stopped twisting the cold wet side of the glass round and round with his fingers and looked straight into the other man's bright black eyes.

"I'm out of my depth," he said briskly. "I need advice, and I need it from a Japanese. And I have to ask you to use your own judgement about what you do with what I tell you. You could certainly get me into serious trouble. I don't know about yourself." He paused, and Takamura nodded silently, encouragingly. Walker slumped back in his chair, his long legs awkward under the little table, and told Takamura about the incongruous people at the condolence visiting ceremony, about the reappearance of two of them seemingly under Otani's eye at the cemetery, and about the substantial total of the incense money. When he mentioned the round figure, Takamura confirmed with a little whistle of surprise that it was undoubtedly a remarkable sum.

There was a lengthy silence before Takamura spoke again. "Andy, I almost wish you hadn't told me this," he said at last. "One thing's for sure, I can't use any of it. At least not yet. It smells complicated, and it smells of the mobs. But how could Murrow have got mixed up with them, for heaven's sake?"

Walker shook his head and gave a little sigh. "I'm hanged it I know," he said. Then he smiled briefly. "If it had been his brother James I could believe it. But James looks such a perfect small-time crook that he *must* be innocent." He went on to describe James to Takamura at some length, breaking off only when he realised that he had lost his attention. Takamura was nodding encouragingly from time to time, but his thoughts were clearly elsewhere.

"Sorry, Ken," he said. "James is quite irrelevant, I realise that. Tell me more about your contact in the police."

Takamura shrugged. "He's not a lot of use at the moment," he said. "He's just an ordinary Joe in the criminal investigation section, and he was the one who tipped me off in the first place. Kimura has his lips buttoned up: wouldn't even take a call from me. Normally their cases are kept about as confidential as a billboard on the Takashimaya Department Store building. But it seems Otani has taken personal charge of the case and even cut out my con-

85

tact's own boss. You say you called on Otani. What did you make of him?''

Walker thought for a moment. "I hardly formed an impression," he admitted. "He seemed very stiff and formal, and I was concentrating on interpreting for the Consul General anyway. And later on at the morgue, well, I must admit, I . . . well, I remember the other one better. Kimura.''

Takamura nodded. "Kimura-san's a sharp cookie," he said. "But don't underestimate Otani. Kimura's only half as smart as he thinks *he* is, but Otani's twice as smart as most think *he* is.''

Walker smiled. "That takes a little working out," he said.

Takamura got up. "Maybe, but bear it in mind all the same. Let's go find some food.''

It was no use. Hanae put down the women's magazine she was pretending to read and slipped quietly out of the room. She made herself ready for bed, then went upstairs and took the folded quilts out of the big cupboard in the fine old room in which they slept and received guests on formal occasions. It took only a few minutes to smooth the fitted bottom sheets and place the small hard pillows with their frilly covers on them. Then the light summer top quilt with its snowy white cover, and the small electric lamp directly on the tatami mat beside the bed, and she was almost ready. A new insecticide tablet in the tiny low-power electric gadget which was so much less trouble than the old smouldering mosquito rings; then, after a momentary hesitation, a few paper handkerchiefs tucked under her pillow.

Hanae was lying flat on her back in her side of the bed, her kimono smooth about her, when Otani came up half an hour later, and she said nothing as he moved about, had his usual minute or two at the sliding window looking out at the black water so far away, and finally stripped off his own yukata to get into bed beside her. She reached out an arm and switched off the lamp, then waited until her eyes had become accustomed to the darkness and she could see the dim outlines of the room.

Then she turned and very gently peeled the cover down to Otani's knees. He lay absolutely still, only the smallest sigh escaping him as the warm lips moved over his chest in little fluttering kisses, ever downwards inch by inch towards his belly. Hanae felt happy for him as she neared her destination. It never failed.

Thursday

JAMES MURROW WAS ALREADY UP AND DOING WHEN Walker emerged from his bedroom. He was in fact frying an egg, sipping a mug of instant coffee as he did so. He greeted Walker with a positively cheerful smile. "Morning," he said.

"Good morning. What time did you get back?" Walker enquired.

"Oh, I don't know. About one, I suppose. They drove me back. Nice people the Endsleighs. Took me out of myself. Heather's a nice woman, I thought."

The egg was done and he bore the plate to the kitchen table, on which he had already placed the toaster, bread, butter and marmalade. While he made his own breakfast and Murrow tucked in to his, Walker told him about Bernard's letter and explained that normally the Consulate General would expect to prepare an inventory of the contents of the house. However, things could be greatly simplified since Murrow was here with what amounted to a power of attorney to dispose of his brother's effects.

Breakfast over, Walker began to wash the dishes, then remembered it was Thursday, one of the two days each week when Fujita-san came to clean to flat for him. He shared the services of this fierce old woman with a colleague who lived nearby and had small children. Though Walker met her only occasionally, the arrangement worked well. Fujita-san was wrinkled and brown-skinned, looking more gipsy than Japanese, with a toothless cackle that would have earned her the role of witch in the average Western child's demonology. Her cleaning techniques were a mixture of sporadic intensity and almost Mediterranean nonchalance, but she could certainly be relied on to leave the dishes sparkling clean. This baffled Walker, since Fujita-san haughtily spurned both hot water and detergent; but he gladly abandoned the task scarcely begun, and the two men set off for Murrow's house.

It was not yet nine in the morning, but the day was already sultry and close, and the precipitous hills above the suburb of Ashiya were purplish and misty against a dead grey sky. The faces of the people in the streets were shiny with perspiration, and the young mothers with babies spreadeagled on their backs in cloth harnesses looked miserable in their resignation as they made their way to the shops and markets. Only the old people, the old ladies and even the occasional man in kimono, looked relaxed and coolly leathery and unflustered, ambling calmly along or stopping for a good gossip with a neighbour.

The car was like an oven. Ever after rolling down all the windows, Walker winced as he slid on to the hot plastic of the seat. It was a relief when they started moving and a reluctant soupy airstream cooled things off a little. Walker avoided the main roads wherever possible, and they accomplished the drive to Murrow's house quite quickly.

Japanese houses are hardly ever completely unoccupied, and Murrow's looked blind and dead as they slid the gate to behind them and approached the entry porch. The house looked less mysterious than when Walker had first visited David Murrow in the cold darkness of a winter evening, when the path had been illuminated by candles in little white paper lanterns; and a little shabby now that it had been stripped of the sombre but stately mourning trappings of two days previously.

Walker unlocked the door and they entered. The atmosphere was close and still heavy with the smell of incense, and he slid all the outer screens open to admit as much air as possible. Then he turned to Murrow, who was mopping his face and neck with a grimy handkerchief. "I suggest we start upstairs and go through the house. We can bring things down and collect them in the living-room if you like."

"Suits me," said Murrow, still curiously cheery. They went up the narrow wooden stairs to the small upper floor, but their initial haul was a small one, since all the cupboard contained was a pile of bedding. They carried it and a few small ornaments downstairs, and Walker was struck again by the austerity of classical Japanese furnishing. The upper floor now contained literally nothing. There were no curtains, no chairs or tables; just the polished wood of the frame of the room, the dull roughcast of the earthen walls and the firm resilience of the fitted tatami floormats with their dull golden sheen and brocade edging, illuminated by the diffused light which came through the translucent rice-paper of the window screens. Yet a few cushions, a single hanging scroll and a coolly lucid flower arrangement in the alcove would be all that would be necessary to prepare it for the most ceremonious social occasion.

The contents of the downstairs rooms were almost equally sparse. Even the kitchen boasted only a modest collection of pots, pans and other utensils, though Walker caught his breath at the beauty of the tea bowls, platters and dishes ranged in the cupboard.

"These are really lovely," he said to Murrow.

"What, those soup bowls?" Murrow replied incredulously. "They don't even match. You can have them if you like."

Walker could have wept. "No, they're valuable. At least, some of them are. I couldn't accept them, much as I'd like to."

Murrow seemed surprised at both statements. "Well, I wouldn't give you a quid for the lot. No good to me. Anyway, we shall obviously have to get rid of all this stuff. Ridiculous to think of sending it to England." They moved on, but amassed only a modest heap of articles from the entire house.

Walker had explained earlier that most of David's belongings would be in his Western-style study, but it still came as a surprise to see how little had been needed to equip the rest of the house. The study was Aladdin's cave by comparison; though it too was tidy and uncluttered.

Along one wall were perhaps five or six hundred books, neatly arranged. Half of them were obviously the tools of Murrow's trade. All the standard works for the teaching of English as a foreign language were ranged against sets of the classic authors so unexpectedly popular in Japan. Shakespeare and Milton, of course, then the Brontë sisters, Dickens and what looked like a complete run of Thomas Hardy. There was a good deal of Somerset Maugham, and several Iris Murdochs.

Next to the fiction were several shelves of books about the Japanese language, the history, geography, religion and sociology of the country, and a considerable collection of well-worn dictionaries. The remaining books, nearly all in English, seemed to bespeak a well-furnished, wide-ranging mind. There were volumes of poetry and philosophy, history and biography, travel and reminiscences. Walker pulled out a handsomely bound volume of T. E. Lawrence and glanced through the pages, enjoying the smell and feel of a well-made book. As he put it back he noticed lives of Wilde, Roger Casement and Lytton Strachey nearby. Mildly intrigued, he looked more closely at the shelves of biography and belles-lettres and noted the predominance of Bloomsbury and its fringes. The contents shaded off towards Cocteau, Genet and the moderns and not illogically, Walker reflected, to English translations of the novels of Yukio Mishima. Strange to think that such an evidently fastidious and cultivated homosexual should attract gangsters to his funeral.

He would dearly have liked to browse through the books at leisure, but tore himself away and went instead to the fitted wardrobes on the opposite wall. Several conservative Western-style suits were hanging in an orderly row, and in the shelves at the sides were shirts, socks and a considerable collection of Japanese clothing. The sombre colours of kimonos and *haoris* made the neckties hanging nearby look gaudy and ridiculous. There were no shoes—these would be in the proper cupboard in the entrance hall—and in general there seemed to be little of the impedimenta one would normally expect to find in a man's room. The only apparent concession to sport was a badminton racket propped in one corner. With his height and reach, David Murrow must have been a terror on the court.

While Walker was looking through the wardrobe, Murrow had seated himself at the desk and opened the top drawer. Walker went over and watched as he scrabbled through the papers in it. They consisted of material obviously connected with the university. Students' essays were neatly assembled in a folder, and there were some draft lecture notes and what appeared to be an outline for an essay by Murrow on the origins of the tea ceremony.

The next drawer down contained only miscellaneous stationery—paper clips, envelopes, a ruler, rubber bands, odd pencils and ballpoint pens. The big drawer at the bottom was locked, and Murrow gave a bad-tempered grunt as he tugged at it uselessly. "I suppose we'd better force it," said Walker, then immediately corrected himself. "No, of course David would have had the key on him. All the things he was carrying are still with the police. I'll tell them we need the keys."

Murrow contemplated the locked drawer moodily for a while, then produced a small penknife from his pocket. "No need for that," he muttered as though to himself. "Take me two minutes to get in there." He took a plastic calendar inscribed with the compliments of the Dai-Ichi Bank which was lying on top of the desk and cut a strip off one edge of it, then straightened a paper clip and bent one end of the wire into a ninety-degree angle. Then ponderously he knelt in front of the drawer and worked the penknife blade into the crevice at the top to force a small gap. Into this he slid the strip of plastic, holding it in position with the thumb of the same hand. With the other he inserted the bent paper clip into the keyhole and gently manipulated it. Within a very few seconds there was a sharp click and Murrow beamed expansively as he opened the drawer.

It was empty.

* * *

"Well, what *about* the British?" Otani demanded testily as Kimura stood at the window staring out at the cranes on the skyline of Kobe harbour.

Kimura was minding his manners that day. "Well, sir, we can't withhold Murrow's papers from them for much longer. The Consulate General will be entitled to take over his bank account and other assets. And then there's the brother."

"I saw him at the cemetery. With that tall young fellow who came here on Saturday night." Otani got up himself and went over to his favourite hot weather position by the electric fan. He had been using a hand fan printed with the compliments of Suntory Whisky at his desk, and getting nowhere.

"Yes. Well, I had a call put through to British Airways in Osaka. He has a return reservation for Saturday. The day after tomorrow. They'll want to clear up as much as possible before then."

Otani nodded. "One thing's sure, we won't have an arrest for them for a long time yet, if at all," he said morosely.

"I wonder how much we ought to let the British know at this stage," said Kimura, edging up to the subject again. "We can't do anything about hushing up the money, and they aren't fools. They'll begin to work things out."

"Any word from Ninja?" said Otani abruptly.

Kimura shook his head. "There's hardly been time," he said reasonably, risking another glare. "When he does call in I want to be told personally. At once." Otani's belligerence was interrupted by the buzz of his telephone intercom. "You get it, Kimura," he snapped. He hardly ever left off the familiar "kun" and Kimura jumped to it. "If it's Tsunematsu or the Governor, I'm out. I'll speak to the Emperor or my wife. Nobody else."

Kimura spoke for a few seconds, then listened for a while, then asked the caller to wait. He cupped a hand over the receiver and looked up at Otani. "It's Mr Walker, sir. The

Vice-Consul. Wishes to speak to you personally. Shall I handle it?"

Otani thought quickly, then shook his head, relaxing a little. "No, I'll talk to him. He's not the Emperor, but he represents the English Queen. Almost as good." Kimura grinned as he handed him the receiver. That was much more like it.

It was only after many delays and repeated explanations to subordinate officials at the police headquarters that Walker was finally put through to Otani, who identified himself and expressed his dismay at the continuing hot weather. He hoped it would not mar the pleasure of Mr James Murrow's stay in Japan. Walker was equally fulsome in his response, countering that the nightly thunder was getting nearer and that rain would be bound to fall soon and make the heat less oppressive. He added that Mr James Murrow was of course much occupied with his late brother's affairs and that they were indeed at that very moment at Mr David Murrow's house and unable to find any personal papers. He wondered if the Commander could offer any advice to them in their predicament.

There was a lengthy silence, after which Walker distinctly heard Otani suck in his breath and expel it again with the inevitable time-buying phrase *"So, des'ne . . ."*, which means nothing whatsoever. Then another silence, after which Otani apparently made up his mind, and conveyed to Walker that, though he hesitated to suggest such a thing when they were so busy, Mr Murrow and he might care to come to his office where they could perhaps discuss the problem more conveniently. Indeed, Otani had been hoping to get in touch with the English gentleman that very day, since he understood that Mr James Murrow must return to England before long. It was now just before noon, and Walker made an appointment for two o'clock before ringing off with the appropriate courtesies.

They left the car at the house and walked to the city centre, plunging into the blessed airconditioning of the vast Sannomiya underground shopping centre with its innumerable tearooms, restaurants and smart boutiques. Over lunch, Walker assured Murrow yet again that he was quite certain Otani would throw some light on the mystery of the missing papers. They had searched high and low and found nothing remotely private—no passport, correspondence, cheque book or receipts, and Murrow's previously amiable mood had soured completely. He attacked his food savagely and scowled at the other customers at nearby tables.

"By the way," Walker remarked in an attempt to lighten the atmosphere, "I was most impressed by your technique with that lock. Wherever did you learn it?"

It worked, and Murrow's heavy face cleared as he smirked complacently. "Never you mind," he said mysteriously. "Call it a hobby of mine if you like. But that was nothing. A kid could have opened that. Easy when you know how." It was quite obvious that he was hoping Walker would quiz him further; and for this reason Walker dropped the subject.

They arrived punctually at police headquarters and were shown in at once to Otani's office. The electric fan stirred the heavy air, and Otani himself looked fresh and dapper in his neat summer uniform. He maintained an appropriate solemnity as Walker introduced Murrow, who had relapsed into the settled ill-humour which seemed most natural to him and made no pretence of paying attention while Walker interpreted Otani's polite clichés.

A police constable brought in a tin tray on which reposed three open bottles of Pepsi-Cola and three tumblers, and eventually they were settled in armchairs, the preliminaries over. Walker felt that the substance of their meeting could now be broached, and explained his and Murrow's consternation at having found no personal papers at the house. He was not particularly surprised when Otani embarked on a long and especially flowery speech which boiled down to the statement that the police had searched the house on the night of the murder and taken away any articles which they thought might be of interest or importance to them. Nor was he unduly puzzled by Bernard's failure to mention the fact.

However, when he summarised Otani's remarks to Murrow it provoked a minor explosion of vague but menacing

95

protests about search warrants, intrusion and bloody nosey-parkering coppers. Whether or not he understood any English, Otani could not possibly have failed to sense the drift of Murrow's outburst, but smiled calmly and politely throughout. Walker cobbled up an explanation to the effect that Murrow was upset by his brother's death and was overcome with fury towards the unidentified murderer; and Otani nodded sympathetically.

He then explained to Walker that the police had completed their examination of the dead man's property and were ready to hand over all but one item which they would like to retain, with Mr Murrow's permission. He crossed to his desk and spoke briefly into the telephone, and almost immediately a uniformed officer entered smartly, trundling what looked remarkably like a tea trolley. On it were a number of plastic bags which Otani transferred to the glass-topped coffee table between them with a "help yourself" gesture.

It was in the main an unimpressive and predictable collection of documentation of the kind without which nobody can hope to live and work in any sophisticated country, let alone a foreign one. Passport, international vaccination certificate, driving licence, foreign resident's identity card—all the essentials were there. Then there were a few letters, which bore British stamps and which Murrow leafed through quickly and then tossed back on the table. "From my mother," he said, then turned to a cheque book and a little collection of bank statement sheets, tidily clipped together. These he passed to Walker, who raised his eyebrows as he looked at the figures. Otani spoke.

"Mr David Murrow was a wealthy gentleman," he said quietly. "He seems to have kept a large current account but not trouble to open a savings account which would have earned him a good deal of interest. Over the past year he had never less than three million yen in the bank: yet his salary from the university was two hundred and twenty thousand a month. I wish I could keep a year's salary on hand like that." Otani suddenly beamed expansively, then reverted at once to dignified solemnity. "He also kept a good deal of cash in the house." As he said this he opened another of the plastic bags and tipped out a solid stack of banknotes held together with a rubber band. Murrow's jaw had dropped open, and he gaped like a fish at the sight of the money.

Otani took a piece of paper from his uniform jacket pocket. It was apparently an inventory and from it he read the figure; 605,400 yen. "About twelve hundred pounds," Walker said to Murrow. "And the current account stands at around six thousand." As Murrow absorbed the information, Walker felt he ought to take an initiative. "I take it that there is no question about Mr James Murrow's entitlement to this money?" he asked.

"None that I am aware of," Otani replied. "The bank will transfer the proceeds of the account to the Bank of Japan on the instructions of the Consulate General."

"What is the item you mentioned earlier—that you wish to keep here?" Walker was shaken and knew that his Japanese was becoming clumsy and inaccurate. Otani reached and pulled the trolley to him. On it was a nest of six small plastic drawers. "Do you know what these are?" Otani's Japanese too had changed, becoming perceptibly blunter and less ceremonious.

"Yes of course," Walker replied. "They're for storing *meishi*." He turned to Murrow to explain. "Everybody in Japan uses visiting cards, and they're printed in standard sizes, large for men and small for women. Quite a few people keep the ones they're given and file them in one of these plastic boxes. Makes a useful card index of addresses and phone numbers of everybody you know." Murrow nodded, still looking dazed and glancing frequently at the pile of money as if expecting it to disappear in a puff of smoke.

Otani spoke again. "Several hundred cards in each drawer; six drawers. Over two thousand possible suspects, Mr Walker. It will take a long time to check them all." He smiled again, grimly this time. "Though some may be excluded immediately. Yourself, for instance." Walker reached for the nest of boxes. "May I?" Otani nodded assent. "In the last drawer," he said.

Walker pulled out the bottom right-hand drawer and saw the alphabetical dividers from A to the combined XYZ. He pulled the W divider forward and saw one of his own visiting cards immediately behind it. Many of his diplomatic colleagues adhered to the old formal European style and proffered elegantly engraved copperplate cards to their Japanese acquaintances. Japanese receiving them were hard put to it not to smile at their size, correct for the chancelleries of the West but ludicrously small to their eyes. In Japan they resemble the tiny name-cards, often perfumed, used exclusively by geisha and other women of the demi-monde.

Walker, being aware of this, had provided himself with a supply of proper Japanese cards, printed in English on the face and Japanese on the reverse. He stared at the one in his hand, its very familiarity incongruous in a police chief's office:

ANDREW WALKER
BRITISH VICE CONSUL
HM CONSULATE GENERAL
OSAKA KOBE

"Turn it over," said Otani with an odd expression on his face. Walker did so, and gave a distinct start as he saw that the Japanese side was annotated in small but clear handwriting:

Met soon after his arrival Kansai Oct 76. Encounters at parties, receptions. Came to dinner, pleasant evening. Durham Univ: history. Language attaché at Tokyo previous. Unmarried, straight. Intelligent, long-winded, will become pompous.

Walker was aghast, and his confusion was intensified when he saw the corner of Otani's mouth working and guessed that he would have had the note translated. Otani made no attempt to break the silence, and eventually Walker's brain unfroze. He turned to Murrow. "They want to keep this card index. It has names of practically everybody David knew: perhaps the person who murdered him. The thing is, though, David seems to have made notes on them all. I think we ought to insist on taking it away. His personal comments on his friends are no business of the police."

Murrow pondered for a while. "Well, we want them to catch the bastard, don't we? It's no skin off my nose if they . . ." Their discussion was cut short by Otani, whose eyes had been flickering from one to the other of them and who now spoke with chilling authority. "Mr Walker," he said formally. "You should know that we have of course made photocopies of all these cards. My own translators are working on Mr Murrow's notes. I shall not release the original cards to you, however, because there are comments about some important Japanese citizens which it would not be correct for you to read."

Walker finally decided that James Murrow was basically stupid when, after they left police headquarters with the re-sealed plastic bags, Murrow decided against accompanying him to the Consulate General to put them in the safe there, announcing instead that he would go shopping for souvenirs and find his own way back to Ashiya. Moreover, he would amuse himself in the evening too.

Relieved and perturbed in roughly equal measure, Walker made his way back to the house to collect his car, and arrived back at the Consulate General just before four. He went straight through to the Consul General's ante-room where Jill Braxon, his personal assistant, sat buffing her nails. She looked up at Walker with mild distaste, having long since written him off her list of eligible potential partners. In re-lation to Jill, Walker pursued a policy of determined courtesy and asexuality, tinged with a hint of the embarrassment he almost always experienced in the company of women of his own age.

"Hello," he now said with an ingratiating smile. "CG in?"

Jill gazed levelly at her fingernails. "You could say His Lordship is in, yes," she murmured. "You might indeed say that His Holiness has just finished giving me a stinking rotten annual confidential interview."

Walker felt himself flush with unease. He had not exactly

99

held back when the others had occasionally over lunch capped each other's complaints about Jill's inefficiency and general surliness. Osterley, more robust in his opinions, was inclined to suggest that Jill would be the better for a gang bang by the England rugger team and had been known to admit that he, Osterley, wouldn't be averse to standing by as a substitute in case of injuries. Jill's present remark made Walker remember that he was himself due for a personal interview with Endsleigh before long, and he muttered an incoherent but vaguely sympathetic comment as he tapped on Endsleigh's door, opened it and peered round the edge.

The Consul General was sprawled in one of the armchairs provided for visitors, feet on the low coffee table, reading *Private Eye*. He scowled at Walker. "Come in, come in. Shut the door. Bloody woman." Walker hovered hesitantly just inside the door. "Don't dither, Andrew. Sit down, for the dear Lord's sake. All too soon you will be giving annual confidential interviews to witless, incompetent manhunting secretarial assistants. I wish you joy of it."

He flung the magazine down and rearranged his handsome features into their habitual sculptured repose. "And how are you progressing with our good Mr Murrow?" Walker hesitated, then gave a clear and, for him, brief and economical summary of the day's events. As he spoke, Endsleigh sat motionless and silent, his eyes fixed on Walker.

At the end of the tale he scratched his nose thoughtfully, then apparently off-handedly remarked, "Do you know what Heather said about our fat young visitor? She said he made a violent and quite incompetent pass at her while I was having a pee after dinner yesterday evening. I observed that he was flushed and sweaty when I returned, but attributed it to my brandy, not to his having been inflamed by Heather's charms. She was quite flattered when she told me about it later. I can't think why."

Walker always enjoyed Endsleigh's style, and in spite of his confused state of mind chuckled as he visualised Heather struggling perfunctorily in Murrow's clumsy embrace. "I'm astonished that Heather doesn't have to fight off such advances every hour on the hour," he said gallantly.

Endsleigh smiled sweetly. "We'll make a diplomat of you yet, my boy," he said. "I shall report that remark to my wife without fail. Now what do you make of all this?"

Realising that as yet Endsleigh knew nothing about the incense money and had probably noticed nothing odd about the observers at the funeral, Walker enlarged on these aspects of the affair and, after some hesitation, gave him the gist of his conversation with Takamura. Endsleigh listened attentively, and a long silence fell when Walker finished. When the Consul General did speak, it was incisively and with authority.

"Andrew, I am considerably impressed by the way you are coping with all this. I think it will be more productive in the end if I do not take too obvious a personal interest at this stage, but I should like you to continue to concentrate on it, to the exclusion if necessary of your other work. If I may make the suggestion, your first priority should be to get James Murrow off your hands. Saturday, I think he said. Get him to sign whatever papers are necessary, and give him an official assurance that the money will be transferred in full as soon as possible. He mustn't hang about here. And Andrew," he added as Walker uncurled his lanky body from the chair, "get some of your considerable intelligence to work on the question whether David Murrow was personally acquainted with the overly generous donors of incense money and the gentlemen attending the funeral. I did notice them, and assumed they were anxious to discover the name of my tailor." He smiled briefly and resumed his scrutiny of *Private Eye* as Walker left the room. "Don't forget the reception tomorrow evening," he called after him. "You can bring Murrow if you can bear it."

Ninja Noguchi spent much of the day mooching about the Amagasaki slum area of Osaka, a bottle of cheap *shochu* rotgut protruding from his scruffy jacket pocket. He passed an hour or so in a *pachinko* pin-ball arcade and lost two hundred yen, and late in the afternoon shuffled up to a pay telephone in Osaka Station.

Kimura was with Otani when the call came through.

Otani had overruled Kimura's suggestion that he should be present during the interview with Walker and Murrow, on the grounds that he wanted to force Walker to use Japanese and that Murrow was unlikely to say anything of significance during any exchanges in English the two of them might have. Kimura had not been too happy, and had hovered in the vicinity of Otani's office in case he changed his mind.

Though not at all confident that Otani's understanding of the Western mind was anything like as profound as his own, Kimura listened to Otani's subsequent account of the meeting with interest, and had to admit that the Old Man seemed to have taken the right line. He could get nothing from Otani's occasional brief comments during the conversation with Noguchi and sat fondling his incipient moustache as it went on for rather a long time. He was still puzzling over the initials HL which appeared on a number of the foreigners' cards in Murrow's shorthand notes.

The figures which could not be dates all fell within the range between thirty and one hundred, and were always followed by one of a comparatively few words. "Punctual", "careful", "difficult", and so on. Kimura had almost decided that the figures referred to sums of money in thousands of yen. Substantial but not astronomical sums. The sort of money one would pay for a night with one of the handful of good class call-girls in Osaka, as Kimura knew from occasional personal experience. The very few American and European girls who were on the fringes of the game charged more. HL . . . HL. Of course.

"Home Leave!" he almost shouted in English as Otani finally put the phone down.

"What are you raving about?" Otani enquired. He looked reflective but pleased.

"Sorry, Chief. I've just worked out Murrow's shorthand. It's dates, then a note when the *gaijin* went off on vacation every year or so, then the amounts he paid and whether he paid up promptly or whatever." Otani nodded rather too perfunctorily for Kimura's taste. A word of praise might not have come amiss.

"Yes, well, it makes sense," said Otani. "Now listen to this. Ninja is fairly sure it was a rub-out job done by a group on the edge of the Yamamoto-gumi. Old Yamamoto always claims never to touch rough stuff. But he makes such a thing of being a patriotic Japanese that he might possibly have made an exception for a foreigner, I suppose." He looked up with a touch of excitement at Kimura. "I might just have to go and have a word with him. Now that *would* be interesting."

Friday

IT PROVED SIMPLER AND QUICKER THAN WALKER HAD EX-
pected to complete the official procedures necessary to es-
tablish Mrs Murrow's title as next of kin to her murdered
son's estate, and to register James Murrow's signature as that
of her legal representative in Japan. A simple power of attorney from Murrow in turn to the Consulate General tied it
up, and Walker was able to report to Endsleigh before the end
of Friday afternoon that the formalities were complete. This
prompted a sour remark by Endsleigh that he proposed to arrange a series of murders; they led to such a marked improvement in office efficiency.

James Murrow too had shaken off his lethargy and indecisiveness, and buckled to with great effect, giving clear and
brisk instructions about the disposal of his brother's material
possessions. The clothes were to go to the Salvation Army,
the books and records to the Kobe Club.

In the late morning they paid a formal call on the president
of the university at which David Murrow had taught. The
haggard, defeated-looking old man received Murrow and
Walker with courtly gravity and added to Walker's sense of
financial confusion by handing over a cheque for the equivalent of a year's salary. This was both as an expression of

104

institutional sympathy and in respect of the improvements David Murrow had made to the house, which remained the property of the university. As they left, it had been Murrow who pointed out that they knew from occasional letters that David had spent far more than a year's pay on what Murrow described as titivating it up.

Walker had now been in Murrow's company pretty continuously for nearly four days without managing to draw him out about the family background, and as they made their way to the Endsleighs in the early evening he was still speculating with mild persistence, like being unable to stop exploring with the tongue the socket left after having a tooth pulled. What kind of family could produce as brothers the fastidious, scholarly David with his perfectionist quest for an authentic Japanese life-style, and the sloppy, crude James?

He had occasionally noticed hints of a detached intelligence in the petulant, flawed face; almost as though a sardonic stranger looked out through James' shifty eyes. But these were mere glimpses only, and Walker concluded as he found a parking space within a reasonable distance of the Consul General's residence that he knew Murrow no more and liked him no better than when he had set eyes on him for the first time on Tuesday morning at Itami airport.

The cocktail party was a large, impersonal affair in honour of a party of visiting British members of Parliament. They were already there, exchanging schoolboyish jokes about each others' party allegiances in loud voices. They struck Walker as being both ill-informed and stupid. Not that the Japanese politicians who arrived a little later were any great improvement. The Governor moved about like a diminutive whale surrounded by a shoal of sycophantic attendants while other guests glanced furtively over shoulders as they spoke, busily establishing an inexorable order of importance among those present.

Walker wandered off to a corner where he had noticed Ken Takamura standing quietly appraising the scene, a small smile on his lean face. "There must be a better way to make a living," he observed as Walker approached. "Ever think of that, Andy?"

"Frequently. When my friends at home envy me the life of a diplomat I tell them it's more or less the same as prostitution, without the fun." They stood in companionable silence for a minute or so, then Takamura raised his glass to his lips and emptied it.

"I need another," he said, and turned to move towards the bar. As he passed in front of Walker, he spoke very quietly. "I hear interesting rumours. Go easy, Andy. And keep in touch."

Before they arrived at the house, Walker had warned Murrow of his own protocol obligation to remain until all the Japanese and other guests had left, leaving only the British diplomatic staff behind. The MPs were borne away early by the Governor and his entourage. The other British guests, bound by an equally rigid self-inflicted pecking order, trailed away in the wake of the President of the British Chamber of Commerce. Walker had recently received a number of heavy hints from this worthy about his claims to inclusion in the Honours List and reported them to Endsleigh who had yawned theatrically and removed an invisible thread from his sleeve but shown no other reaction.

When only the Endsleighs, Murrow and Walker were left, Murrow marched up to the Consul General with hand outstretched. "I'm off in the morning, sir," he said with unusual grace, "so I must make my farewells and thank you and Mrs Endsleigh for your kindness." Endsleigh took the proffered hand. "My dear fellow," he said without a flicker of expression, "I'm sure my wife joins me in wishing we could have done more for you."

Heather choked a little on the drink she was finishing, and with difficulty resumed her professional hostess face. "*So* nice to have met you," she cried. "Have a *lovely* flight home, and try to forget all the horrors." Still stiff and formal, Murrow had not finished. "Mr Endsleigh, I feel Andrew Walker here has done far more for me than he needed to. I'd like you to permit him to accept from me the gift of my brother's tea bowls and ceramics. As an expression of appreciation," he added unnecessarily.

Endsleigh looked at him. "That's extremely handsome of

you, Mr Murrow," he said in a voice which sounded surprised. "I can assure you there's no official objection whatever." Walker was almost speechless, and barely managed to mutter conventional thanks to Heather for the party. Then they left.

"Look," Walker protested as soon as they were out of the house, "those things are valuable. I appreciate your kindness, but you did agree this morning that they at least ought to go to England. There's a terrific market for them among collectors there." Murrow shook his head, but said nothing until they were in the car and rolling down the steep hills of Nishinomiya. When he did, it was quietly and pleasantly, with much of the habitual harshness of his voice suppressed.

"Andrew," he said, "I'm a disagreeable sort of bloke, and you've been very patient with me. I don't pretend to be indifferent to having a brother murdered, but I never liked Dave and the longer I'm here the less I'm enjoying what I'm finding out about him. You probably wouldn't think of it to look at me, but the family are well off at home. My mother's already said she doesn't want a penny of Dave's. It's all to come to me. And I want to give those bowls and things to you. I'll still get a hefty whack of money I didn't expect, and it's going to give me the chance to do some of the things I've always wanted."

"What are they?" Walker asked.

Murrow assumed his secretive face and shook his head. "That would be telling," he said, and for the rest of the evening would say nothing about his mysterious ambitions. When Walker asked for his address in England Murrow merely replied that anything care of his mother would find him.

The following morning Walker recalled their conversation as he stood on the observation platform at Osaka airport, waving pointlessly as the British Airways plane took off for Hong Kong. Then he shook his head with an amused smile as he went back inside the airport building. Anyway, the tea bowls were lovely things, and perhaps Nicole would be available over the weekend. He could do with a day off.

WEEK TWO

Monday

"**I**'VE MADE UP MY MIND," SAID OTANI FIRMLY. "IF I'M
going to be pressurised by the Governor and by the Foreign
Ministry, then at the very least I want to know what I'm being
pressurised *about*." The three of them were sitting over lunch
in Otani's office. Otani himself was eating from the lovely
old black and gold lacquered box which had belonged to his
father and which Hanae prepared for him most days except
when he had lunch with the Rotarians. Noguchi and Kimura
had plain flimsy wooden boxes with throwaway chopsticks
brought in from the sushi shop near police headquarters. Noguchi was washing his food down with Ozeki *sake* drunk cold
from a tumbler, Kimura had a bottle of his usual Kirin beer,
while Otani stuck to the green tea he drank by the pint day in
and day out.

Noguchi picked his teeth slowly and thoroughly before
trying again. "Can't see the point of it," he grunted at last.
"The whole organisation runs on cut-outs. I'm not saying
Yamamoto wouldn't see you. In fact he'd probably enjoy it
as much as you would. I can't see him even admitting any
knowledge of the job, though, let alone telling you why he
let his people do it. If he did."

Kimura produced a clean handkerchief and fastidiously

wiped the moisture from his hands after refilling his glass from the cold beer bottle. "Ninja's right, Chief," he conceded judiciously. "It's a back-to-front sort of case. Ninja's found out who did it—not the actual individual, but that's not significant—and we're fairly sure of the motive. But the motive belongs to Mister X. Mister X paid Mister Y indirectly to commit his murder for him. You can't really expect Mister Y's employers to tell you who Mister X is." He paused to collect his thoughts, having slightly confused himself as he spoke.

"Yes, yes, I accept all that," said Otani a little testily. "And I'm also aware that your Mister X could be any one of half a dozen or more of the people on your list. But we can narrow it down. It *has* to be a politician. With the election in a few days' time and Tsunematsu and the Governor wetting themselves in case we crack it too soon, I think I can reduce the field to three. And I can try the names on old Yamamoto. You never know, I might get a reaction."

"Suppose you do," said Kimura curiously. "What would you do then?" Otani stared at him grimly. It was a point. They were all public officials, and firmly located in the framework of society. If, as now seemed to be clear, Murrow had been a petty criminal murdered by another as the penalty for moving into a game too big for him, did it matter very much in social terms? If he could "solve" the crime in the ordinary sense of the word, should he precipitate what could be a national crisis by shouting the fact from the house-tops?

He slowly and carefully wiped his inlaid lacquer chopsticks on a paper handkerchief and laid them in the empty box on his knees, then replaced the lid. "I don't know," he said simply, at last. "But I'm going to see Yamamoto. I should be glad if you would arrange it, Ninja."

Noguchi lumbered to his feet and dropped his empty lunchbox and *sake* bottle into the wastepaper basket. "If you say so. I'd better come with you. Probably can't fix it before tomorrow."

Otani shook his head slowly. "Tomorrow would be alright. Thank you, Ninja, but I'll go alone."

Noguchi stood a moment longer looking down at them, and belched. "Sorry," he said briefly, and was gone.

It had been a relaxing Sunday, with Nicole at her most agreeable, and Walker was rather enjoying a routine sort of Monday in the office. From a purely administrative point of view there were a number of things he ought to have been doing in connection with the Murrow affair, but he put them on one side during the morning and browsed instead through an accumulation of office circulars to give his mind a rest. He was looking forward to a similarly idle afternoon as he made his way back upstairs after lunch, and the message waiting for him on his desk constituted something of a nuisance. In her careful handwriting, little Miss Tsuchida had noted that a Mr Stoneham had telephoned a quarter of an hour earlier. There was no message, except that he would ring back a little later.

Walker sat back and wondered what had prompted Terry Stoneham of all people to try to get hold of him. He wasn't the sort of person one was likely to forget altogether, but it had been weeks since his and Walker's paths had crossed. This was no great deprivation, since they had nothing in common. Indeed, Walker had disliked Stoneham from the first moment he had set eyes on him, at a fire ceremony conducted by the order of mountain priests near Kyoto late the previous autumn.

Walker had himself approached the occasion in a frame of mind perhaps midway between the simple piety of the country people who had toiled up the two-hour ascent by the narrow rocky path in the early evening, some with babies on their backs, and spent the next few hours in prayer and superstitious gossip; and the slick cynicism of the tourists festooned with cameras and of the television cameramen who clambered everywhere with total disregard for the intricate symbolism of the ritual.

He recalled it vividly. It had been bitterly cold up there at night, enough to make him grateful to pay an outrageous price for a beaker of steaming porridgy *amazake* with grated ginger from a wrinkled and cunning-looking old woman, enormous

113

in a variety of cloaks and blankets. It made his nose run, but perked up his spirits amazingly.

Then a proud old priest, savage and strange in his tight breeches, short robes and coloured pompoms on a kind of stole round his neck, sounded a conch shell, its strangled wailing echoing in the clear night. Amid the nasal chanting and invocations, arrows were shot into the black sky, and a huge bonfire of logs covered with a shaggy coat of green pine needles was started. A great cloud of aromatic smoke rose into the sharp brilliant night, hazy in the flickering of torches and the glare of television lights, followed soon after by the fierce flaring of the tall leaping flames.

All too soon the timber was consumed and tumbled into a throbbing pile of white, yellow and autumnally red embers, which were raked into a winking cherry carpet about ten feet long by six wide. Without the slightest hesitation the chief priest, his feet completely bare, walked steadily and resolutely from one end to the other. The other dozen or so *yamabushi* priests followed in close succession, and after these the faithful laity, stripping off their footwear and carrying it with them for all the world as though they were paddling in the sea.

In a comparatively short time so many feet left a black path across the still glowing embers and it was possible to imagine that even without the support of faith and autosuggestion it would be possible to cross without great discomfort. Many of the tourists in fact did so, and the dignity and impressiveness of the ritual rapidly deteriorated. Even so, the behaviour of an odd little group of three men, one European and two young Japanese, struck Walker as being in poor taste. They lurched across, slapping at each other, giggling and striking extravagant and ludicrous poses on the way.

Walker had not himself ventured across but had positioned himself at the far end in order to watch the faces of those undertaking the fire walk. As a result of a particularly violent piece of horseplay, the European stumbled as he reached the end, and grabbed at Walker's arm.

''Whoops! *Sumimasen*,'' he cried, then looked up to see that his involuntary supporter was a fellow Westerner.

114

Walker looked down with distaste at a flushed and spoiled-looking baby-face. The man was rather short, but stocky and solidly built. He wore a fashionable car-coat with a fur collar, and a pair of ankle-boots dangled from his free hand. "A friend in need," he twinkled roguishly. "My dear sir, I am most grateful to you. A port in a storm indeed. American perhaps? Your first visit to one of our quaint and colourful local festivals? Stoneham's my name, Terry Stoneham." He continued to lean heavily on Walker while putting on his socks and boots, ignoring his two companions who had by then arrived and were standing grinning and panting by his side.

At that time Walker was still very new in his first real diplomatic post, and it was with special gravity and stiffness that he identified himself, wobbling slightly under the impact of the heavings and hoppings of the appalling Stoneham. "No, I'm not a tourist, nor an American. As a matter of fact I'm the British Vice-Consul in Osaka. Walker." He deliberately used his surname only. Stoneham released his arm at last, stood back in mock awe and sketched a military-style salute.

"My God," he said. "The dear old FO. Like stout Cortés, silent on a peak in Darien. Allow me to present my companions, Your Honour. On my right, the Crown Prince, on my left, the Mayor of Kyoto."

The two young Japanese simpered uneasily, and Walker had an uncomfortable feeling that he was coming out of it all rather badly. He decided to descend from his high horse and grinned at Stoneham. "All right, I deserved it," he said. "But I hate being taken for an American tourist."

Stoneham too adopted a more reasonable attitude. "So do I, oh, so do I. But you can't blame the Japanese, after all, it's not so very many years since all the Westerners here *were* Americans, practically speaking." He stuck out a hand in a man-to-man gesture of conciliation. "Have a drink," he said, and produced an expensive-looking leather-covered pocket flask from inside his coat. Unscrewing the silver top, he poured a liberal helping of brandy into it and handed it to Walker. Feeling slightly ashamed of accepting Stoneham's hospitality while still thoroughly disapproving of him, Walk-

115

er gulped the welcome liquid down and felt the warmth reach to his very fingers and toes.

They walked down the mountain path together by the light of electric torches held by Stoneham's two acolytes, who fell silent after a few half-hearted attempts to join in the conversation. Stoneham chattered gaily throughout, obviously delighted to be talking about himself. The descent was much quicker than the climb but still took over an hour, and by the time they reached the bottom Walker felt he knew a good deal about Stoneham. He knew that he was an artist by training and that he had lived for several years in Japan. That, needless to say, he earned his basic living by teaching English, but supplemented it handsomely by advising an Osaka advertising agency on English-language layouts for their international business. Stoneham was obviously a born drifter, but a drifter with style who had arranged a very comfortable existence for himself.

They parted amicably enough when they reached the village at the foot of the mountain where the better-heeled visitors to the fire ceremony had left their cars, and encountered each other subsequently once or twice at impersonal occasions, the last having been a grand reception given for the Consular Corps by the Chamber of Commerce. Then Stoneham had been very much on his dignity, wearing a neat dark suit and in deferential attendance on the president of his advertising agency. Walker recalled that they had done no more than nod rather distantly at each other, and if he ever thought about Stoneham at all, supposed that his own distaste was reciprocated.

Walker had to wait only a few minutes for the promised second call, but its effect was merely to add irritation to his former mild puzzlement. The voice at the other end was bland enough, if a shade insistent. "Mr Walker? Terry Stoneham. There's something I'd like to discuss with you if I may. It's rather urgent."

Walker glanced at his desk diary and replied in tones of greater enthusiasm than he felt. "Gladly. Nice to hear from you. I've nothing particular on my plate this afternoon. Could you drop in?"

116

There was a pause. "I wonder if we could make it this evening? Perhaps at your place? I looked you up in the Japan Directory and you're not far from me. I could be there any time to suit you." Another pause, then, "I'd really be very grateful."

Walker ruefully rubbed his eyes, the vision of his precious free evening dissolving as he briefly entertained—then, out of his better nature, dismissed—the temptation to invent a previous engagement. "All right," he said less warmly. "I'll expect you about eight, after dinner." Stoneham thanked him and rang off, leaving Walker vaguely ashamed of his churlishness in so pointedly not offering to eat with the man.

On the tiny stage a sullen girl perfunctorily marched round in small circles to the sound of a raucous pop song played at full volume on a tape recorder. She was dressed in shiny red knickers with a tasselled black fringe and absurdly high platform shoes, and from time to time approached the two or three men in the front row and squatted in front of one of them for a few seconds. By way of a climax to her act she sat astride a gold-painted wooden chair and pretended to masturbate for a while, grimacing in simulated ecstasy before getting up in a matter-of-fact way and walking off, taking the chair with her.

There were no more than eight men in the shabby little theatre, most of them quite respectably dressed and staring at the stage with silent intensity. Noguchi and his companion were the only ones sitting together, murmuring quietly under the cover of the racket from the tape recorder. The music changed and a different girl came on, this time in a kimono.

"All right," said the man next to Noguchi. "But don't blame me if it goes sour. You're sure he really will go on his own?" He was a sharp-featured, youngish man in shirtsleeves and a clip-on bow tie, and he looked at Noguchi with a half-curious, half-admiring expression on his face.

"Told you already," said Noguchi, scratching his belly as he prepared to go. "Three o'clock then. At the office."

The girl on the stage had removed her sash and now opened the kimono to reveal one breast, which she hefted about in her hand as though estimating its weight, and started twiddling her nipple as Noguchi left the smoky little room through the curtained doorway. He paused at the cashier's box and bought a packet of cigarettes from the old woman in charge, then went out into the street, blinking slightly in the hazy brightness.

Though he spent a good deal of time there, Noguchi disliked Osaka. He could perfectly well have telephoned, but instead made his way to the Hanshin railway and took the interurban electric train to Kobe, and was back at headquarters well before six. He met Kimura in the entrance, and looked him up and down. His colleague was apparently as fresh as a daisy, and Noguchi sucked his teeth morosely. "Off to enjoy yourself?" he enquired.

"Of course," said Kimura cheerfully. "I generally do."

"What's her name?"

Kimura shook his head. "You must be kidding," he said. "You're supposed to be a detective. Find out. Have a useful afternoon?"

"Not bad," grunted Noguchi. "Went to a strip show." Kimura stared after him as he shuffled into the building, then shook his head and skipped lightly down the stone steps.

Still mildly remorseful, Walker set out a particularly lavish drinks tray when he got home having eaten on the way, and opened a tin of imported Twiglets in Stoneham's honour. Punctually at eight the bell rang, and Stoneham almost stumbled in his eagerness to enter when Walker opened the door. He looked ghastly, and Walker hurried him to an armchair. "You look as if you could do with a drink," he remarked mildly, and Stoneham nodded, his eyes closed.

"Whisky and water, please. No ice."

As Walker poured a generous drink for him and a lighter one for himself he looked at his self-invited guest. Stoneham was wearing a short-sleeved open-necked shirt like himself, and a few bristly hairs showed at the opening. He sat gulping like a fish, his Adam's apple bobbing up and down, then abruptly pulled from his trouser pocket a large and very white handkerchief with which he wiped the beads of sweat from

118

his nose and forehead. He accepted the tumbler Walker put in one hand and telegraphed his thanks with the other, eyes still closed, then drank deeply.

Interested and perturbed by Stoneham's evident distress, Walker was nevertheless determined not to break the silence first. Instead he sat quietly, sipping his own drink and watching a little colour come into Stoneham's greyish skin. From outside the open window came the sound of thunder, quite nearby. When Stoneham did speak he astonished Walker. He opened his eyes and in a calm, level voice said, "Have you any reason to suppose this place is bugged?"

Walker stared at him curiously, then shrugged. "I very much doubt it. Anyone who might be remotely interested, Japanese or otherwise, would be perfectly well aware that we don't have anything worth knowing down here. But I don't guarantee it." Realising as he did so what a pointless exercise it was if his flat was in fact bugged, Walker rose and closed the window just as a flicker of lightning outlined the hilltops immediately to the north of Ashiya.

A wretched suggestion of a smile appeared on Stoneham's face. "Well, you are about to hear something worth knowing. And on reflection I don't suppose it matters in the slightest if you are bugged. At least, not by the Japanese." He drained the last of his whisky and held out the glass in a supplicant gesture to Walker, who poured him another, this time less potent. Stoneham took it and straightened a little in his armchair as he began to speak.

"I don't know how much you've heard about David's murder," he began. "But you wouldn't need x-ray eyes to see that I'm homosexual, or much imagination to guess he was. There are quite a few of us here, and in the days when the law was different in England . . . you're probably too young to realise that people really *were* sent to jail for it . . . well, anyway. People even came and found work here because the Japanese have always been civilised about it. They aren't hung up about sex of any kind the way we are. It was almost like belonging to a good club. We called it the Chrysanthemum Chain, and had friends and contacts all over the Far East."

A particular loud clap of thunder made the lights flicker, and Stoneham glanced towards the window before continuing. "Well, David had this theory that gay tourists and business visitors who come to Japan aren't much interested in the sort of people they can just as well meet at home—people like us—but want to make it with Japanese boys. Am I disgusting you?" Walker shook his head. He was rather shocked, but not particularly disgusted. Stoneham went on. "Of course, you can go to any drag bar in Japan and pick up *something*, but what David did was to build up what amounted to a call-boy service. He used really nice boys; actors, TV people and so on. He was a grasper, you know, and once the money started rolling in he began to enjoy it more and more. The rest of us didn't go for this business of his—we really didn't—but oddly enough it wasn't illegal and there wasn't much we could do about it. Besides, David could be such a very delightful fellow when he chose."

Walker had a sudden vision of Murrow excusing himself to go to the telephone while he himself sat pleasantly fuddled with *sake*, warming his hand over the glowing charcoal on top of the great bowl of ash in the living-room and talking to Bernard. Stoneham went on, as though unable to stop talking. "What I've come to tell you is that David had a number of Japanese clients as well as foreigners. Prominent men, some of them, married men who couldn't let it be known even here that they're interested in other men. The law is civilised, but it's not done to be gay if you're in public life. A lot of Japanese are AC/DC, you know. Well, I've heard rumours that the police theory is that David was blackmailing one of these people and that he was killed on that person's instructions, to shut him up."

Walker sat in silence, his mind alternately racing and seizing up in stupefaction. "You mean a sort of Murder Incorporated?" he asked at last.

Stoneham nodded. "Exactly. There are any number of hoodlums in Osaka and Kobe who will gladly dispose of somebody for a fee. They mostly kill other gangsters, of course."

After doing his best to absorb this startling information,

Walker asked what occurred to him as the obvious question. "But where do you come into it? You haven't been doing any blackmailing, have you?"

Stoneham leaned forward. "No, emphatically not. But I'm very much afraid that whoever is behind it may be trying to eliminate the group of us closest to David, who knew about the call-boy business. And I'm scared, and I want the British authorities to know what's been going on."

Walker laughed out loud. "I'm sorry, but that's the most farfetched idea I think I've ever heard. I don't mean the blackmailing bit, but the rest." Stoneham's face remained grim and set, and Walker went on to try to reassure him. "I can quite understand your being overwrought, but please don't let it obsess you. There's not a shred of evidence that you may be in any danger."

Stoneham picked up his leather document case from the carpet beside his chair and took an unfamiliar newspaper out of it. "Think so? This is today's *Shikoku Shimbun*," he said quietly as he handed it over. A small paragraph was ringed in red, and Walker held it to the light to decipher the blurred newsprint. As he peered at it and tried to identify the proper names, Stoneham spoke again. "I'll save you the effort. It says that a body has been found in Takamatsu Harbour. It was identified as that of Hirata Sei ichi, a student. Bernard, to you and me."

Noguchi very rarely indeed raised his voice, and his roaring was terrible as he confronted the quaking young constable standing before him in the untidy little office he so seldom used. It was bad enough that Kimura had given Hirata leave to go back to his family home in Shikoku after the funeral without mentioning it to anybody; worse still that the idiot hadn't even required him to report daily to the police there. And now the cocky lunkhead had gone off whoring somewhere for the evening, leaving Noguchi to brief the Old Man about the following day's meeting with Konnosuke Yamamoto, and to mention in passing that the Criminal Investigation Section had just received routine notification of the death of Hirata either by murder or suicide in his home town on the other side of the Inland Sea, in a totally different prefecture.

"All right, son!" he bellowed at length. "I'm not blaming you, you stupid-looking apology for a man! You did right to come to me. Now go home to your mother. And before you do, leave a message for your pig-headed boss. Tell him Noguchi has taken on his responsibilities until he sees fit to come back to work. Inspector Sakamoto should have informed the Commander about this, not me. And I'll kick his arse for him next time I see him." Dismissed at last, the terrified young man scuttled out of the door, recovering his wits just in time to saunter into the office he shared with the other clerks and junior detectives and boast about having been in conference with the legendary Ninja.

Noguchi himself consulted a greasy and tattered notebook which he took from a drawer in his desk, then sat in thought for a long time. Eventually he picked up the telephone and dialled a Takamatsu number. The conversation was brief, and he sat back for a moment after putting the receiver down and before walking round to see if Otani was in his office. He always greatly preferred to talk to him face to face, and this would be a tricky one to handle.

Walker was an intelligent, well-read man, but there had been many times during the course of what he now thought of as the Murrow Business that he had been made abruptly conscious of his inexperience of death, violence and crime. Stoneham's recital had up till then excited his intellectual interest; he had felt himself to be a sophisticated and knowledgeable man of the world. The news of Bernard's death now hit him like a physical blow. A wave of nausea swept over him and a sense of worthlessness seized his imagination. He stared at Stoneham, speechless and horrified; and Stoneham stared back.

The storm had finally broken, and gross, heavy raindrops hit the window fatly, streaming down in silvery trails against the blackness. The hissing of the rain emphasised the tension of the silence between the two men. A hint of damp coolness crept into the sultry atmosphere and Walker shuddered, sud-
122

denly aware of the stickiness of his own skin, and the cotton of his shirt sticking to his back.

When he spoke his voice came out at first in a hoarse croak and he had to begin again. "Do you have any idea which of these clients of David's might be behind it?"

Stoneham made an almost imperceptible questioning gesture. "No. The police may. But the rumours reaching me haven't been specific." Walker shook his head violently as if to clear away a fuzziness, and grasped at a straw of practicality. "But what on earth can any of us do?" he asked despairingly. "We can't do the job of the police for them. Why did you come to me? Why not go to them and ask for protection?"

Stoneham continued to stare fixedly before him, talking rationally but as though over a vast distance. "Because I dare not," he said dully. "If I go to them obviously knowing what I do, I can't be sure that this man hasn't got police contacts too. In fact, I should think he probably has. I might be offering my head on a block." He continued to speak evenly, as though reciting a speech committed to memory beforehand. "I came to you because I want the British authorities to know about this, and to get it across to the Japanese somehow. So long as it remains a Japanese case, I'm in danger. But if they think a foreign government is taking an interest, I'll get protection. I'm sure of it. I know the Japanese better than you."

Walker found his powers of judgement gradually returning as he absorbed the force of Stoneham's argument. Then all at once he felt very tired, very young and very determined to extricate himself at least temporarily from the muddy waters in which he felt himself to be floundering. He got up, crossed to the telephone and dialled the Endsleighs' number, bracing himself wearily to deal with Heather.

A dull sense of relief followed as he heard the Consul General's firm and polished voice giving his number in correct but heavily accented Japanese, then his name. Endsleigh knew enough of the language to identify himself and to say "please" and "thank you". Nothing more. Stoneham's earlier talk about bugging had made Walker uneasy. He found himself using roundabout ways of expressing what he wanted to say, after he had announced himself and heard Endsleigh's courteous "My dear Andrew, how pleasant to hear from you."

"I wondered if you might be free by any chance this evening, sir? There's something I'd like to consult you about." There was a silence, and Walker knew that Endsleigh was pondering the significance of his use of the word "sir". Then he spoke.

"Where are you ringing from, Andrew?"

"Home, sir. I have a visitor with me."

Another pause. "Do I know him?"

Walker agonised for a moment before arriving at the right form of words. "Yes, sir. He's registered with the Consulate General." He gave Endsleigh time to absorb this, waiting till he heard the Consul General speak again. "It's rather late, but if it can't wait till tomorrow you'd better come over. Perhaps your visitor should come too."

Walker put the receiver down and turned to Stoneham. "That was the Consul General. I think you'd better come with me and go over this again. The more of us in the picture the better." The rain had slackened and the evening air felt soft and clean as they left the apartment block. Stoneham's car, a smart Nissan saloon, was parked outside. "Mind if we use your car?" Walker said. "Mine's in the garage."

"By all means," said Stoneham. He unlocked the door on the driver's side, got in and reached across to unlock the passenger door. Walker gave brief directions, then sank back, enjoying the rare pleasure of being driven by someone else.

The distance from Ashiya to Nishinomiya is not great, and there are several roads running roughly parallel. Traffic was light, and it was less than fifteen minutes later that Stoneham swung over to the right and took the side road running up to the Nishinomiya foothills and which follows the suburban branch railway line, running beside a narrow stretch of open parkland with large trees. They had almost reached the small fire brigade post which stands by the roadside to the right when the accident happened.

The surface of the narrow road was slippery from the rain,

and the car behind them had held its position quite unremarkably until all at once it put on a burst of speed and began to overtake. At the same moment a big car with headlights blazing bore down on them from in front. The overtaking car cut in dangerously and Stoneham wrenched at the wheel and braked violently. They swerved and skidded over to the left and Walker involuntarily cowered as a huge tree loomed up beside him. They missed it by a whisker and the car came to a halt on the soft earth at the side of the road, undamaged. The other two cars had not stopped, and they were again alone in the damp summer evening.

Walker looked at Stoneham, his heart pounding. Stoneham sat rigid, gripping the wheel, sweat pouring down his face. He did not resist when Walker got out, opened his door and motioned him to slide across to the passenger side. As he settled himself and cautiously backed the car on to the road again, he was relieved to find that it seemed to have suffered no damage, and was reminded of his own reactions after identifying Murrow's body in the morgue, when Endsleigh had insisted on driving.

He drove slowly and carefully the last mile or so to the Consul General's residence, ready to stop instantly at any sign of danger. Neither of them spoke until Walker swung the car into the parking space beside the big house and switched off the engine. "Could have been pure coincidence," he said at length.

Stoneham shrugged and got out. "I don't think so, and neither do you," he replied.

Otani had a curious relationship with his son-in-law, which had begun ten years earlier when, as a divisional Inspector, Otani had felt obliged to arrest him during student disturbances on the campus of Kobe University. Of all the factions which hived off from the All-Japan Students' Federation at the time, that led by Akira Shimizu was far and away the most efficient and the most troublesome; mainly because of Shimizu's own qualities. During the long hours of questioning he had been by turns mute, belligerent, ideologically blink-

125

ered, impervious to reason, eloquent, charming and persuasive.

It had been all the more exasperating because of his own daughter Akiko's passionate attachment at the time to the particular interpretation of Maoism professed by the Shimizu faction, and her insistence that the similarity between their given names indicated that their *karma* were obviously intertwined. When Shimizu had finally been released from police custody, Akiko had been one of a number of girls in jeans and sweatshirts daubed with slogans picketing his own police station and giving the young man a hero's welcome. And no doubt, as Otani had hinted with a grim smile to Hanae at the time, his choice among them in the way of feminine companionship.

He now looked across with quiet affection at the man sitting opposite him in the best room upstairs. Otani was in his yukata, Shimizu in light slacks and a sports shirt, and they were both enjoying the clean smell of rain-washed air from the open window. From down below the voices of Hanae and her daughter floated faintly up. Otani reached across to pour his son-in-law some more *sake*. "It was nice of you to look in, Akira-kun," he said. "Especially as you must be very busy at the office now that you're a section head."

Shimizu smiled. Having in former years flung all manner of epithets at Otani he had never, even as a respectable citizen, quite been able to bring himself to address him as "Honourable Father-in-law". Otani found it a little like talking to Ninja Noguchi. There was a mutual respect, but an avoidance of conventional courtesies.

"I know you've never been in business," the younger man said. "But you really ought not to be taken in by all that stuff about the long hours people work. Some of them stay late because they enjoy playing *go*, or they don't like their wives, or they think it might impress the boss. But they don't really work very hard, you know. When I've done what needs to be done, I go. Aki-chan and I just thought we'd drive by after orchestra practise to see if your storm shutters were up. We thought you might both be out, but you weren't, so . . . ." He reached for the *sake* flask and refilled Otani's cup. "I sit here

126

drinking your excellent *sake* wondering why you look so worried.''

Otani was startled. "Worried? Do you think I look worried?''

Shimizu corrected himself. "No, perhaps not. Preoccupied, rather. You have an expression that reminds me of the times when I thought I might just be making a dent in your self-respect.'' Otani smiled, genuinely relaxed. "And you did, Akira-kun,'' he conceded. "And I did my best to make a dent in yours. But I'd never have guessed that we'd be sitting here tonight like this or that I'd ever see my daughter's legs in a skirt again.'' He paused, then straightened up and looked Shimizu straight in the eye. "I *am* preoccupied,'' he admitted. "Tell me, what do you think will happen in the election?''

Shimizu shrugged. "Same as usual. Big majority for the left in the cities, while the right keeps the countryside and an overall majority. It won't change unless hyper-inflation sets in. So what?''

"How important do you think the corruption issue is, really?'' asked Otani insistently.

Shimizu looked at him curiously. "Lockheed? Bribery? That sort of thing? It leads to a few resignations when something big comes out, but it doesn't alter the balance of politics, I'd say.''

Otani nodded slowly. "I suppose you're right. I'm sorry I can't tell you exactly what's on my mind. It's just that I have a tricky meeting to handle tomorrow, and I can't stop thinking about the way to do it. Have some more *sake*, you renegade revolutionary, before your wife comes to take you off home.''

Endsleigh opened the door to them himself. He showed no surprise at seeing Stoneham, and greeted him normally and by name before leading them to the large, untidy sitting-room. There was no sign of Heather, and as if reading Walkcher's mind, Endleigh said, "Heather's in Tokyo for a few days. You must forgive my messiness.'' When they were all seated he took over completely, abandoning his habitual

127

lazy, sardonic manner. It was clear that he did not much like Stoneham.

"Right," he said briskly. "Here you are, looking like a couple of ghosts. Let's have it, please." Walker collected his thoughts. "I think somebody just tried to kill us in a car crash," he said mildly. "Following us really, to see where we were going, and did a bit of quick thinking when he saw another car coming down the hill rather fast. But it's better if you hear it all from Terry Stoneham. This last little unpleasantness just brings the story up to date, as it were."

Endsleigh turned to Stoneham, who seemed to be recovering some of his composure, and spoke sharply. "Well, Stoneham, what's all this about?"

Stoneham told his story lucidly and with reasonable brevity, almost exactly as he had done to Walker. Endsleigh sat quite still and listened, making no comment of any kind. When Stoneham eventually concluded with an account of their near-accident on the way to Nishinomiya, silence fell for a few moments. Then Endsleigh spoke.

"Andrew's right. You could have been followed, but it was sheer chance the other car came along. Nobody could have known you were on your way here: certainly not in time to set up a two-car trap. Anyway, most unlikely to be effective. If you had hit that tree you'd probably only have been cut and bruised. Stoneham, my advice to you is to go away for a little holiday to Hong Kong till all this is cleared up. I take it I can't persuade you to leave Japan for good?"

Stoneham gaped at the Consul General in silence for a while, then seemed to pull himself together. "I honestly hadn't thought of running away," he said slowly. "No, I don't want to leave Japan permanently. I have a work permit, and a good life here. I suppose I could go to Hong Kong for a while. But wouldn't that be as obvious as putting an ad in the *Kobe Shimbun* saying that I know something?"

Endsleigh stroked his nose thoughtfully. "Don't think so," he said in his smoothly modulated voice. "Nothing unusual about a foreign resident in Japan going off to Hong Kong at short notice. Anyway, the whole object of the exercise would be to buy us a little time to put the Japanese au-

128

thorities in the picture. That's my job: yours is to make yourself scarce. Are there any other Westerners like yourself at risk, d'you suppose?''

Stoneham considered, then shook his head. ''I really don't think so. The only other person I can think of is an American who's home on six months holiday anyway. But if I go to Hong Kong how long should I stay? I really can't afford to just take off from my job.''

The Consul General reached across to his scribbling pad which lay on the coffee table in front of him, a slender silver propelling pencil at its side, and scribbled a few lines on the top sheet which he tore off and handed to Stoneham. ''Go and see that chap in the Colonial Secretary's office in Hong Kong Government when you arrive. Give him that piece of paper, tell him where you're staying and keep in touch with him. He'll advise you when to come back here. I'll see there's no difficulty about your job with the advertising agency. Now when can you get away?''

Stoneham took a small diary from his back trouser pocket and turned the pages. ''I need some time to cancel various lessons and organise myself a bit. The day after tomorrow.''

Endsleigh nodded, his face set. ''Do that,'' he said curtly. ''And for God's sake don't walk down any dark alleys before then. Now you'd better get home. Andrew, I'd like you to stay here for a while. I'll run you back later myself.''

The constrained atmosphere remained as Stoneham with obvious reluctance took his leave. Walker sank back in his armchair as he heard a few murmured remarks exchanged by the other two men at the front door, then the sound of Stoneham's car starting and driving away down the hill. He must have closed his eyes, unthinkingly, for on opening them again he realised that Endsleigh had come back into the room and was standing by the door, staring at him with an odd expression of distaste on his handsome face. Walker felt himself colour with an obscure sense of guilty embarrassment, and began to babble apologies which Endsleigh cut short with an irritable gesture. Then he spoke with all his customary ease.

''It's a lovely cool evening now, Andrew. Come, let's have a stroll. I'll walk you down to the Hanshin railway and you can go home by train.'' Baffled and mortified, Walker got to his feet, feeling like a schoolboy dismissed for the headmaster's study. It was indeed blessedly cool after the thunderstorm, and there was even a hint of breeze as he walked at Endsleigh's side down the hill. The silence remained unbroken for a dull five minutes until Endsleigh suddenly swore colourfully and uncharacteristically. Walker listened in amazement, then felt he ought to apologise again. ''I really am sorry to have disturbed you. But it seemed such a convincing and worrying story . . .''

Endsleigh gave him a friendly punch on the shoulder, and smiled. ''Shut up, you pompous young ass,'' he said, ''and listen to me. I'm not swearing at or because of you. It's because there are certain aspects of my job which I find extremely distasteful. One of them is the whole nasty business of intelligence work. I consider it a degrading waste of time and money, and I don't like the kind of people that the Friends tend to recruit as agents. People like Stoneham for example.''

It took a little time for Walker to register Endsleigh's words. Then, in a dazed voice, he asked if he had understood him correctly. The Consul General marched on for a few more paces before answering. ''Andrew, for an intelligent young man you sometimes give a remarkable impression of feeble-mindedness,'' he said in a mild voice. ''Yes, Andrew. The reason why we are walking down this dark and damp hill instead of sitting comfortably in my living-room is that your repulsive acquaintance Stoneham has for some years been one of our sources in Japan.'' He paused to let his words sink in before going on.

''And why, you ask yourself plaintively, did they not tell me in Security Department what a source is? I will answer your unspoken question. Because no thinking person can concoct any satisfactory explanation of why we employ sources at all in a country like Japan. Stoneham is a perfectly genuine freelance teacher-cum-English-language-consultant to the Miyazaki Advertising Agency. That is how he earns the comfortable income which enables him to live agreeably and to indulge his highly personal proclivities. Which I do

130

not condemn, my dear Andrew, don't think that. We all have our funny little ways."

Walker found himself slowing down as the lights of the main road came into view. He was completely riveted by what he was hearing, and needed time to assimilate it. Endsleigh went on. "But in addition to this, Stoneham hoovers up and transmits to the head of our Japan station a quantity of information about the world of Japanese business. This is added to other scraps of gossip of various kinds and made the subject of reports which are read without much interest by people in London who, if they could contrive a little patience, could read much the same thing a week or two later in *The Economist* at the cost of a few silver coins. For this pointless snooping Stoneham—with others like him in most countries of the world—receives a modest but acceptable tax-free supplement to his monthly income and does his bit to sustain the great world of Intelligence."

Endsleigh was warming to his theme. "Intelligence, Andrew, is the great con-game of our time. God knows how many tens of thousands of Stonehams prod about nastily on behalf of ourselves, the Americans, the French and for all I know the Peruvians, keeping in employment an even greater number of chaps on the other side identifying and keeping tabs on them. And when they do very occasionally fish up an interesting gobbet of information, it's either filed away or viewed with great suspicion as a probable plant. Keep away from them if you can, Andrew. I'm an old-fashioned diplomat. Heaven knows, the profession is hardly respectable: but I'd rather show the flag openly than poke about in other people's dustbins. I almost wish the tiresome fellow would get himself murdered. But if a British agent, however unimportant, is killed in suspicious circumstances the thing could get out of hand."

Walker's fascination and mortification had grown in equal measure throughout Endsleigh's monologue, and he made a valiant attempt to re-establish himself. "I'm sorry to have been so dim," he said briskly. "It has been rather a confusing business all round. What can I do to help?" They were now no more than a few hundred yards from the little sub-

'urban station, and Endsleigh looked at him speculatively. "Have you still got the incense money envelopes? They have the names of the senders on them, don't they?" Walker nodded.

"Right. Make a list of the names, and underline any that aren't obviously colleagues from the university, neighbours, other straight forward ones. Check up particularly on any public figures. I have a feeling that our man wouldn't have been able to resist the temptation to add a little personal touch to the funeral he arranged. Get your friend on the *Kobe Shimbun* to see if he can spot any gangsters on the list. Then when you've whittled the thing down, we'll see if Intelligence can display any. Goodnight, Andrew. Don't let your imagination overheat. But do realise that it's not only in books that this kind of thing happens. See you in the morning."

Endsleigh abruptly turned on his heel and strode back the way they had come. Walker bought his ticket from the automatic machine at the little station and checked the time. Ten to eleven, and the next train would be along at two minutes past. There was just time for a bottle of beer at the tiny restaurant near the entrance. He felt he needed it.

Tuesday

IT WAS A LOVELY MORNING: STILL HOT BUT WITH A CLAR-
ity very different from the muggy haziness of the previous
days. Otani felt lighter and more cheerful, though when Hanae had commented happily on the fact over breakfast he had
been hard put to it to think why. They always had a Western-
style meal: toast and jam, coffee, sometimes even bacon and
egg. Otani had never like miso soup, rice and seaweed at that
hour, and had converted Hanae, pointing out that even the
Emperor himself was reputed to start the day with English
marmalade.

It must be the weather, he thought to himself as Tomita
wove through the mid-morning traffic towards Ambassador
Tsunematsu's office in Osaka. They were using an unmarked
car, and Otani was in a neat lightweight civilian suit. Tomita
seldom had the chance to wear plain clothes and rather over-
did it when the occasion arose. That day he was sporting a
loud check sports shirt which was obviously brand new, in
that it stood out from his skinny frame stiff with the original
dressing, like cardboard. It also gave off the sort of smell
characteristic of menswear shops, but the windows were all
open and it was not troublesome.

The news of Hirata's death had been infuriating, certainly,

and Kimura had been thoroughly and rightly sheepish when they met first thing. Ninja Noguchi had been oddly angry over what he insisted on representing as Kimura's dereliction of duty. Needless to say, he had already been in touch with one of his cronies in Takamatsu and was able to report that the police there were pretty certain that it was a case of murder, not suicide. Kimura's defence was that Hirata's own innocence had in any case been established without doubt and that there was no reason to keep him in Kobe. Further, that since events had shown that he was clearly vulnerable, it was not unreasonable that he should be allowed to distance himself from the danger area. The fact that the long arm of the Yamamoto gang reached as far as Takamatsu was simply extremely bad luck for Hirata.

Otani's dressing down of Kimura had been sincere but not too protracted, and Noguchi went off in what might have been an ill humour, though one could never really be quite sure with him. Otani promised himself that he would make a point of lunching alone with Ninja in the near future, but in the meantime his blood was up and he felt the better for it.

The head of the Osaka Liaison Office of the Ministry of Foreign Affairs received him in his elegantly furnished office with courtly dignity. He was, as always, dressed in a style thoroughly appropriate to his personal rank of Ambassador, from the tips of gleaming black shoes to his striped trousers and black jacket and waistcoat. The gold-rimmed glasses on his aristocratic nose glistened, and even his thin grey hair had a polished look. Otani greeted him warily, wondering as he did so whether Tsunematsu had any moisture in his body whatsoever. He was prepared for some complicated sparring, and put up with the Ambassador's long-winded preliminary courtesies with fortitude, waiting for the first probe.

It was as though Tsunematsu regretted having made his early telephone calls about the Murrow case, since he made no attempt to broach the subject. Though he began a number of sentences with the words "Frankly speaking . . .", they turned out to be banal statements about the latest news on the international scene and other generalities until Otani looked at his watch ostentatiously and took the initiative.

134

"Mr Ambassador," he said firmly. "We have had a number of dealings over the years; and I believe you know that I have always done my best to co-operate with your Ministry to the best of my ability."

"Your very considerable ability," Tsunematsu murmured, gravely inclining his head. "And I for my part have expressed my appreciation most sincerely on a number of occasions."

"It has not always been easy," Otani continued bluntly. "There have been times when my work and that of my men would have been greatly facilitated if you had seen fit to take me more fully into your confidence."

Tsunematsu's thin face was a mask as he sat very still in the big armchair opposite Otani, his delicate hands on his knees. Having dropped the pretence of courtesy, Otani pressed on. "I was therefore grateful to have this opportunity to come to see you, if for no other reason than to make it very clear to you that I intend to pursue the investigation into the murder of the Englishman Murrow as vigorously as possible."

The Ambassador removed his glasses and polished them unnecessarily with a snowy handkerchief. "I would expect nothing less of you, Superintendent," he said. "I confess that I am a little surprised that you seem to suggest that I am in some way seeking to hamper your investigations."

Otani shook his head hastily. "I must apologise for having implied such a thing. You have expressed a—dare I say—particular and perhaps unusual interest in the case, but it would be quite wrong to suggest any more than that. On the other hand, I must tell you that I am receiving hints from the Governor's office which it would be ridiculous not to interpret as requests for a delay."

"Do your investigations lead you towards any possible explanation of any apparent embarrassment in official circles?"

Otani nodded grimly. "We are not complete fools, Mr Ambassador," he said. "There is quite obviously a political dimension to all this, and that that embarrassment as you put

135

it should become evident during the closing stages of an election campaign is hardly coincidental."

Tsunematsu looked at the ceiling. "We live in uncertain and confused times, Superintendent," he said after a while. "The fabric of our society is tough and flexible; but it is not indestructible. We need a period of political stability as much as ever. It is no part of my duty to try to dissuade you from yours. I think we understand each other. May I ask before you go if you expect an early conclusion to your enquiries?"

Otani stood up, and something in his face brought the Ambassador to his feet too. "I expect to know the identity of the person who brought about the Englishman's death this afternoon," Otani said quietly. "Whether I shall be able to prove it before he is returned to office again is another matter." He bowed quickly and left the room, and after a moment Tsunematsu crossed to his desk and picked up the telephone.

Walker had been so tired when he arrived home the previous night that he had felt distinctly relieved that the condolence envelopes were in the safe at the Consulate General; but he was at the office bright and early in the morning. As he sat at his desk and slipped off the rubber bands which held the stacks together he reflected that he had indeed quite possibly bowed in formal courtesy to the murderer or his agent at Murrow's house on that hot, dusty, incense-laden afternoon the previous week. Lord, it felt like months ago.

His task was simplified by the Japanese custom of writing not only names but professional affiliations on formal occasions, and he began by sorting out and setting to one side the considerable heap of envelopes which bore the name of Murrow's university. He also set aside another pile, all from people who lived nearby and were probably members of Murrow's *tonarigumi* or neighbourhood association. The sums of money donated were neatly written on the reverse of the envelopes in the classic Japanese style and the amounts here were small; five hundred or a thousand yen, a pound or two.

This left about forty envelopes which fell into no particular category. For want of a better idea, Walker turned them over

136

and sorted them by amounts. Most went on to a five thousand yen and under pile, but a few were still left, which Walker scrutinised with mounting puzzlement. Why on earth hadn't he thought of doing this earlier? One, for seventy-five thousand, made him purse his lips in a silent whistle. Close on a hundred and fifty pounds was a handsome tribute by any reckoning, and there were others approaching that.

He stared at the beautiful calligraphy but the names meant nothing to him. All the addresses seemed to be of commercial firms; mostly in Osaka and Kobe, but there were two from Nagoya and three from Tokyo. Walker took a sheet of plain paper and a black felt-tip pen and copied out the names and addresses of the particularly generous donors, taking great care to reproduce the brush-strokes of some of the Chinese characters used for proper names which were unfamiliar to him. The envelopes themselves he put into a separate pile and slipped a rubber band round each of the stacks as he had rearranged them before returning them all to the safe. On his way back to his own room he glanced into the Consul General's ante-room, but there was no sign of Jill, and Endsleigh's door was open so that Walker could see that he too was away from his desk.

Walker picked up the paper from his desk and studied it indecisively. The obvious first thing was to find out which if any of the names meant anything to Ken Takamura. Indeed that was exactly what Endsleigh had told him to do. After that, he'd implied, somebody on the spooky side of the Embassy might have a view, and Walker mused glumly that it would be tedious to be relegated to the sidelines just when things were becoming interesting, especially as he'd had to do all the donkey-work so far.

He heaved a sigh, stretched his arms and rubbed the end of his nose, looking out of the window at the first blue sky for some days. If Takamura had any sense he'd be out and about somewhere; but he reached for the telephone anyway. One ought at least to go through the motions, even though he found himself rather hoping that Ken wouldn't be available. He wasn't, and the girl Walker spoke to at the *Kobe Shimbun* was vague about when he might be back.

Walker looked again at the list of names, not all of which he knew how to read. Some were fairly easy. Fujikawa Kosaburo for instance—a Mister Wisteria River, with an address in Nagoya. Walker's restlessness mounted to the point where he found it impossible to keep still, so he wandered over to the window to ponder the seductive motion of taking a train to Nagoya and prodding around a little.

Nagoya was not much more than an hour away and within the consular area: he didn't need permission to go there in official time. Mr Fujikawa seemed to be head of some kind of travel agency, so he ought to be fairly accessible. A courtesy call perhaps? To thank him on behalf of the Murrow family. That might be intriguing, and would certainly be better than sitting twiddling his thumbs in an empty office until such time as he could get hold of Takamura. It would be a pleasant jaunt, harmless enough, and might yield up an impression of one at least of David Murrow's more generous friends.

Distinctly taken with his idea, Walker made sure that he had enough money on him to pay for his ticket, then went back to Endsleigh's office. There was still no sign of him, nor of Jill. He looked at the open book on her desk and saw that Endsleigh had engagements outside the office until late afternoon. Reflecting that he had at least tried to carry out the CG's instructions, Walker slipped out of the building in a pleasantly truant mood.

He was at New Osaka Station within half an hour, buying his ticket and watching the computerised machine stuttering out the details, including seat number. Walker travelled on the famous bullet trains dozens of times, but this particular piece of organisation, handling trains which went in each direction at intervals of twenty minutes or less from early morning till late at night, still struck him as verging on the miraculous. He had only a few minutes to wait on the platform, and occupied them in watching a farewell ceremony taking place near one of the market sections where the first-class coaches would draw up. A plump, well-tailored businessman was conversing curtly with three or four underlings,

138

solemn younger men. As if at a signal they all began to bow, and their superior inclined his head in acknowledgement.

Punctual almost to the second the streamlined train drew in, smart in its blue and cream livery, the driver and his deputy gazing ahead with glassy-eyed dedication. It slid to a halt, the pneumatic doors precisely aligned with the appropriate lines and arrows painted on the platform, and Walker entered at the opposite end of the same coach as the businessman and found and settled himself in his comfortable gold-upholstered airline-style seat.

Meantime the Japanese dumped his briefcase and cloth-wrapped bundle on his own seat nearby and remained standing, staring impassively at his little band of supporters outside, now ranged in a neat semicircle facing the window. The doors sighed shut and the great train began almost imperceptibly to glide forward. As it did so all the little group outside bowed in unison and a fraction of a second later the great man returned their salute, remaining bent at the waist for a few seconds before stowing his bundle on the rack and settling down in his seat.

It could have been a significant event like a departure on transfer to another company office in a different city, but the absence of flowers or other symbols of a special occasion led Walker to suppose that he had been witnessing the send-off for a perfectly routine business visit by a department head. As he mused on the fascinating combination of ceremony and ruthlessness which seemed to characterise Japanese business operations, the super-express gathered speed and was soon streaming through the Vale of Yamazaki. Walker saw the Suntory whisky distillery on his left, then almost at once the lofty pagoda of the Toji temple on the southern outskirts of Kyoto. This was the only stop before Nagoya, and the whole journey of more than a hundred miles took only just over the hour.

Most major Japanese cities offer sharp contrasts between their business sections, with high office blocks, hotels and department stores all in the most modish Western style, and the muddle of jerry-built blocks on the outskirts, with the occasional row of traditional wooden houses putting up a brave

139

shabby show among them. The line of demarcation is particularly clear-cut in Nagoya, with the steel and glass cliff of the New Takaido Line extension on the south side of the original railway station rearing up like some monstrous spaceship out of the jumble of little shops and slum housing beyond.

The wrong side of the tracks indeed, Walker thought to himself as he emerged into the hot sun from the airconditioned underground complex beneath the fashionable north side of the station where he had lunched early off a bowl of buckwheat noodles and chicken in one of the innumerable little restaurants there. He now felt ready to brave the unknown hazards of the quarter of the city called Tanaka-cho, which is where it seemed the Fujikawa Travel Company, Limited, had its office. He wondered if Mr Fujikawa would be there in person.

In more fanciful moments during his wanderings through the principal towns of western Japan Walker had often enough tried to visualise the days before reinforced concrete and earthquake-proofing, when daily tremors forced builders in brick to accept the inevitability of cracks and fissures. How much more suitable the simple old-style wooden structures, which swayed and yielded to the heavings of the earth, often caught fire, but were easily rebuilt and housed people whose austere way of life was rooted in a social integrity which constituted its own form of defence against the cruelties of nature.

There had always been outsiders, though. Extraordinary to think that the Japanese could replace a word like "outcast" with a bureaucratic euphemism like "special people" and yet accept that the areas of the cities where the *burakumin* live are as rigidly defined as they have ever been. There are no physical barriers: one may pass freely across the invisible but effective frontiers. As long as the Japanese system of birth registration remains, however, it will be just as difficult for an outcast to enter respectable society as for a black African to pass for white in Pretoria.

There was no sense of menace in the air as Walker made his way through the alleys of Tanaka-cho. The unmade roads were not more unkempt than those of any other urban backwater, and the little shops, bars, and eating houses looked quite ordinary. In the immediate neighbourhood of the station he passed through a sleazy little night-life area and good-naturedly fended off a few perfunctory invitations from girls leaning from upper windows, and one rather more pressing line of sales talk from a sharp-featured young tout standing in the entrance to a massage parlour.

Deeper into Tanaka-cho there was nothing of that. Instead there were little knots of men standing about at the corners who stared at him curiously, but listlessly and without a hint of aggression. Their dress was shabby but unremarkable. Their skinny chests were clothed in threadbare but reasonably clean singlets, and woollen belly-bands in purple or blue protruded above the waistbands of their trousers. On their feet they wore cheap rubber flip-flop sandals, except for one or two older men who looked like wizened oriental jockeys in a kind of riding breeches tucked into leggings, and the quaint rubber-soled socks with a separate compartment for the big toe.

Unless it happens to be on the outskirts of town, a Japanese *cho* or city block is rarely very large in physical extent, and Walker was able to judge fairly well when he had penetrated to roughly the centre of this one. There was nothing in the appearance of the area to suggest that a travel agency would be likely to do much business in the neighbourhood; but this came as no great surprise to Walker. He stopped at an open-air sweetshop, little more than a covered stall but colourful with its brightly wrapped selection of Morinaga chocolate bars and packets of chewing gum.

An elderly woman presided, her light summer kimono loose round her wrinkled neck, bright black eyes darting over the tall young foreigner in his lightweight suit, incongruous among the local men. Walker chose a packet of chewing gum at random; it had a shocking pink wrapper with a picture of a popular television cartoon character on it. He handed the woman a hundred-yen note and, as she fumbled for the change in a shallow wooden drawer, asked her in Japanese which he deliberately made as plain and direct as possible whether she could direct him to the Fujikawa Travel Company. She looked up sharply, the shrewd eyes alive with interest.

"Fujikawa *nani*? Fujikawa what?"

"The Fujikawa Travel Company," Walker repeated patiently.

The woman gave him an unexpectedly cheery and youthful smile. "That's a good one," she observed. "I can tell you where Fujikawa Kosaburo Sama lives, if you like. Don't know about a travel agency, but he's Mr Big around here." She used the word *oya-bun*, one colloquialism with which Walker was thoroughly familiar, though he would have found it hard to explain the subtle relationship between *oya-bun* and *ko-bun*, patron and dependent, without a long disquisition on Japanese history, religion and psychology. He consulted his list of names to confirm once again that Kosaburo was indeed the given name of the self-styled President of the Company. He must indeed be Mr Big if she referred to him as "Sama".

"Yes," he said to the sweetshop woman. "He's the one I want."

"Well, let's hope he wants you," she said, still with an odd hint of amusement in her voice, and gave Walker what for a Japanese were remarkably concise and simple directions. He thanked her and walked off, and was staggered to hear her call after him in English, "Come back!" He turned back to see her holding out her hand with some money in it. "Change," she said laconically. "Thank you, English gentleman."

"Thank you," Walker murmured, distinctly dazed. He walked off again, troubled by the small mystery until it dawned on him that the woman had almost certainly in her past worked as a bar hostess or prostitute and picked up a few English phrases in the process. What really smarted was that she had accurately identified his accent in speaking Japanese.

Fujikawa's house was about ten minutes' walk from the sweet stall, and Walker felt hot, sticky and dirty when he arrived at what must be his destination. It would have been difficult to visualise anything less like a travel agency. Tucked neatly between a cheap eating house on one side and a *pachinko* pinball amusement arcade on the other was a high and

142

very solid wooden gate set into a short wall of stone; great blocks of granite matched and cemented into a barrier with a certain crude vulgarity, but giving the impression of great power and not without a swaggering dignity. At the side of the formidable gate was a simple wooden slab with the two Chinese characters reading "Fujikawa" carved deeply and picked out with gold paint.

There was no bell-push and Walker was wondering what to do for the best when the gate opened silently and apparently without human agency, disclosing a flagstone path freshly watered in the Japanese manner. This led through a small but exquisite formal garden to the front door of a large house built in Western style, of reinforced concrete. Walker suddenly wished devoutly that he had thought of persuading Ken Takamura to come with him; and immediately dismissed the idea as absurd. Here he was, clothed in the armour of diplomatic status, in broad daylight in one of the principal cities of a civilised modern state, about to pay a courtesy call. Why did he suddenly feel so chilly under the hot summer sun?

Squaring his shoulders and telling himself that electronically operated gates were becoming a commonplace in Japan, Walker stepped in and made his way up the path, noting in spite of his unease the immaculate beauty and harmony of the little garden. A tiny waterfall fed a balanced bamboo tube, closed at one end so that it emptied itself and fell back with a hollow click every ten seconds or so. It was about to tip over under the weight of the water, and Walker paused to watch. The click coincided exactly with that of the gate closing behind him.

Otani's long-awaited interview with Konnosuke Yamamoto was developing along interesting lines. Punctually at three o'clock Otani had presented himself at the unremarkable head office of the Yamamoto Construction Company, which was in a good, if not the best, location near the main business centre of the city. The construction company was in fact only one of the many enterprises whose offices seemed to be in the same six-storey building, judging by the names

143

listed on a large and beautifully-lettered sign inside the main entrance.

The lobby was furnished expensively, but with modest good taste, from the quiet design of the thick carpet underfoot to the comfortable black leather armchairs in the small waiting area which was marked off by a teak-enclosed trough in which grew a number of indoor plants. Behind a desk of the same wood sat a well-groomed and well-spoken young woman receptionist in fashionable Western clothes, a single telephone in front of her. She smiled warmly at Otani as he entered.

"Mr Otani?" He inclined his head, noting with some interest the civilian mode of address. "You are most welcome, sir. If you will please take a seat for one moment, I will inform Mr Yamamoto that you are here." She picked up the telephone and depressed three buttons in its base. Otani heard the smallest and most discreet chirruping sound came from it, and decided there and then to arrange to have one installed in his own office. Whoever answered at the other end did all the talking, the receptionist merely saying, "Yes, certainly," before putting the phone down again. She then stood up, smoothing her skirt as she did so and revealing a trim bosom under her silk shirt, and approached Otani.

"I apologise for having kept you waiting, Mr Otani. Will you please come with me?" There were three lifts at the back of the lobby, only two of which had call-buttons. Beside the third was a small panel with a little door in it, which she opened to reveal a set of buttons not unlike those on her ultra-modern telephone. The receptionist tapped out a sequence of numbers and the lift doors slid open. She stood courteously to one side to allow Otani to precede her, and he stepped into the lift, which was carpeted in the same design as the lobby.

There were only UP and DOWN buttons apart from the usual red emergency stop, and one of the intercom telephones which are not uncommon in lifts nowadays. There was no way of judging how many floors they ascended; Otani supposed it would be natural for the old man to occupy some kind of penthouse office, and the movement of the lift was smooth and quiet. When it stopped, he was a little surprised that the receptionist took up the intercom receiver and said "Otani Tetsuo" into it. The use of his given name in such circumstances was most unconventional, and apart from the obvious security device of the coded call-button in the lobby, was the first mildly disturbing reminder that he was after all entering the private domain of an extremely powerful man.

The lift doors opened and he found himself in another small lobby, but with a very different atmosphere from the neutral modernity of the ground-floor entrance. The girl who was waiting for him was also quite unlike the smart receptionist from downstairs, who now disappeared from view with a final bright, twentieth-century smile as the doors closed on her. Otani found himself standing on a small silken mat placed on highly polished dark wooden boards, and quite without conscious reflection slipped his shoes off as naturally as he would have done on entering his own home.

He had never previously seen anyone dressed as this girl was, except on the stage in a kabuki play, or in one of the waxwork tableaux at Nijo Castle in Kyoto. Come to think of it, she was dressed more like the figure of the Lady Murasaki they displayed at Miidera Temple near Lake Biwa, kneeling at her low desk in the throes of writing *The Tale of Genji*. The girl was perhaps seventeen or eighteen, and was got up in the style of a medieval court lady—one of the concubines of the Emperor, perhaps.

Her glossy black hair was absolutely straight, falling from a central parting like a river of spun silk over her shoulders and halfway down her back. Otani reflected that it was just as well the building was airconditioned: the child must have been wearing at least five or six under-kimonos in delicately contrasting colours, as well as her principal richly-embroidered robe and a heavy silk sash which trailed on the floor behind her. On her feet were snow-white *tabi* of soft thick cotton. Even her face looked as though it came from a former century. The pale mask-like effect and the painted eyebrows at least an inch above the plucked area where nature had placed them were similar to those Otani had seen often enough on modern geisha; but this girl's fine features had not been obliterated under a heavy plastering of white pancake

145

make-up, and her very bone-structure looked different from that of modern girls.

She bowed very humbly to Otani and murmured greetings in archaic classical Japanese. He bowed in return, part of him wanting to smile at the sheer ludicrousness of the whole charade, part awed by the remote dignity of the girl. She raised her head, keeping her eyes lowered, and continued speaking, one little hand in front of her mouth in the old polite manner. Otani wouldn't have sworn to it, but it looked as though her teeth had been blackened too, just like the old courtesans. It was quiet in the building, but just at that moment an ambulance must have passed in the street outside, for the sound of its siren penetrated into the corridor; and for the merest fraction of a second the girl's eyes met his in a weirdly eloquent flash of communication.

She indicated a sliding fusuma screen door at Otani's right, then knelt beside it herself and slid it open, bowing again to the floor as he approached it. The effect of the décor was such that Otani found himself using the old-fashioned phrase. "I apologise for the intrusion," he said, bowing and stepping on to the tatami-matted floor of Yamamoto's room.

It would have been a mistake to call it an office, though there were papers littered over the softly gleaming surface of a low black lacquer table. The room was designed in a purely classical style, the tokonoma alcove marked off by a lovingly polished cryptomeria wood pillar. There must have been conventional windows behind, but they were concealed by shoji screens of light wood and the most delicate parchment paper which bathed the room in diffused light. On one wall was a hanging scroll framing a piece of boldy-brushed calligraphy which Otani was quite unable to decipher, immediately or later.

There were three objects on the glowing wooden shelf of the alcove. One was a samurai sword mounted on a display stand, the second a plain lacquer box, the third a flower arrangement of great beauty and simplicity in a coarse ceramic bowl. Konnosuke Yamamoto himself looked positively out of place in his conventional business suit.

Otani knew that he was in his seventies; and he looked it.

He was sitting cross-legged on a brocade cushion behind the lacquer table, his thin dry hands reposing quietly on its surface. When he moved his head the leathery folds of his thin neck twisted freely in the white collar that seemed much too big for him. Like that of many elderly Japanese, his skin was much yellower than that of younger people, and was blotched with patches of darker pigmentation.

"Sit down, Superintendent," he said. The voice was firm and resonant, and might have belonged to a man thirty years younger. "You will take some refreshment?" Otani demurred, but only to the most token degree demanded by common courtesy. He had no intention of missing the chance of experiencing this man's hospitality. Etiquette acknowledged, the old man clapped his hands. The sound was hardly audible even to Otani, but almost immediately the fusuma door again slid open and the same girl reappeared, entering the room on her knees, sliding the door to before approaching with a lacquer tray on which were two bowls of ceremonial tea and two small sugar-cakes. After the girl had served them and had withdrawn, Yamamoto popped his own cake in his mouth and picked up his tea-bowl, nodding at Otani, who followed suit. They drank their tea noisily, in the correct manner, and exchanged a few conventional clichés about the weather.

"We'll have some whisky later," said Yamamoto somewhat to Otani's surprise as he put his bowl down. "Well, Superintendent, what's on your mind?"

The directness of the question was unexpected. Otani had put himself into something of the mental state he found most useful in dealing with Ambassador Tsunematsu, and being put off guard by Yamamoto he said the first thing that came into his head. "Several things. But mainly where on earth do you keep her outside office hours?" he asked.

Yamamoto laughed with what seemed to be genuine amusement. "I like that, Superintendent," he said after a while. "I expected questions from you, but hardly that one. You might have expected me to favour the old ways, surely?"

Otani pulled himself together. It would be absurd to have to tell Noguchi and Kimura that his conversation with Yamamoto had boiled down to trivialities. He adopted a stiffer manner. "I've read reports of your speeches," he said. "I'm very well aware that you are a right-wing extremist. And that often goes with a sentimental romanticism about the past. But in my official capacity I haven't noticed any reluctance on your part to squeeze as much money out of the modern world as you can."

The old eyes glinted in the shrunken face. "I am a businessman, Otani-san," he said. "There have been businessmen in Osaka for centuries; and they have usually been valued supporters of the government and, through the government, of His Majesty."

No point in beating about the bush, Otani thought. "So far as I am concerned, you're a crook," he said bluntly, wondering momentarily whether he was overdoing his own response to Yamamoto's forthright approach.

Yamamoto seemed unconcerned. "You may use these meaningless words if you wish. I was interested when you requested this meeting. Some of my associates regard you as a man of ability. I have no quarrel with the police myself. What is your business with me?"

Otani got up and looked more closely at the hanging scroll. The brushwork was fine, but he couldn't make head or tail of the meaning. He spoke without looking at Yamamoto. "Your associates, as you refer to them, are for the most part men with criminal records. Records acquired in the course of carrying out your instructions. I am concerned with one particular criminal act at the moment. It was committed by a rank-and-file member of your organisation. You will tell me you haven't the slightest idea of his identity and you will almost certainly be telling the truth: I imagine the chain of command through which the order was transmitted is long and complex. What I want to know from you is the name of the man who commissioned you to have the Englishman Murrow and the Hirata boy removed."

Yamamoto did not answer immediately. Instead he got up too and crossed to the tokonoma. He picked up the samurai sword and drew the blade from the scabbard. For one wild moment Otani thought he was about to be attacked and pos-

148

sibly decapitated. It was a fine sword, the blade glittering and obviously well cared for. "Come over here," said Yamamoto inconsequently, and Otani approached him carefully. "This belonged to my son," the old man said, turning the blade back and forth a few times before returning it to its scabbard. He bent with unexpected grace and returned the sword to its stand, then picked up the lacquer box. He held it out to Otani, who took it and opened the lid. "Do you know what it is?" Yamamoto asked.

"Of course," said Otani quietly. "I was in the Navy myself." He carefully took out the folded white silk scarf, inscribed with signatures done in black Indian ink which had blurred and faded over the years. "Was your son a pilot?" he asked.

"Yes. Not kamikaze, or I would scarcely have these things now. But he had volunteered for the kamikaze corps. He died gallantly on board his aircraft-carrier. His commander gave me the sword and the scarf. His commander is still living, a man distinguished in public life." He took the scarf from Otani, re-folded it and returned it to the box. "There are few things I would not do to help a man who has proved himself in war and peace to be a true patriot."

Otani looked him up and down as Yamamoto stood in a pathetic parody of military stiffness. It seemed almost cruel to attack a slightly deranged old man. Yet Yamamoto was not simply one bereaved father like thousands of others up and down the country, mourning the passing of an era and the loss of a son in early manhood, dressing up his sorrow in dreams of a pure fire of dedication that never was. He was a gangster, a racketeer and a cynical manipulator of the small and furtive vices of his fellow-men. He was also a murderer, at no matter how many removes.

"You realise that you have given me enough to identify him?" Otani said at last.

Yamamoto's thin lips twisted contemptuously. "Do you seriously imagine that I would repeat any of this, or admit I said it?" There was scorn in his voice. "I will confirm only what you yourself accepted earlier. That I have not the remotest idea who killed the Englishman. Or his catamite." He

149

almost spat out the last word, then relaxed and reverted to his earlier almost affable manner. "Now, what about that whisky?" he enquired.

Otani looked at him with distaste. "I think not, thank you," he said curtly. "I am grateful to you for allowing me to call on you. Now I have work to do."

Yamamoto himself led the way to the lift and summoned it while Otani put his shoes back on. There was no sign of the girl as the two men bowed stiffly and in silence to each other and the doors closed on Otani. He pressed the DOWN button, and speculated briefly as he descended about his prospects of being let out at the bottom. He was, by the same glamorous receptionist who had conducted him up. It was a pleasure to be back in even this high-gloss kind of normality after the unreality of the last half hour, but even better to go out into the familiar smells and noises of down-town Osaka on a hot afternoon in July.

The front door of the Fujikawa residence was painted a sober blue and was opened by a young man who clearly modelled himself on the classic television stereotype of the promising younger criminal of the executive class. His hair was elegantly styled, and he wore sunglasses. His suit was expensive, of nubbly black silk, and he wore a plain knitted silk tie with a very white shirt. The sightless black lenses moved slightly as he looked Walker up and down, but he remained silent. Eventually Walker found his voice, and spoke in his most formal Japanese. "I am sorry to intrude. Is Mr Kosaburo Fujikawa at home? My name is Walker, from the British Consulate General in Osaka."

The young Japanese spoke curtly and rudely. "Your business?"

"I wish to convey on behalf of the late Mr David Murrow's family their thanks for Mr Fujikawa's generous donation of incense money. I therefore come on official British Government business."

Walker's last remark in particular seemed to give the bodyguard pause. He hesitated for an instant, then spoke in a slightly more gracious tone. "Please wait a moment." The

150

door was closed again in Walker's face, but gently, and for something less than a minute a hot summer silence fell, broken only by the hollow click of the bamboo waterspout and the trickling of the water as it refilled. Then the door was opened again and the Japanese in the dark suit stood back politely.

"You are welcome, Mr Walker. Please enter and come this way." Walker followed him, with a nagging feeling that he had seen him before. It could only have been during the condolence visit afternoon at Murrow's house the previous week, but the sunglasses made it impossible to be sure. The entrance hall was opulently furnished with expensive reproduction French antique pieces, and what looked like an Aubusson carpet. An original landscape in oils hung on one wall. It was a pleasant picture in a style vaguely familiar to Walker. No natural light entered the hall: it was discreetly illuminated by wall lights, and the whole house seemed to be centrally airconditioned to an arctic chill which made Walker shudder involuntarily.

His guide led the way through a large living-room furnished in the same style as the entrance hall, but with curtains of deep burgundy velvet. The only apparent concession to the twentieth century, apart from the airconditioning, was the same subdued lighting and an elaborate stereo record-player. The Japanese opened a panelled door in the far corner. *"Soryojikan no Waruka-san,"* he announced. "Mr Walker from the Consulate General," and Walker entered the presence of the President of the Fujikawa Travel Company.

Fujikawa's room was a pleasant, book-lined study, still cool but gentled by the view of sunshine on a stretch of moss and an azalea hedge beyond through big generous windows. The desk was large but untidy and a little battered. On it, apart from scattered papers, stood an unpretentious portable typewriter and a single, quite ordinary telephone. Behind it sat a slender, middle-aged man in a light sweater under a well-cut but shabby sports jacket. His features were light, the bone structure delicate. The eyes were intelligent and humorous, hooded in repose by heavy lids. His small hands rested lightly

151

on the typewriter, and he made no move to get up. Instead he smiled and spoke in educated English.

"Come in, Walker. Come in and sit down, my dear fellow. I feel quite honoured to be the first on your visiting list."

He sounded disconcertingly like Endsleigh, and Walker could do little but gape at him as he sank into a comfortable armchair facing the desk. "How did you know you're the first?" he asked in a strangled voice, seizing on the only point he could make sense of.

Fujikawa smiled even more broadly. "Because if you had already been to see any of the other gentlemen whose names and addresses you have on the piece of paper in your right-hand jacket pocket, I should have heard about it. That's why." The door opened and a girl of about nineteen entered, carrying a tray with Western-style cups and saucers, milk jug and sugar bowl and a plate of biscuits. She wore jeans and a T-shirt with a likeness of Beethoven on her small breasts and flashed a quick smile at Walker as she put the tray down and left again, without having said a word. Fujikawa gestured to the tray between them and gazed steadily at Walker as he helped himself to milk and sugar and took a biscuit. They were Bath Olivers. Then Fujikawa took a cup of tea himself, adding milk only, and sipped, still keeping his eyes fixed unnervingly on Walker.

Walker busied himself with his teacup, playing for time. He felt like a schoolboy called upon to answer questions without having done his homework. He had not come to Nagoya with any very clear expectation of what he would find, but the reality was completely bewildering. Eventually Fujikawa broke the long silence, his slim body still relaxed and contained.

"You told my assistant that you had come to thank me for the condolence money. That is very kind." The drooping eyelids suddenly opened wide. "Why did you really come?"

Walker gathered up the shreds of mental discipline and replied. "That is the only reason, Mr Fujikawa. You and a few others were the only ones who were not either colleagues or neighbours of David Murrow, and his brother particularly asked me to express the family's appreciation to David's

152

friends." He decided to try to put Fujikawa just a little on the defensive.

"Do you operate your travel business from your house, sir?" he asked politely. The smallest suggestion of a smile passed rapidly over the older man's face. "I operate *all* my business from this house, Mr Walker," he replied equably. "I have to." Walker felt a sick sensation in his stomach as Fujikawa continued, "The reason I did not rise to greet you was because it's a complicated business for me to stand. Not having any legs, you see. A regrettable consequence of a demarcation dispute with another *oya-bun* some years ago." He pushed the typewriter to one side and leaned forward, fingers linked, as he continued.

"Mr Walker, I'm not sure that you are quite as silly as you like to pretend. I met a good many young men like you when I was up at Cambridge." He raised a hand as Walker opened his mouth to speak. "Yes, I was at Cambridge. There are one or two members of your Embassy in Tokyo who can tell you the circumstances, if you're really interested. A lot of odd things happened at the end of the war."

He took a biscuit and nibbled delicately at its edge. "Mr Walker, you are setting yourself up as an amateur detective. That is unwise on your part. There is no secret about the fact that Murrow was murdered. The investigation of the crime is a matter for the police, not for a foreign diplomat. Let me assure you that the police will quite certainly find the murderer. In due course."

The power of Fujikawa's personality was enormous, and Walker found himself almost hypnotised by the shining jet eyes under the drooping lids. With an effort he jerked himself upright in his chair. "The police may find the person who knifed Murrow," he said. "I'm not at all sure they'll do anything about the real murderer."

For the first time Fujikawa betrayed a hint of tension. He put the biscuit down and passed a hand quickly over his lower face; and several seconds passed before he spoke again. "No, you really aren't as silly as you pretend. Very well, let us suppose—just for the sake of discussion—that whoever killed Murrow and the person you refer to as the 'real murderer' are

153

different. What is that to you, other than a matter of idle curiosity?''

"It's the job of British consular representatives to protect British subjects resident in other countries. I want to leave nobody in doubt that we know quite a lot about the circumstances of Murrow's death. Too much to make it practicable to silence anybody else who was close to him." Fujikawa's eyes were now wide open, and seemed to look beyond Walker into another dimension.

He remained silent, and Walker went on. "It really was an extraordinary thing to present those large sums in incense money. Especially if the idea was to keep things quiet."

Fujikawa spoke quietly. "Be very careful, Walker," he said. "There are interests involved which would have no hesitation in arranging your removal if you become a serious nuisance. For all your diplomatic immunity."

The bland voice angered Walker, who stood up with a sense of outrage. His voice choked. "I'm not afraid of you or your thugs," he stammered. "If anything happens to me the whole lousy story will be given to Reuters and your clients can try gagging the whole Western press."

Fujikawa sighed gently. "I'm afraid you've got it all hopelessly wrong, Walker," he said patiently. "It isn't me you have to be afraid of or otherwise as the case may be. I would simply advise you, very earnestly, not to pay courtesy calls on any of the other people on your list.''He smiled. "At least until after the General Election." He pressed a concealed bell-push under the edge of the desk, and Walker heard the door behind him open almost at once. "Our visitor is leaving," said Fujikawa in Japanese. Then he held Walker's eyes for a long moment before reverting to English. "My daughter will show you out. I repeat. Do nothing for a day or two, until you receive a message from me."

The girl in the Beethoven T-shirt held the door open for Walker and gave him a wide, happy girl-next-door smile as he went through. He gave a last glance back at Fujikawa through the closing door and saw him reaching for the telephone, his face sombre and the eyes no more than glittering slits in the reflected sunshine. There was no sign of the young
154

man in the dark glasses, and the girl opened the front door, admitting a solid wedge of heat into the chilly, quietly lit elegance of the entrance hall. She spoke for the first time, in beautifully cultivated Japanese, using the conventional polite phrases.

"This way, please. You must honour us with another visit in the future." Feeling slightly silly, Walker found himself replying with the absurd formula prescribed even when one has just left the presence of the person referred to. "Please commend me to your honourable father." He bowed, the girl bowed; and then there was just the hot sunshine in the garden, the closed front door and the click of the bamboo tube. As he turned, the front gate swung open, and Walker made his way out and into the shabby slum street beyond.

On the way back to Kobe by train, Otani went over and over the situation as it now revealed itself. There was no chance that he would be able to fend Noguchi off and keep the evening to himself to ponder what to do, or use Hanae as a sounding board for his thoughts. Noguchi had fixed the meeting with Yamamoto: not, he supposed, an easy thing to do. And he would be lying in wait to hear all about it. So would Kimura, presumably. And he owed it to them to talk through the possibilities for action. Yet their job was virtually done. He, Otani, now knew all he needed to know to make an arrest.

"Except that you can't prove any of it," said Kimura an hour later as the three of them sat in the visitors' easy chairs in Otani's office. Noguchi had indeed just happened to be passing through the entrance hall when Otani arrived back, and the relief in his battered face at seeing his chief return safe and sound had made Otani momentarily ashamed of his earlier half-formulated plan to give him the slip. Nor had it taken many minutes for Kimura to materialise, natty in a new pale blue safari jacket with matching trousers. Otani looked at them both affectionately after he finished his recital, to which they listened in total silence. A conceited popinjay, undeniably clever but with a shocking record of misjudgements and blunders, and an operator of genius whom one couldn't possibly take along to Rotary. What a pair to trust and depend on so completely! Yet the correct and predictable Sakamoto—still presumably sulking in his tent—would have been no use whatever in this situation; or any other, come to think of it.

"That, Kimura-kun, is precisely the conclusion I came to myself on the way here," Otani said heavily. "My line is to the Prefectural Commission and then to the Governor, and it's been made very clear to us where *he* stands. I can just see him even trying to get access to the Prime Minister at this stage of the election."

Noguchi picked up his half-empty bottle of Pepsi-Cola from the ancient tin tray on the table between them and looked at it with disgust before pouring some more into his tumbler. "Could let the Minister know directly that we're on to him, maybe," he growled.

"What good would that do?" said Kimura reasonably. Noguchi glared at him. "Don't misunderstand me, Ninja," he added hastily. "I don't doubt you could do it. But he'd simply deny everything and then we're back to the beginning again." He turned to Otani, pulling a face. "I think we're stuck, Chief," he said glumly.

"For the moment, perhaps," Otani agreed. "Let's all sleep on it and meet here first thing in the morning. Anyway, gentlemen, I compliment you both on your efforts . . . and particular thanks to you, Ninja, for arranging an afternoon I shan't forget in a hurry. He's crazy, you know," he added as though the thought had struck him for the first time.

Noguchi lumbered to his feet. "Yamamoto? Of course. Crazy. And nasty. You shouldn't have gone without me."

"Stop grumbling, Ninja," said Otani more cheerfully as he and Kimura stood up and they all made for the door. "They'd never have let you in unless you bought a pretty new suit like Kimura here. And even if they had, you'd have scared Yamamoto's little girlfriend out of her wits."

"Jesus," said Takamura, and took a long pull at his whisky. "Why in hell didn't you ask me before you went to see him?" He and Walker were again in the bar of the Oriental Hotel in Kobe, and Walker had just finished giving a pretty well complete account of his interview with Kosaburo Fujikawa. He had not yet reported to Endsleigh, and felt an odd impulse to talk it over with Takamura first. The more he had to do with Takamura, the more he trusted him. It was a purely instinctive trust, and yet he realised that he had this faith partly because Ken Takamura *was* a rôle-player, acting out the part of a Pulitzer prize-winning investigative reporter. He felt confident that Takamura would never compromise the integrity of his performance, and liked him for it. "How much do you know about Fujikawa, Ken?" he asked.

Takamura produced a crumpled packet of Hi-lite cigarettes from his pocket, lit one and blew out a great cloud of smoke before replying. "One. He's about the biggest man west of Tokyo. Two. He has fantastic political pull among the *burakumin* all over Japan, because he made good. He was an ordinary enlisted man in the Japanese army during the war, part of the occupation garrison in Java. Even though he was a *buraku* outcast they saw he had something special, and he was in an intelligence unit attached to an internment camp where they held some Dutch, British and other Europeans. The story goes that he disappeared at the end of the war, then turned up again working with the British when they were between the Indonesian liberation people and the Dutch trying to get back."

He signalled the barman, pointed at their two empty glasses and waited for the fresh drinks to arrive before going on. Walker sat quietly, in no mood to interrupt the flow. "Well, it's not too clear what happened then, except he got paid off by the British and they say he went to college in England. Anyway, he must have come back to Japan in the early fifties, because he's been kind of Robin Hooding in Nagoya for the past twenty years. He runs the political machine, he runs the rackets and he takes care of his *ko-bun*. He's the most popular crook in Japan. Do you know he even gives interviews on TV, for heaven's sake? About juvenile *delinquency*?" Takamura raised his eyes to the ceiling and attacked his drink.

157

"How did he lose his legs?" asked Walker.

"Car accident," said Takamura. "They say it was the last round but one in his fight with the guy who used to run Nagoya. Fujikawa was in hospital for months . . . his wife was killed. But the one who apparently fixed the accident was dead within a week. Don't know how. Must be going on ten years ago."

"What do you think I ought to do?" Walker's heart felt distinctly unsteady as he looked at Takamura. "What do you think he meant about waiting for the election?"

Takamura shook his head indecisively. "If Fujikawa told you to wait for a message, my advice to you is to wait. Don't cross him, Andy. As for the elections, it adds up. Maybe Dave Murrow was putting the bite on a politician. Anyway, who are the others on your list?"

Belatedly, Walker remembered Endsleigh's advice to him to check the names with Takamura. He pulled the paper out of his jacket pocket, reflecting as he did so that the sweetshop woman in Nagoya must have given a remarkably full and accurate account of their meeting, presumably by telephone, during the few minutes it had taken him to follow her directions to Fujikawa's house. He handed the list to Takamura, who looked quickly over the names. Then he pulled out a felt-tip pen and made small marks against three other names, passing over that of Fujikawa at the top of the list. Two had Tokyo addresses and the third lived in Osaka. The second Nagoya name on the list he left unmarked, but pointed to it with the pen.

"It was a bit of luck you went to Fujikawa first in Nagoya," he commented. "This other man used to work for Fujikawa, but there was some kind of disagreement and I've heard he's off the payroll now. Fujikawa could have run him out of town, but he let him stay. He's linked up with some Tokyo interests now—maybe Fujikawa lets him stick around for the sake of the information he can pick up from him. Now the three I've marked are very interesting. The addresses don't mean much, but I recognise the names. They're all active politicians, and all running in the elections."

Takamura pointed to one of the Tokyo names. "This one

is trying for the Lower House, and the other Tokyo man is trying for prefectural Vice-Governor, I think. Our friend in Osaka is running in the national constituency because he's pretty well known as a baseball promoter and thinks he has friends all over the country. They all belong to the Government party . . .'' Takamura leaned back and wrinkled his long face, comically scratching his head in the gesture so common among Japanese schoolboys trying to avert the wrath of teachers by a show of modesty and charm.

Walker watched him, amused in spite of the excited tension he felt after his visit to Nagoya, and sipped his drink, crunching a small piece of ice between his teeth as Takamura straightened himself up and lit another cigarette. ''One of the other Osaka names I *didn't* mark is a mobster. Not the biggest—that's an old guy called Yamamoto—but pretty high up in Yamamoto's crowd all the same. Thank the Lord you didn't take it into your head to call on him. You might not be sitting here this evening if you had.''

Walker's amusement rapidly drained away as Takamura went on. ''The only sense I can make of these gifts is that they were intended not so much out of generosity to Murrow's family as to register in a kind of code *to each other* their interest in the murder and how much they knew about it, or thought they did. Kind of a language of flowers, Andy. You see, even though you didn't take much interest in the amounts at the time, you can be quite sure that if this murder had been done on somebody's orders, Mr Somebody had a man placed somewhere near the centre of the funeral arrangements. It was a way for various people to signal that they either knew something and needed to be bought off, or just know something and had to be reckoned with.''

Walker felt as though he were stumbling through a quicksand. ''But why politicians, Ken? Surely, with an election on, the last thing a candidate would want to do would be to draw attention to himself in the context of a murder?''

Takamura dragged hungrily at his cigarette and expelled the smoke through his nostrils, eyes closed. ''Depends who they were trying to signal to. It could have been the police, Andy. It just could have been the police.''

Abruptly he stood up, crossed to the bar and paid for their drinks, waving aside Walker's ineffectual efforts to beat him to the bill. "C'mon, kid," he said in a grotesque parody of Humphrey Bogart. "You and I are going out on the town." He led Walker almost at a run up from the basement bar to the main hotel lobby and through the automatic doors. Several taxis stood waiting, and as the driver of the first in line saw the two men he touched the remote control lever which made the back door of the car swing open invitingly. Takamura dived in, speaking quickly to the driver as he did so. Walker followed, scarcely having time to settle himself before the door banged shut behind him and the taxi jerked into movement, tyres screeching as it turned into the main road headed for the Sannomiya amusement district.

"What's the hurry?" asked Walker.

"No hurry," said Takamura, smiling blandly. "I guess he just likes to drive this way." He muttered something in coarse colloquial Japanese and the driver replied in what was obviously similar vein, finishing with a shout of good-natured laughter which showed off three gold teeth to full advantage.

"Did you get that, Andy?" asked Takamura, and Walker shook his head. "Only a word or two. Depressing."

Takamura explained. "I asked him whether the kind of guy who usually uses the Oriental generally goes where we're going, and he said yes, and they're generally in one hell of a hurry. Then he suggested a few reasons why that might be so." Walker smiled weakly, conscious of the fact that he was rarely the life and soul of the sort of party that it appeared they were about to go to.

The taxi veered away from the main road and entered a maze of little streets seemingly much too narrow for a car, but barely slackening pace as it negotiated the many twists and turns. They were in an area of tiny bars, cheery with their brightly and imaginatively illuminated signs. Suddenly the taxi shuddered to a halt, and Walker feared there must have been an accident. But the door swung open as before, and the driver cheerfully wished them a pleasant evening.

This time Walker was ahead, and paid off the taxi while Takamura stretched, looked around him and sniffed the air appreciatively. The bar to which they had been brought was obviously airconditioned, since its door was closed against the sultry night air. It had a discreet and quite tasteful illuminated black sign, with the woman's name "Yasuko" in cursive phonetic script picked out in a pleasant lavender colour. The door was of heavy opaque black glass.

Takamura led the way into the cool interior, where they were at once greeted by a friendly "You are welcome" from the young man behind the bar, dapper in a white jacket and black bow tie as he handled a cocktail shaker like a new and experimental percussion instrument. Two elegantly made-up girls slid from stools at the bar, smiling as they approached the two men, and led them to a table. Takamura was clearly known in the bar, and greeted the girls by name. The taller of the two, dressed in a Western evening gown, was called Reiko; her companion, who wore a light summer kimono in palest green, was Teruko. Teruko sat next to Walker, seemingly delighted to discover that he spoke Japanese.

Takamura was not only known but must have been a habitué of the place. He ordered drinks from what he referred to as his own bottle, and the barman reached behind him to a shelf on which there were perhaps twenty or thirty bottles of various types of whisky, each neatly labelled with the owner's name. The girls asked for Violet Fizz, a drink made from a Japanese liqueur called Crême Violette, with soda water. Its alcoholic content was modest, and it looked and smelt like cheap hair lotion. Walker had once tasted a sip, and wondered ever after why it was so popular with Japanese bar hostesses.

They sat there for a while, the girls chattering gaily and with every appearance of genuine enjoyment. Walker nursed his drink and Takamura sat back, eyes narrowed above drifting wisps of cigarette smoke, holding hands with Reiko. All at once, as though he had come to a decision, he sat up straight and murmured something into Reiko's ear. She nodded, got up at once and disappeared.

Her place was taken after a minute or two by another woman, considerably older and with great elegance of manner. She too was in kimono, of a darker shade appropriate to

161

her age, and she bowed with formal dignity before sliding into the vacant seat beside Takamura. As she did so, Teruko rose, excused herself and disappeared in turn. Walker guessed that this was the Mama-san or owner of the bar, and Takamura confirmed it by introducing him to the lady with considerable formality. She was indeed Madame Yasuko herself, and was obviously a person of consequence.

Good as Walker's Japanese was, he was unable to glean very much from the rapid conversation which followed in undertones between the other two. At one point Madame Yasuko's eyes widened with surprise and she shot a quick glance at Walker, wary and interested, before resuming the conversation. She glanced at him once or twice more during the rest of the conversation before nodding decisively. She then flashed a smile of great brilliance at Walker and clapped her hands, rising to her feet as she did so. Reiko and Teruko came back almost at once and took her place, taking up the conversation, such as it was, where they had broken it off. Walker forced himself to join in, longing to get Takamura on his own to find out what was going on.

Notwithstanding the airconditioning he felt warm and a little dizzy, and paid less and less attention to Teruko's delicately seductive questions about whether or not he had hair on his chest, as foreigners are supposed to have. It was with some surprise that he noticed that she had in fact undone two of his shirt buttons and was finding out for herself. It was after eleven, and Walker had had a long and demanding day. He had no desire to spend another hour or so in frustrating erotic teasing with Teruko, even at Takamura's expense—or, more likely, that of the *Kobe Shimbun* newspaper.

He morosely for another fifteen minutes, enjoying the pressure of Teruko's thigh against his but with a great longing for sleep coming upon him; and was relieved when Takamura suggested that they should go.They were seen fondly to the door by the two girls, and after protracted expressions of courtesy on all sides found themselves outside at last in the narrow street, quiet now except for the occasional pedestrian. They walked out to the main road, in silence at first, until Takamura began to talk quietly.

162

"Yasuko's a retired geisha. She used to be good, very good. Her last patron was a top politician. He's now a Minister. No, he isn't on your list, in case you're wondering. He set Yasuko up in that bar three years ago and they parted good friends. Often happens that way. Reiko's her daughter. Not by him, by a previous patron."

Walker wondered whether he was being stupid or had just drunk too much. He could see no relevance in all this. "So what did you find to talk about so busily?" he asked.

Takamura stopped walking and looked him full in the face. "Well, you see," he said, "I got to thinking. Those guys on your list are essentially second-line. And second-line politicians have to have support from above as well as below. That's why you have quite formal factional groupings within parties. They don't necessarily have differences over policy, they just group around particular individuals. It's the Japanese way."

Walker was tired and fed up. "So what?" he said with a touch of irritation.

"Don't get touchy, Andy," said Takamura reprovingly. "I'm coming to it. Yasuko's Minister's a married man of course. But there are whispers that he may be the other way inclined. Some say that he even took up with Yasuko as a kind of investment in his reputation. A guy doesn't usually go to the expense of keeping a top geisha just because he enjoys her conversation. It's a kind of public demonstration of *machismo*."

The open air was helping to clear Walker's head, and he began to put two and two together, or thought he did. "Why did he pay her off with that bar, then?" he enquired.

"That's what I was trying to find out. It wasn't easy, and Yasuko certainly wasn't about to say anything about his sex life. I wouldn't have dared to ask. No, I just said that some prominent politicians seemed to be particularly worried about the murder of the Englishman and that you were naturally puzzled, being officially concerned in the investigations. I didn't say a word about her ex-patron, and I simply don't know whether she got the message. But she did volunteer that she kept out of politics nowadays. She mentioned his name,

163

and said it got so that he was too busy to come down from Tokyo often enough to make it worth while their going on, and that she wouldn't have been allowed by the guild to go to work as a geisha in Tokyo.''

They walked on in silence a little longer, then Takamura spoke again. ''She wouldn't have referred to him unless he was on her mind. And my guess is that she's on the phone to him right now to tell him about our little talk.''

Wednesday

HER HUSBAND HAD ONLY JUST LEFT WHEN THE TELE-
phone rang at about eight-thirty, and when she heard the ag-
itation in Ambassador Tsunematsu's voice Hanae very nearly
ran out of the house to see if the car was still in view. She
suppressed the idea almost immediately; partly through consciousness of being still in nothing but her light sleeping kimono, but mainly because she disapproved entirely of what
seemed to be becoming Tsunematsu's habit of intruding into
their domestic privacy. Such a thing ought to have been un-
heard of; and in any event must be stepped on at once.

There was no hint of her displeasure in Hanae's voice as
she offered profound apologies for the inconvenience to
which the Ambassador had been put in finding him gone after
doing her husband the honour of telephoning him at his home
at such an early hour; but her meaning was clear, and an
expression of very slight hauteur settled on her normally
gentle face as Tsunematsu belatedly apologised. Then, mollified, Hanae pointed out that Otani would almost certainly
be at his desk by nine if the Ambassador would be so kind as
to telephone him there. With a renewed flurry of apologies
Tsunematsu rang off, and Hanae put the receiver down with
some satisfaction as well as a lingering curiosity.

Hanae was a woman given to reflection, and her pensive mood persisted as she cleared away and washed the breakfast things, then dressed. The after-effects of the thunderstorm of Monday evening were still in evidence, and the heat was definitely more acceptable with a little blue sky to go with it. Rather than going down to the small local shops for a few essentials she decided to venture rather further afield, so she picked out a favourite Western-style summer dress and set aside a soft woollen cardigan to put on if she should venture into the airconditioning of a department store.

It was nice to wear Western clothes quite a lot of the time. Even though she was careful not to choose anything too outrageous for a woman in her forties she had a good deal more freedom of choice than when buying kimonos, and it was specially nice to be able to show off her white arms and pretty shoulders in the summer. She slipped into a rather daring bra she had bought quite recently in one of the shops in Kobe that dealt mainly with foreign women, thinking it rather a pity that it was most unlikely that Tetsuo would ever see it on her, especially as he was a little unusual among Japanese men in taking pleasure in breasts. This triggered off a little reverie about their honeymoon in the hotel in Miyazaki twenty-five years before: oh dear, how very awkward and complicated it had all seemed, and how much nicer now. Even though their daily routine was such that she almost never nowadays seemed to dress or undress in front of him. But perhaps she might give Tetsuo a little surprise this evening . . .

How strangely he was reacting to this case of the foreigner. It must be important, for Kimura-san to have brought him in on it from the very beginning like that. Not to mention Ambassador Tsunematsu, a distinguished gentleman but a little two-faced. She had thought that on the one and only occasion he had actually called at the house, even though it had been New Year and the Ambassador all sweetness and light.

At least Tetsuo was now treated as a person of distinction; a very far cry from his early days as a junior officer stubbornly making a career in a necessary but despised profession, looked down upon by other professional people because he was a non-graduate. Unless, Hanae reflected with a little

166

smile as she put the final touches to her make-up, they happened to know he was the son of old Professor Otani. Well, anyway, he always enjoyed taking personal charge of a case on the rare occasions he decided to do so nowadays. And Hanae knew that at such times his habitually almost unnervingly even temper would give way to occasional black or disagreeable moods. She smiled again as she left the house. No problem really; she generally knew what to do about *them*.

"I'm surprised, too," admitted Kimura with some reluctance. "I would certainly have expected him to wait and insist on speaking to you personally. But he said he had to go and make an early official call . . . it could only be on the British, I'd say." Otani nodded thoughtfully. It was shortly before nine-thirty, and he had been surprised on walking into the building twenty minutes earlier to find Kimura hovering in the entrance hall, bursting with the news that Tsunematsu had been on the telephone at a quarter to nine demanding to know whether the police were aware that a member of the British consular staff resident in their area was on friendly terms with Kosaburo Fujikawa of Nagoya.

"What did you tell him?" asked Otani.

"Well, I explained that he'd got the right man anyway, because as head of the Foreign Affairs Section I have the job of keeping an eye on these people and liaising with my opposite number in Osaka. Then I asked him who he was talking about. He didn't want to say at first, but realised after a while what a ridiculous position he was putting himself and us into. It's Walker, the Vice-Consul."

"Walker? Wasn't he the young man who came to the morgue? I saw him at the funeral, too." Otani recollected the tall young man with the big ears quite well.

Kimura nodded. "Yes. The Japanese speaker." Assimilating this new information, Otani buzzed for his clerk and asked him to see if Inspector Noguchi was in the building. Noguchi came into the room almost immediately and listened in grim silence as Kimura repeated his news on Otani's instructions.

"I told him no, I'd no evidence that Walker had any doubtful contacts, let alone a man like Fujikawa,'' Kimura concluded. ''And he rang off suddenly, as though he regretted making the call in the first place.''

Otani turned to Noguchi, who was massaging one cauliflower ear as he listened. ''What's the connection between Fujikawa in Nagoya and Yamamoto in Osaka, Ninja?''

''Hate each other's guts,'' said Noguchi briefly. ''Different type of operation. Old Yamamoto—political nut. But just a hobby. Spirit of Yamato, samurai stuff. Can you see him working with an outcast like Fujikawa?'' He used the old, forbidden word ''*eta*'', rather than the official ''*buraku*'', and Kimura winced delicately.

Noguchi continued, in what was for him a burst of eloquence. ''Fujikawa's a decent crook. He's carved out his own piece of action. More of a politician than anything. And he does a lot for his own. Tough as hell, mind you. Doesn't do to get in his way.'' He paused and sucked his teeth, then looked at Kimura. When he spoke again the cunning old eyes were locked on the younger man's. ''I've heard things. You should have.''

''What things?'' said Kimura uneasily as Otani looked from one to the other of them with interest.

''If you were really as smarty-arse as you act, you'd know Fujikawa spent years in England,'' Noguchi said with affable contempt.

''And the English Consul has dealing with him, it seems.'' He wheeled round and addressed himself to Otani. ''Suggest anything to you?'' he demanded.

Walker treated himself to an extra hour in bed after his late night and eventually set out for the office still feeling distinctly hung over, but with a pleasant sense of anticipation as he looked forward to telling the Consul General about his exploits of the previous day. The staid offices above the bank, with their formal Notices to British Subjects, cheap COI prints of colour photographs of the Royal Family in kilts at Balmoral and commercial handouts from the Overseas Trade Board, seemed very dull after the sort of surroundings in which he had been playing detective, and he settled down to look through his in-tray with a sense of anticlimax.

Endsleigh was not normally an early bird, and in any case liked to devote himself to his papers for the first hour or so of the day. In spite of his own late arrival, Walker waited impatiently a full half hour before dialling Jill Braxon's number on the internal line. "Yes?" came the tired voice. "Morning, Jill. Andrew CG in yet?"

"Been in bloody hours," said Jill sourly. "Like a bear with a sore head, too."

"Is he free?" asked Walker.

"No. Ambassador Tsunematsu's with him."

Walker was surprised. He could think of no reason why the liaison officer of the Japanese Foreign Ministry would be calling on Endsleigh that morning, or indeed at all. Apart from the routine courtesy calls at the beginning and end of tours of duty on both sides, contacts with the Japanese authorities were relaxed and informal. The liaison officer's role in relation to the Consular Corps was mainly ceremonial, and official communications of a day-to-day kind were generally by telephone or letter.

"Let me know when he's finished, please, Jill," he said, and after hearing a mutter of what could have been assent, put the phone down and began to shuffle through his papers. He couldn't seem to settle to work, though, and was relieved when his phone rang a few minutes later and on answering he heard Jill. "He wants you. Now," she said without ceremony.

As he went out into the corridor Walker saw the neat and elegant back of Ambassador Tsunematsu disappearing into the lift. As he watched the doors close Walker wondered why the Consul General had not extended the usual courtesy of escorting him to the lift, and experienced a vague sense of unease as he went into the ante-room. He returned Jill's sour look with a tentative smile as he passed her desk, tapped on Endsleigh's door and went straight in.

The smile faded from his lips as his eyes met Endsleigh's and he saw the look of icy dignity on the Consul General's face. Endsleigh stared at him in silence, and tension built up until Walker found his voice. "Is something wrong?" he asked.

Endsleigh spoke quietly. "Sit down, Andrew. I blame myself for this. Tsunematsu rang me at home this morning setting up a meeting first thing. I've just had him in here lodging an official complaint about your activities. Claims the police have had you under observation and that you've been consorting with known criminals. Warned me that if it continues the Ministry will summon our Ambassador and have you PNG'd.''

Walker could hardly believe his ears. To be declared *persona non grata* in some countries could amount to very little: a tit-for-tat face-saving device used by an unstable or touchy government which nobody at home in the FCO would take seriously. But to be expelled from Japan, the country to which he hoped to devote most of his diplomatic career, a country scrupulously correct in its interpretation of the Vienna Convention, would shatter his future in the service. Endsleigh saw the distress in Walker's face and smiled at him sadly. "Be of good cheer, Master Walker," he said. "It hasn't happened yet, and probably won't. Nevertheless, you'd better tell me what you've been up to that's upset them so badly.''

Walker blinked a few times, straightened his tie and told the Consul General exactly what had happened the previous day, from the time he arrived in Nagoya to the time he parted from Takamura late at night. Endsleigh listened attentively, lips pursed, whistling noiselessly as Walker described his meeting with Fujikawa and Takamura's conversation with Madame Yasuko. When the young man had finished Endsleigh leaned back, fiddling with a paper-knife bearing the arms of the City of London, the gift of a visiting alderman.

"And Takamura thought it possible that the incense money could have been a signal to the police?" he said at last. Walker nodded, and Endsleigh looked round his airy, comfortable office. "Well, my dear fellow," he said more cheerfully, "I must say I rather hope the boys in blue have a little bug recording all this. You are a perfect chump to have gone barging off to Nagoya without either asking or telling me. Let me make that quite clear. All the same, it seems to me that if a

170

high government official comes trotting round here the morning after you've paid an unexpected and perhaps worrying call on a top Nagoya crook who happens also to carry a good deal of weight in political circles, to say you must mend your ways or be booted out . . . well, I should say you're on the right lines. And I should also say," he continued in his clear, polished voice, "that if they do call in the Ambassador, he should invite the Minister of Foreign Affairs to cast an eye over a draft message to be given to all the wire services the same day, with a bit of background about the election campaign. Would you think that a good idea, Andrew?"

Walker began to feel a little better, even though the confused thoughts and emotions racing round his brain did little to help his residual headache. Endsleigh spoke again, in a more natural manner, the note of concern back in his voice. "You're a grown man, Andrew, in a responsible post. I've asked you to use your discretion over all this, and can scarcely complain when you do. All the same, I've been reproaching myself ever since it dawned on me what Tsunematsu was burbling about. Would you like to be let off the hook?"

Walker shook his head decisively. "No, thank you . . . Joe. I realise it was a bit rash to go yesterday, but I feel much clearer about it all after talking to Ken Takamura. And in any case, Fujikawa warned me off the other people in the list. Till after the election. So I can't really get into any more trouble before the weekend, can I?"

Endsleigh considered. "Polling day Sunday, of course. Mmm. I wonder why we always have it Thursdays at home? Very well then, Andrew. You go on using your discretion. I really feel the other chaps, whoever they may be, have the most to worry about for the present. And I certainly don't think the Foreign Ministry could possibly make a convincing case for a PNG on the basis of what you've done. So don't let it spoil your lunch."

He nodded to Walker and smiled as he left the room, then spent a long time staring thoughtfully at the closed door before picking up the telephone to talk to the Head of Chancery in the Embassy in Tokyo.

Walker for his part went back to his office in something of a daze, and spent what was left of the morning aimlessly pushing his papers about, achieving nothing. At noon he went out into the hot city bustle of Midosuji Boulevard and strolled down to the canal which separates the inner city island of Nakanoshima from the rest of central Osaka. The foetid water stank in the hot sun, but the bustle of traffic was muted slightly, and Walker watched a barge move slowly past on its way down to Osaka Bay.

It felt odd, frightening but distinctly exciting to have come by the awareness of a mixture of fact and innuendo which could, it seemed, conceivably bring down the government of one of the most sophisticated and industrially powerful countries in the world. In an age in which the function of a diplomat had become more and more emasculated, to the point sometimes of seeing oneself as nothing more than a well-paid messenger boy in occasional fancy dress, a strange thing had happened to Andrew Walker, a lowly Grade Seven Vice-Consul in his first substantive post. He had become, Walker told himself, a personage of consequence, a man to be reckoned with.

He was honest enough to admit to himself that he was very scared. The day had taken on a dream-like quality which even the heat and sunshine of high noon could not dissipate, and he wandered aimlessly along the canalside, half thinking he ought to do something about lunch, but not wanting to go into any of the busy little snack bars and tearooms now full of office workers taking their brief midday break.

The streets among the skyscraper buildings were full of the "new" Japanese; the men in neat white shirts and ties, the girls in cotton summer dresses chatting animatedly in twos and threes, often quite unselfconsciously holding hands as they sauntered along. There were hardly any man-woman couples, but the thought did not occur to Walker, preoccupied and in any case accustomed to the scene as he was, until a young man and a girl did come along together, avoiding physical contact but with their eyes locked on each other in obvious absorption.

The sight in an odd way helped Walker to see his problem

in perspective. Endsleigh's encouragement had done something to allay his first sick feeling of apprehension on hearing of Ambassador Tsunematsu's threat. And, as he had already pointed out, he fully intended to follow Fujikawa's advice, at least for the next few days. Finally, whatever sickness and corruption there might be all around, the young man and his girl had looked happy in each other's company.

Slightly heartened, but though still not really having any appetite, he went into a quick lunch bar and had a sandwich and coffee; then made his way back to the familiar cool orderliness of his office. There was a message on a slip of paper on his desk. A Mr Suzuki had telephoned, and Walker was requested to call back, on an Osaka number. Suzuki is a very common name, and Walker had met several Suzukis during his time in Japan. He speculated idly about the identity of his caller as he dialled the number on the paper. He heard the ringing tone, then a quiet male voice answering in the peculiarly unhelpful Japanese manner. "Yes?" Walker gave his own name and asked in Japanese for Mr Suzuki. He was a little surprised when the man at the other end spoke in quite fair English.

"Thank you for calling back, Mr Walker. Mr Suzuki is out just now. This is the Osaka office of Fujikawa Travel Agency." Walker stiffened and felt a bead of sweat trickle down his back as the voice continued politely. "Mr Suzuki wished to invite you to see the famous cormorant fishing in the old Japanese tradition at Gifu. He would like to arrange it for one evening this week if you are free. You know this is the time of the year for this famous tourist sight."

Walker tried to keep a cool head. "Thank you," he said. "But I have already seen the same kind of cormorant fishing at Arashiyama near Kyoto." There was a pause at the other end of the line before he heard the voice again, quietly insistent. "The Fujikawa Travel Agency would be very honoured if you would accept, Mr Walker. I think you would find it very interesting and colourful at Gifu. Mr Suzuki would like to suggest this evening, as a matter of fact. If you will please take the Kodama express train leaving Shin Osaka Station at ten minutes after four this afternoon, you will be met at Gifu

Station. Your seat reservation has been made and the ticket will be delivered to your office within the next half an hour."

There was a click as the connection was cut, and Walker replaced his own receiver suddenly rather short of breath and with his stomach churning. How could he be sure the message really was from Fujikawa? Gifu. Less than half an hour from Nagoya by road. Fujikawa territory, certainly. Better ask Joe Endsleigh's advice. Then Walker heard himself firmly declining to be let off the hook. Use your discretion. A chump to go barging off to Nagoya without asking or telling.

Walker indecisively stood up and almost unconsciously walked through to the Consul General's ante-room as he continued to debate with himself. There was no sign of Endsleigh or of Jill. Probably both at lunch. Walker looked at the desk diary in which Jill noted all engagements and saw that Endsleigh would be out for virtually the whole afternoon at a meeting of the British Chamber of Commerce. There was nobody else to whom he could explain the situation, so he scribbled a message on a piece of paper:

Jill: Pl tell CG I've gone out for continuation of yesterday's meeting. Back in the office tomorrow. AW

As he straightened up from Jill's desk the Japanese receptionist hurried up to him, an envelope in her hand. "A man just brought this for you, Mr Walker," she said. "He said you were expecting it."

"What did he look like?" Walker asked, taking the envelope. The girl looked puzzled. "Just ordinary," she said hesitantly. "Like a messenger."

Walker smiled at her dismissively. "Thank you," he said, and took the envelope back to his own room. He ripped it open there and found a ticket with a first-class seat reservation for the train the man on the telephone had specified. Fujikawa had said that Walker had nothing to fear from him. He was intrigued, keyed up and more than a little scared. But he decided to obey the summons to Gifu.

* * *

Otani had decided to attend the regular weekly meeting of his own Rotary Club, Kobe South. He was tempted to give it a miss and make up at another club later in the week, but there was no real reason why he couldn't go along to the New Port Hotel and eat the lunch he had already paid for rather than paying a second time elsewhere. Besides, he need not pay attention to the weekly talk, and could instead sit quietly and ponder the implications of Tsunematsu's extraordinary behaviour.

The man must obviously be under enormous political pressure to act in such a hamfisted and ill-considered way. He was as good as admitting that Otani's own politician-gangster-murderer equation was right. That was of little help in itself; as Kimura pointed out, it was all very well knowing who the guilty man was, quite another to prove it. The anxiety about the young Englishman's contacts with Fujikawa, whatever they might have amounted to, was something else again.

Otani sighed inwardly as he prodded with his spoon at the inevitable crême caramele which was provided with an accompanying cup of coffee as the conclusion to the hurried meal. The Secretary was already shuffling the cards of visiting Rotarians from other clubs and tapping the microphone unnecessarily as a prelude to introducing them. Tsunematsu was a wily old bird and Otani had been irritated by him—and even lost his temper with him—more than once in the past, especially when Tsunematsu had quite obviously been in possession of information which either had, or to which he had decided to attribute, a security classification.

If there had been anything in Ninja Noguchi's dark hints, the situation was back to front this time. It seemed hard to credit that Fujikawa might maintain links with British security; still less that Tsumematsu and his contacts in the Security Agency wouldn't know if he did. Otani traced spirals on the starched white tablecloth as the visiting speaker droned on and his own thoughts revolved round the central issues. It was absurd to think of that amiable young man with the jug ears as a British spy, even if he did speak Japanese quite competently. Another thing. Suppose, just suppose, some piece

175

of hard evidence came his way to demonstrate beyond any question the involvement of the Minister in the murder plot. He was a senior police officer, and also a responsible citizen. He also owed a certain personal loyalty to the Governor who had appointed him.

Not a political loyalty, of course, Otani mused as the meeting ended and he automatically bowed and waved at a few special acquaintances in the rush for the doors. As a matter of fact the Governor might well be slightly surprised if he knew the pattern of his prefectural police commander's own voting habits over the years. Never mind. It was still loyalty.

When he arrived back at headquarters Otani summoned Kimura. "You're an educated man, Kimura-kun," he began, and Kimura looked at him warily. Otani frequently teased him, occasionally complained testily about him, and once in a while blew him up with imperial rage. But he rarely indulged in sarcasm. "I'm serious," Otani reassured him, noticing the look on the younger man's face.

"You know we were talking yesterday afternoon about the difficulty of actually pinning this thing on to the right man?" Kimura nodded.

"Well, I'm quite prepared to have a try. Two people—at least—seem to have been killed to preserve his public reputation. It's going to be a very long and messy case in the courts, and the police might not win even in the end. But my real problem is this. Is it right to pursue this man *immediately* in the absence of hard objective evidence, and very probably affect the whole course of the election?"

Kimura nodded slowly, flattered to be consulted. "I see what you mean, Chief," he said. "Then again, we're not absolutely sure it isn't one of the other two or three people we extracted from Murrow's card index. We could possibly put together just as convincing a case for suggesting that one of them did it. You've really only Yamamoto's indiscretion to go on."

Otani shook his head. "Not really. How else to explain Tsunematsu this morning? Somebody high up is obviously putting the heat on him."

The two men sat in glum communion for a few moments

longer, then Otani got up wearily and crossed to the window to look at the ever-changing harbour skyline. Kimura remained in his chair, studying his carefully manicured fingernails but with genuine absent-mindedness. "There's a technical problem, anyway, Chief," he said at last.

Otani turned to him moodily. "Oh? What's that?"

"He's in Tokyo. You'd have to talk to the police there, and their prefectural prosecutor, into agreeing to an arrest. And I doubt if they would," said Kimura. "What's more, in view of everything that's happened I doubt very much if you could even persuade *our* prosecutor to agree, always assuming you could lure our man down here somehow. Unless you could pose him with a knife in his hand dripping blood while he dictated a confession on to video-tape in the presence of witnesses."

"You're right, of course," said Otani. "I don't know whether to feel sorry or relieved. Shouldn't get carried away, I suppose. But we carry on, Kimura-kun. I'd like to get that man, however long it takes." He looked at Kimura with mock impatience. "All right, don't sit there loafing," he barked. "Get to work. Find out why the devil that young man has anything to do with Fujikawa."

The boat drifted nearby on its fourth pass along the reach of the Gifu River, the flaring brazier suspended over its stern making the black surface of the water ruddy and alive, and enhancing the velvety quality of the night around them. One fisherman leaned out of the old-fashioned boat, banging its side with a heavy billet of wood and shouting in a hoarse, rhythmic chant. The cormorant master stood at the bow in a short, tightly belted cotton happi-coat, the leading strings in his hands, playing them like a puppeteer with never a tangle as the ungainly birds bobbed and plunged in the water ahead.

With a clumsy flapping of its great wings the senior bird fluttered back to its master, who grasped it while it disgorged the silver *kisu* sweetfish from its gullet into the basket at his feet, then released it to perch proudly in its allotted place on the prow. In succession the other birds under the master fisherman's control surfaced, delivered their catches and perched

177

with hieratic dignity in their due positions, as serenely conscious of their station and duties in life as domestic servants in Victoria's England.

A noisy party of Japanese men on the periphery of the light from the brazier on the fishing boat sang in ragged chorus as the gaudy bar-girls with them refilled their *sake* cups, the paper lanterns decorating their flat-bottomed boat a kaleidoscope of pinks and reds. Other similar boats, each carrying ten or a dozen spectators, floated here and there on the same stretch of river, sculled perfunctorily by elderly boatmen to keep them within view of the fishing. Walker was filled with a strange but by no means unpleasing mixture of bewilderment and content. The day which had begun so disturbingly and had developed so mysteriously seemed to be moving towards a most promising conclusion.

Gifu is not a large city, and its railway station, though sizeable, is not a kind which generates the life and excitement of a metropolitan terminus. As his train pulled in late in the afternoon Walker had half expected to be met by the young man who had acted as Fujikawa's doorkeeper and henchman at the house in Nagoya. He had been knocked completely off mental balance when he saw Fujikawa's daughter, the girl with the Beethoven T-shirt, waiting on the platform. The face and the happy, intelligent expression were as he remembered from their earlier brief meeting, but her general appearance was transformed by the fact that she was wearing Japanese dress; a light summer kimono in cool shades of blue, a gossamer silk fan in one hand.

She came forward as Walker stepped out of the train, gave a little bow and smiled at him. "You are welcome," she said in Japanese in the formal manner. "I'm glad that you could come to see our famous Gifu cormorant fishing."

"I am very glad to see you again," replied Walker with perfect truth. "It must be very inconvenient for you to come all the way from Nagoya to meet me, though."

The girl smiled again, and with a delicate gesture indicated the way to the exit. "My father asked me to show you the fishing," she said as they walked along. "Afterwards Suzuki-san would like to talk to you."

They emerged from the station and she led Walker to the car park, where to his further astonishment she produced a set of keys from her kimono sleeve and unlocked a stylish Mazda sports car. She slid into the driving seat and reached over to unlock the passenger door, starting the engine at the same time. As Walker got in beside her he felt the cool freshness of airconditioning, and with a mental shrug settled himself comfortably, amused by the incongruity of the spectacle of the slight, delicately feminine Japanese in her classic dress in command of this complex and expensive assemblage of modern machinery.

"Fujikawa-san," he said as they moved off. "Can you tell me what all this is about?"

"My name is Mitsuko," she said irrelevantly, "but you can call me Mi-chan. Everybody does." Walker didn't know what to make of this offer of intimacy. To address a child as "chan" was normal and natural, but she was a distinctly adult young woman, of an apparent breeding which would justify the use of the suffix only by her immediate family or by close friends from schooldays.

He passed it over for the time being as she drove the car out of the station precincts and swung it expertly into the mainstream of the traffic. She negotiated two or three junctions and soon they were driving beside the river, towards a cluster of inns and waterside restaurants. Walker tried again. "You didn't answer my question," he said. "I would like to know why I'm here."

Mitsuko smiled, very much to herself. "To see the cormorant fishing," she said simply.

Walker gave up, and looked out of the window. After a while Mitsuko pulled in to the forecourt of an inn near the jetties where the passenger boats were being made ready for the evening's festivities. It was after six-thirty, and the short dusk of Japan was beginning to soften the greenery of the opposite bank of the river and the hills beyond. Mitsuko led the way into the inn, where they were greeted with great ceremony by a male receptionist and led to a lounge furnished in comfortable Western style.

Mitsuko smiled at Walker without a trace of embarrass-

179

ment. "There is a men's room through there," she said, pointing. "Please refresh yourself after your journey. We shall be on the river for at least two hours." Walker felt the beginnings of one of his maddening blushes, and hurriedly went in the direction indicated. The facilities were lavish in the extreme; he took his time and rejoined Mitsuko in the lounge feeling relaxed and in a pleasurable glow of anticipation.

On a table in front of her was a tray bearing a bottle of Johnnie Walker Black Label, soda water and ice. She poured two generous drinks, handed one to Walker and raised her own glass to him. "Your health," she said, and sipped delicately. "I suppose this Walker whisky is made by members of your family? Walker is a very important name in England?"

Walker grinned and shook his head. "Sorry, no connection. I wish there were. But Walker is a very common name—so much so that it had never even occurred to me to connect it with the whisky firm. It's more common than, say, Fujikawa in Japan. More like Suzuki."

He rather hoped that he would be able to lead on from there to ask Mitsuko what the mysterious Mr Suzuki wanted to talk to him later about, but she made no response and a constrained silence fell between them. Walker drank his whisky rather more quickly than he should have done, and Mitsuko poured him another which he also attacked, more out of general clumsiness and embarrassment than thirst for alcohol. She had hardly touched the liquid in her own glass, and her level, amiable gaze was thoroughly disconcerting. Walker was relieved when the receptionist returned, bowed and announced that their boat was ready.

Outside it was almost completely dark. Their boatman was waiting, a bent, shrivelled old man, and he led the way to the jetty, talking almost to himself in a monotone which Walker found quite incomprehensible. Their boat was distinctly superior to those available for general hire and now rapidly filling up with parties of tourists, nearly all Japanese.

It was flat-bottomed like the others, but designed to accommodate no more than four passengers in spacious luxury,

180

sitting on soft cushions round a low central table. On this table was spread a meal which it would have been insulting to describe with the word "picnic". Mitsuko cast little sidelong glances at Walker as he took in the full magnificence of the feast, and settled herself opposite him, arranging the folds of her soft lawn kimono round her slender thighs.

The old boatman poled them away from the jetty and they drifted downstream. Mitsuko indicated the food with a small hand. "There isn't anything much, but please try some of these small snacks," she said absurdly as Walker goggled at the platters of smoked salmon, delicately grilled pieces of chicken, fish, *sushi,* strawberries, melon and other fruit. "It is difficult to arrange for warm *sake* on the river, though there are special restaurant boats which come round to sell it. But my father has sent this wine for us."

So saying, she reached behind her and produced a bottle of what proved to be excellent Moselle, nestling in an ice bucket. Having been listless about food earlier in the day, Walker now found himself ravaged by hunger. The whisky had inspired a degree of tipsy recklessness in him, and Ambassador Tsunematsu's ultimatum vanished from his consciousness for the first time since he had learned of it. At that moment he could think of few more agreeable things than floating in a luxuriously appointed boat with plentiful supplies of good food and drink on a pleasant stretch of river in the company of a remarkably attractive girl.

He ate a lot; Mitsuko only a little, while continually urging particularly appetising morsels on him. She drank her fair share of the wine, though, and her cheeks grew pink and her eyes sparkled in the flickering candlelight of the lanterns hanging round their boat.

They could see clearly from fifty yards away the preparations for the actual fishing as full darkness descended on the river. They watched the lighting of the brazier which would attract the fish to the vicinity of the boat, and the assured technique of the cormorant master as he attached his cords to the rings on the collars at the base of the necks of the haughty birds. They saw a squabble flare up between two cormorants when one occupied a perch in the other's territory; and as quickly end when the fisherman rebuked the upstart and mollified the bird whose dignity had been affronted.

They finished their meal, and Mitsuko quickly cleared the table, which the old boatman stowed away. Then she moved across and sat beside Walker, one slim arm over the side, trailing her fingers through the water. It was about eight-thirty, and the evening's fishing was almost at an end. Walker began to entertain gently maudlin hopes of improving still further on his growing acquaintanceship with Mitsuko, and decided to try out her pet name.

"Mi-chan," he said tentatively, and she smiled at him encouragingly. "Mi-chan, may I ask how old you are?"

"I shall be twenty next week," she said. "Why do you want to know?"

Walker was at a loss for a satisfactory reply. "I don't know, really," he said. "Japanese and Westerners find it hard to guess each other's ages, they say. But I was right about you, anyway. I'm twenty-eight. Do you go to college?"

Mitsuko turned to him with a touch of impatience. "*Buraku* people don't go to college. Well, perhaps a few do, but not one with a name as well-known as mine. No college would take me."

Walker was mortified by his tactlessness, and struck even in his embarrassment by the power of a social tradition that could exclude from higher education the charming and obviously intelligent daughter of one of the most powerful men in Japan. Yet Fujikawa could well afford to send his daughter abroad. Why didn't he do so?

Further thought was interrupted by a shock of physical excitement as Mitsuko slipped her arm through his and sang quietly. "*Che sera, sera,* Whatever will be, will be; the future's not ours to see, *che sera, sera.*" The sound of the English words prompted Walker to abandon Japanese for a moment. "Do you speak English?" he demanded abruptly. At first there was silence except for the gurgling of water at the side of the boat and the diminishing sound of merrymaking in the distance.

"Yes," she said eventually. "My father has always made

182

me study hard. But of course I don't speak it as well as he does. I don't meet many English or Americans to talk to." Walker boldly took her hand in his and squeezed it gently. The sensation was much more electrically erotic than when he experienced Nicole's expert but somehow routine caresses.

"Why didn't you tell me before?" he asked.

Mitsuko giggled "I like your nice funny accent in Japanese," she admitted.

Walker was distinctly nettled. "Well, if it comes to that, you have a nice funny accent in English, too," he said, then laughed as well. "From now on, half and half. Agreed?"

"Agreed," said Mitsuko, releasing her hand from his. Walker was disappointed until he realised that she was delving into a bag behind her. She produced a half bottle of cognac. "You must drink to our agreement," she said, and poured Walker a glass of the brandy. "You too," said Walker, but she shook her head a little sadly. "No, thank you. We are going back now, and I must drive you to the station. I've already had so much wine." They were indeed approaching the lights of the inn, and Walker drank up quickly, glad that Mitsuko had taken his hand again for the last minutes of their ride.

When they disembarked Walker in a fit of expansiveness wanted to give the old boatman a large tip. Mitsuko prevented him. "No, please not," she whispered in English. "He will be offended." A nagging thought drifted into Walker's fuddled mind as they got into the car. "What about Suzuki-san?" he asked. "I've had a lovely evening, but what about the message?" He felt drowsy and amorous. The last thing he wanted to do was talk to Suzuki, whoever he might be. He wanted to hold Mitsuko's hand again; to put his arms round her, to slip the kimono from her smooth young shoulders and find the warmth and softness beneath.

He gazed adoringly and foolishly into Mitsuko's troubled brown eyes as the drug took hold and the waves of blackness swamped his consciousness, then slumped back in his seat, out cold. Mitsuko gave a little sigh, then her mouth tightened and she started the engine. They ought to be in Nagoya well before ten.

Ninja Noguchi watched them drive off. The young Englishman had found himself a pretty classy girlfriend. He noted the registration number of the car. It would be interesting to find out the following day who she was, from the traffic department. Or maybe he could find out more easily right away. He made for the jetty where the old boatman was pottering about tidying up, pulling a bottle of *sake* from the pocket of his sagging cotton jacket as he went.

Thursday

I**T WAS A CURIOUS DREAM. W**ALKER WAS A BOY AGAIN, AT the first concert he had ever been to, sitting in the Royal Festival Hall with his father, listening to Mozart. The soloist in the piano concerto was Ken Takamura, playing with great brio; and his father was not his father but Endsleigh, gravely turning the pages of a miniature score. This perturbed Walker, who feared that the pages would rustle and disturb the performance. His mother, on the other side, sensed his anxiety and put her hand reassuringly on his forearm, pressing it gently, then with more insistent force.

Walker opened his eyes in irritation. The Mozart was real, flooding from the stereo speakers in the elegantly furnished sitting-room of Kosaburo Fujikawa. The hand belonged not to his mother but to Mitsuko. She was again in informal Western clothes, but this time her blue jeans were surmounted by a red and white checked shirt which gave her something of the look of the young Doris Day in spite of her glossy black hair.

Walker pulled himself away and tried to get to his feet, but sank back among the cushions of the sofa on which they were both sitting as a wave of pain and nausea drenched his consciousness. The girl got up and crossed to a side table, returning with a small glass of colourless liquid which she handed to him with her broad, un-Japanese smile.

"I think Walker-san has a great pain in his head," she said in well-bred Japanese. "If he will please drink this, it will soon go away." Walker took the glass, thinking through a mist of pain and sadness that she seemed a very unlikely person to be an accomplice of gangsters, but that the glass could nevertheless very well contain poison for all he knew. Death could hardly be more disagreeable than his present misery, however, so he drank the contents down, noting only a faintly salty taste as he swallowed.

The effect was indeed both rapid and pleasant. He closed his eyes and gradually the nausea passed and the aching diminished. The Mozart piano concerto came to an end and was followed, presumably on tape for Mitsuko had returned to the sofa and was curled up at the other end of it, by Schubert's *Trout* quintet. After a few minutes Walker very gingerly sat up straight, this time without difficulty, and looked at his watch.

The hands stood at ten minutes to ten, and he realised that he must have been unconscious for over twelve hours. He rubbed his face, and felt the growth of stubble on his chin. "Is my watch right?" he said, omitting any of the polite forms the girl had used. "Nearly ten?"

She looked at him over the tops of her knees, her arms hugging her shins. "Something like that," she said with equal lack of formality. "Want some breakfast?"

Walker became aware with some surprise that he was in fact hungry, but the desire to wash, shave and if possible change his clothes was the more urgent. He replied curtly. "First I should like to make myself clean, then to be told why I am here, and then perhaps to eat after that."

Fujikawa's daughter uncurled herself, jumped to her feet and beamed with good humour. "You are more handsome when you are clean," she agreed. "And you smell better, too.

"This way please," she said as she skipped to the door. She led Walker across the entrance hall and through another door, then up a flight of carpeted stairs bathed in natural sunshine and to a well-equipped Western style bathroom with a cool, clean, welcomingly fresh atmosphere. Then, to Walker's relief, she left him. At least, he reflected, she hadn't offered to bathe him.

He stared at himself in the mirror and was appalled by his appearance. No man with a growth of stubble can avoid looking viallainous, but the face that confronted Walker was pale, haggard and ill-looking. His eyes were bloodshot, his mouth tight and strained. He turned away and peeled off his clothes. The shower was copious, the supply of hot water apparently endless, and ten minutes later he felt a great deal better.

Cleansed and freshened, a towel round his waist, he turned to the wash-basin and found a plastic throwaway razor set complete with shaving cream. He dealt with the stubble, then washed and dried his face finally. Hair combed, he looked at his reflection again. It was much improved. The pallor and tension were still there, but he felt and looked alert.

He didn't much relish the thought of putting his soiled clothes back on again and looked with some longing at a neatly folded cotton yukata on a chair. It all depended what was in store for him. He even got as far as shaking out the folds of the garment, but a glance at its totally inadequate length decided him, and he dressed again in his own clothes. To be physically vulnerable in nothing but a cotton wraparound was one thing; to be ridiculous was something else. At least his lightweight suit was well cut and still looked good. The shirt was crumpled but still tolerably clean. It would just have to do.

As he left the bathroom the bars of sunshine gave the house an air of opulent tranquillity. One of them illuminated Mitsuko, who was sitting on the top stair. As he appeared she rose to her feet and went down them, beckoning Walker to follow with the typically Japanese palm-down gesture. She led him to a dining-room bright with sunshine, with a view of the Japanese garden through which he had entered on his first visit. The sound of the bamboo water-spout could just be heard, and it was hard to realise that just beyond the high wall was the seedy slum street and the rest of the sleaziest part of Nagoya.

On the table were the makings of breakfast, complete but clumsily presented. There was an electric toaster and a sliced loaf of bread in its paper wrapper. An electric percolator contained not coffee but hot water to go with the jar of instant coffee powder, the tiny bottle of milk and the packet of sugar. There was butter in a dish, and jam in its jar. Though a far cry from the elegance of the meal on the boat, to Walker it looked magnificent.

A hundred questions chased themselves round in his head, but the power of his appetite subdued them. Without much pretence at good manners he sat down and loaded the toaster with two slices of bread, then made himself a cup of coffee while he waited for them to rise from the machine again. At last they did, and Walker buttered one piece and coated it with jam. Seldom had the characterless pap of Japanese bread tasted so good.

The first pangs allayed, the questions would wait no longer and he looked at the girl, now seated opposite and watching him gravely as he ate. He chewed thoughtfully, wondering how much of his conversation with her father Mitsuko had overheard. Of course, he should have realised that Fujikawa would be proud of his own perfect English and want his daughter to learn.

"You drugged and kidnapped me, Mi-chan," he said plaintively in English. "Why did you do that?" She made no reply, but got up and went to the window, her back to him. Walker finished eating, letting the silence continue. Then, feeling almost normal again but for a sense of light-headedness, he got up and joined Mitsuko at the window, standing in silence while the bamboo tube filled with water and emptied itself twice. There seemed to be no breath of wind outside, and the sky was taking on the grey, hazy quality of high summer noon in the polluted city.

Mitsuko spoke at last. "My father will tell you the answers to your questions," she said. "I know only that you are here for your safety, not to do you harm." It sounded mildly reassuring, and he wanted so much to like her.

"When may I see your father?" he asked, trying not to sound too impatient.

188

"I have told him you woke up," said Mitsuko. "He is very busy just now, but he said he will send Suzuki-san for you soon. Suzuki-san is the one you met when you came here the other day. He helps my father."

Walker well remembered the blank stare of the dark glasses, and found it difficult to see Suzuki in the role of one of his protectors. Further thought, and the uncomfortable silence, was interrupted by the opening of the door. Suzuki entered, still elegantly dressed, but without his sunglasses. The face now fully revealed was that of a man of not much more than his own age, perhaps thirty. He was by no means bad-looking, and had a quick liveliness of expression. Mitsuko obviously doted on him, and Walker experienced an odd and unexpected twinge of jealous irritation as she skipped to him and took his arm.

Suzuki bowed slightly. "Please come this way," he said in Japanese. "Mr Fujikawa will see you now." He released his arm from Mitsuko's, smiled at her and ruffled her hair tenderly as Walker crossed to the door. He followed Suzuki through the handsome sitting-room towards Fujikawa's study, filled again with a righteous sense of outrage over his predicament after the totally uncalled-for display of affection between the pair of them.

"Well, where the hell is he now, then?" demanded Kimura, his customary debonair sang-froid quite exploded by Noguchi's calm explanation that he had decided to tail the young Englishman the previous day. At first he had refused to believe it, wanting to know how Noguchi knew what he looked like. Noguchi patiently pointed out that he had after all been painting a fence immediately opposite Murrow's house throughout the afternoon of the condolence visits and had seen the two Europeans both coming and going. There was only one tall one with jug ears, and he had been the one Noguchi had followed from the Consulate General to Gifu, where he had supped on the river on obviously intimate terms with a nice bit of stuff who had turned out to be Fujikawa's daughter.

"And I suppose you dressed up as a cormorant?" Kimura

189

had suggested bitterly when he finally accepted that Noguchi had scooped him yet again.

Massively unruffled and with the smallest of wrinkles at one corner of his leathery face which might just possibly have been a smile, Noguchi urged Kimura to keep his hair on. "I'm good at some things, you're good at different things," he said amiably.

"Such as what?" snapped Kimura in a rare mood of self-denigration.

"Such as finding out where he is," said Noguchi. "Before we go and tell the old man. Ring up and ask to speak to him. He might be at work where he belongs. It's after eleven. But if you want to know what I think, he's still screwing in some motel. I'm surprised at Fujikawa allowing it, I admit."

Noguchi slowly and sorrowfully shook his bullet head. "He was all over her when they got in the car."

Kimura's spirits rose a little, as they always did when the conversation touched upon sex. "No law against it, Ninja," he said with a certain loftiness. "Yes, I think I'll take your advice. Then I can advise the Commander how to play it next. Thank you for your help, Ninja." Noguchi looked at him in silence, even his solid features betraying a degree of incredulity.

"Kimura, you're a wonder," he said at last, and lumbered to his feet to make his way out of his colleague's little office. Then he gave a harsh bark of laughter. "You do that, my lad," he said affably. "You advise the old man what to do next. I'll bet you a bottle of *shochu* he can hardly wait."

Kimura looked a little wounded as Noguchi's bulky shape passed by the reeded glass wall as he made his way down the corridor, then picked up the telephone and rang the British Consulate General. "Give me Mr Walker," he instructed the Japanese switchboard girl who answered. "Oh? He isn't? Mr Endsleigh, then." There was a longish pause before he spoke again, his voice syrupy and confiding. "Jill? Well, *hi*, Jill. Jiro here. You know, Jiro Kimura? Hyogo Police?" His rising inflection was not quite as Robert Redford did it, but it was getting better. "You bet, Jill. That would be just great. How about next week? Mm? Look, honey, I hate to bother

190

you, but I really wanted a word with Andrew Walker. Just a little leftover routine thing about the Murrow papers. No, they already told me he's out. How about Mr Endsleigh? On his way to Tokyo? Uh-huh. Well, I'll call you real soon, Jill. Mm. Look forward to it. Bye.''

Kimura rang off thoughtfully, then pencilled himself a quick reminder to make a date with Jill Braxon the following week. Not his very top priority prospect among the consular secretaries, but the sullen types were often unexpectedly passionate, and he might get to second base next time. So Walker was apparently out, whereabouts unknown. And Endsleigh on the way to Tokyo. And Jill sounding just a little worried. Interesting.

Fujikawa sat at his desk, wearing the same tweed jacket but this time with a neat check shirt and a plain woollen tie. He was not alone. In an armchair, rigidly upright, was a heavily-built Japanese with a coarse, pock-marked, swarthy complexion. In spite of the coolness of the room his face was shiny with sweat, and his fists were clenched on his fat thighs. Walker stood looking from one to the other until Fujikawa spoke.

"Good morning, Mr Walker," he said in English. "You will have to take my word for it that the gentleman in the chair does not understand your language. We therefore have a considerable advantage over him." He broke into Japanese and introduced Walker to the man in the chair, whose frozen rigidity was relaxed for the fraction of a second it took him to jerk his head in a parody of a bow and mutter his name, "Watanabe."

"Please sit down, Mr Walker," Fujikawa continued in English. Walker did so. "I deeply regret the manner in which I had to have you brought here. It was, however, for your protection. I hope that you have been treated courteously since then." Walker found his voice with some difficulty. "I've heard a good deal about you since I came to see you before," he said with an attempt at nonchalance. "I must say it's a relief in a way to see someone who actually looks like

191

a crook." He glanced at Watanabe. "Your own household seems too much like Happy Families to be true."

Fujikawa grinned with apparently genuine amusement and glanced in turn at the unhappy Watanabe. "How odd that you should take my visitor for a crook," he replied. "He is in fact a highly respectable and successful lawyer, here to represent the interests of a client of his." Startled, Walker looked at Watanabe again. The lawyer gazed back with glum immobility. "I assure you that it's true," Fujikawa continued. "And now, I think, to business." He turned to Watanabe and in formal Japanese asked his pardon for their having spoken in English. He explained that Walker understood Japanese, and that they would continue in that language. Watanabe nodded tightly.

Japanese is not a language well suited to precision, but perhaps because Fujikawa was trying to use relatively straightforward expressions to help Walker, he achieved a model of clear exposition. He began by discounting the possibility that Murrow's murder had been a straightforward act of unpremeditated violence. He appeared to know all about Murrow's reference index of visiting cards, but made no mention of his activities as a homosexual procurer. He said simply that there was a reason to believe that Murrow had accumulated "damaging" information about a number of prominent persons in Japan, both foreigners and Japanese.

With a general election pending, it was not impossible that some of these persons might have had cause to fear a scandal, particularly if Murrow had by chance been seeking to extort money as the price of his silence about "certain matters". Could Murrow have been eliminated on the instructions of such a person? The police had been making enquiries in the course of testing this theory, and had been subjected to what Fujikawa described as "pressure from high political quarters." At this Watanabe looked if anything a shade more unhappy still.

Fujikawa continued by referring in flowery terms to Walker's diligence in very properly making every effort to assist the enquiries into the death of a British subject, with the result that the same "high political quarters" had instigated diplomatic moves to have him expelled from Japan. All this, Fujikawa went on, could only lend support to his theory about Murrow's death. Those concerned, he concluded in states manlike tones, almost as though summing up an academic lecture, were, in acting in an increasingly panicky way, in danger of fomenting an infinitely greater scandal than any which Murrow could possibly have generated.

He switched his gaze from the wretched Watanabe to Walker, but continued in Japanese. "When Mr Walker came to see me recently, I already knew that at least one person close to Murrow—a Japanese—had also been murdered. There seemed good reason to counsel Mr Walker to proceed with caution. This I did. Then yesterday I received certain information which led me to fear that Mr Walker's own life might be in danger. I therefore decided that I must personally assume responsibility for his physical well-being until I receive certain assurances through the good offices of Mr Watanabe here. I need hardly remind Mr Watanabe to mention to his client or clients that I have a certain political influence in this part of Japan, and I am sure that they would not wish to do anything which might put the result of the elections in doubt."

Walker's heart was still thudding as he assimilated Fujikawa's remarks about danger to his own life, and he was astonished when Fujikawa accompanied the last few words with an exaggerated wink which he made no attempt to conceal from Watanabe. Watanabe moved at last, rising stiffly from his chair. He stood in front of Fujikawa's desk and bowed.

"I am confident that there will be no misunderstandings," he said, then turned to Walker. He bowed again and used the formal expression of farewell. "Please extend your favour to me." Walker heard a bell sounding outside, and the door opened to reveal Suzuki, now in the regulation dark glasses of the underworld. Watanabe produced a handkerchief from his pocket and mopped his whole face as he left. The door closed and Walker looked at Fujikawa, who was staring out of the window, two slender fingers tapping the top of the desk.

"Thank you," said Walker humbly.

Fujikawa smiled briefly. "Not at all," he said. "It will be quite safe for you to go back to Osaka now. Do by all means stay to lunch if you have the time, though."

"That's all very fine and large, Ralph," said Endsleigh to Her Majesty's Ambassador, "but I'm damned if I can play it cool, as you put it." The two men were alone in the book-lined study in the Embassy in Tokyo. Outside, a gardener was mowing the immaculate Residence lawn with an old-fashioned hand mowing machine. Cicadas were loud around them, and the rumble of traffic on the main road between the compound and the moat of the Imperial Palace grounds seemed very far away. The Ambassador leaned back in his leather armchair and raised a podgy finger.

"Listen to the mower, Joe," he said benignly. "Reminds one of getting the pitch ready for the big match at prep school, doesn't it?" Endsleigh had known Sir Ralph Dunbridge for years. They had been years of mingled pleasure, amusement and exasperation, and he now controlled his irritation with the skill that came of long practice.

"You know something, Ralph," he said carefully. "Come on, put me out of my misery. Here's young Walker gone missing since Tsunematsu came in yesterday morning to complain about his behaviour; that nasty little poof Stoneham raving about claiming that a bunch of homicidal VIPs are trying to murder him, and you sitting there like a confounded Buddha."

The Ambassador's eyes had been closed in tranquil repose as Endsleigh spoke, and he opened them suddenly. He leaned forward. "When you told me on the phone the other day about Walker's Sherlock Holmes efforts, I thought you were being a trifle rash in letting him prod about the underworld. Not very nice people, you know. Wouldn't ask them round for drinks. So I had a word with Fred. Now as you know, Fred is a businessman and a good one, quite apart from having run this station since you and I were young and innocent."

The bleak, calculating eyes set so unexpectedly in the rubicund face were fixed on Endsleigh's. "Fred knows more about the politico-financial-gangotero setup here than most, and what he doesn't know he no doubt finds out from our American cousins. I don't enquire. Anyway, he confirmed Stoneham's theory and the identity of the culprit. A thoroughly disagreeable man. I've met him several times and I'm not in the least surprised that he has to pay for company in bed, of whichever sex. Then when you rang yesterday and told Oliver about Tsunematsu's call on you, we got in touch with Fred again. He took action, and I can tell you that Walker is safe and sound. I don't know where. Fred didn't tell me and so I can't tell you. But I'm assured he'll surface as right as ninepence in due course."

Endsleigh rubbed his eyes. He felt old and rather sick. "The note he left me was ambiguous. But I inferred that he went off in connection with the Nagoya visit. When I got no answer from his flat during the evening I worried myself sick over the young ass. He didn't answer as late as two in the morning, or at six when I tried again. I had to stop myself getting somebody to ring up this Fujikawa chap. Just as well I came here instead."

The Ambassador nodded in silence. His eyes were again closed. "Very wise, Joe. After all, he could perfectly well have been spending the night with a paramour. He's young and reasonably eligible, in spite of his ears."

Endsleigh's patience ran out. "I'm glad you're deriving some amusement from all this, Ralph," he snapped. "I'm not. I'm glad Walker seems to be safe, from what you say. But am I to understand that you're proposing to let this murderer get away with it, if you're so sure you know who it is?"

"I don't pretend to be happy about it, Joe," the Ambassador said. "Don't be cross with me. But supposing we *did* want to blow it all, there's a world of difference between knowing something and being able to prove it. D'you seriously believe that if I went to the Foreign Ministry and upended this bucket of worms on their carpet they'd thank me nicely and ask the policeman at the door to nip round and arrest the fellow?"

The eyes were wide open again now, boring into Endsleigh. "And there are *raisons d'état,* my friend," he contin-

195

ued. "My American colleague made it very clear to me just yesterday that they regard it as essential not only for the government to win this election, but if possible to do so with an increased majority. The opposition are making quite enough noise as it is without any additional help being called for. There's been a good deal of chat about all this among our masters, Joe. As soon as the CIA here got it they alerted the State Department, and Foggy Bottom didn't waste any time in urging Whitehall to refrain from rocking the boat."

Endsleigh sat slumped in his chair. "What price the honourable profession of diplomacy now?" he said bitterly, half to himself.

When the Ambassador spoke again his voice had an edge to it. "Come off it, Joe," he said sharply. "No hearts and flowers in this room, if you please. You're too old a bird to do it convincingly. We're all forever quoting that thing about being sent abroad to lie for one's country. Well, dammit, you're only being asked to lie low for yours. Murrow's dead. Sad about that, but he was a silly bugger in more ways than one to take on the Japanese Establishment. Some might say he asked for all he got. Then the Japanese boy, whatsisname, Hirata. God knows if he deserved it; I certainly don't. As for Stoneham and his Chrysanthemum Chain or Flower Arrangement or whatever it is, he's had a good fright which will do him no harm whatsoever, from all I hear about him."

"You make it all sound so confoundedly unimportant," said Endsleigh. "At the very least young Walker's had his career wrecked."

"Don't think so, you know," the Ambassador said mildly.

Endsleigh looked up. "How can you say that?" he asked. "We shall have to report the PNG warning, and for all we know they may do it."

The Ambassador smiled fatly, his hands laced over his impressive belly. "Well, actually, I *have* been to see the Foreign Minister. This morning. Told him that HMG will take strong and forthright action if there's any renewal of their complaint about Walker. The 'forthright' bit got him worried, and he assured me that it was all a mistake. Their man Tsunematsu acted hastily on unreliable gossip, and is being withdrawn from Osaka. They have a job for him in one of the stickier African climes, it seems, poor chap. And Walker will enjoy his home leave with a good chit from us and none the worse for his adventures. Send him home a few weeks early; and forget the PNG warning. *I* certainly don't intend to report it.''

He placed his hands flat on the surface of the desk and levered himself to his feet. ''Now,'' he said briskly, ''I dare say that if we ask Priscilla nicely she'll give us some tea. Here's a *real* piece of news for you, Joe. I've been asked to find out how you might feel about Ankara next year. Agreeable post even nowadays, lovely house, and think how Heather will enjoy being Lady E . . . '' Chattering affably, the Ambassador led the way to the small drawing-room.

Friday

"**W**ELL, WHEREVER IT WAS FUJIKAWA'S DAUGHTER took him, he's back now," said Kimura to Otani as he entered the office. Otani was trying to interest himself in routine administration, without a great deal of success, and pushed the pile of papers to one side with relief. Any movement on the Murrow case was better than none, and Kimura looked if anything even more pleased with himself than usual.

"Do you realise, Kimura-kun, that any other officer in this building would have knocked and waited outside until invited to enter?" Kimura looked momentarily uncertain. It was always so difficult to tell with Otani. But he had called him "kun", which was a sign of amiability, so he took a chance. He grinned back cheerfully at his superior's basilisk stare, and miraculously Otani was the first to give in. "All right, all right," he huffed. "You'd better sit down. I suppose every Noh play has its *kyogen* clowns, and you're mine. How do you know?"

"Know what, Chief?" Kimura asked innocently.

Otani raised a finger warningly. "Not too far, not too far," he said.

Kimura simmered down at once. "Sorry. He just telephoned me from the Consulate General."

"Oh?" said Otani. This was indeed interesting. "Why should he do a thing like that?" Kimura explained the excuse he had given to Jill Braxon for ringing in the first place. Walker had simply called back to find out what it was Kimura wanted.

Otani was a little deflated at first, but told himself that he ought to have realised during their conference the previous day that Kimura would have had to invent some reason for checking to see if the young Vice-Consul was at his desk. Kimura went on to say that he had fudged up some tale about another bureaucratic procedure that had to be gone through in settling Murrow's affairs.

"Did he seem suspicious?" Otani asked.

"No. He seemed rather full of himself actually. I didn't get the impression he attached any significance to my original call."

All this seemed to Otani to lead precisely nowhere. "So. He's back at work, and feeling pleased with himself. What's that supposed to mean?"

Kimura got up and went over to the window. It was nearly lunchtime and office workers were already beginning to drift out of nearby buildings. "You remember what Ninja hinted at the other day, Chief? About Fujikawa and a possible connection with the British?"

Otani nodded at Kimura's back. "Yes. It's not like Ninja to make up fanciful theories, but it struck me as rather far-fetched."

Kimura wheeled round and faced Otani, rising up and down athletically on the balls of his feet as he spoke. "I can only guess," he said. "It ought to be my business to know, but as long as I have no direct access to the security service . . ." It was an old complaint.

"I know, I know," said Otani. "You have to go through the Foreign Ministry liaison office in Osaka, and we all know how unhelpful Tsunematsu's people are. There's nothing to be done, Kimura-kun. And stop bouncing up and down like that."

"Yes, well, it's very unsatisfactory. And if they won't give us any help, I don't see why we should offer them any. Especially as Tsunematsu seems to be putting positive obstacles in our way on this case. Well, for what it's worth, I think there may be something in Ninja's idea. A rendezvous on the river with Fujikawa's daughter? How on earth could he have met her in the first place unless he had dealings with her father? *Buraku* girls don't move in consular society, after all.''

Otani nodded thoughtfully. ''There's much in what you say,'' he conceded. ''And if as you say the young man sounded pleased with himself . . .'' His voice trailed off, and after a pause he stood up. ''I didn't bring a *bento* today,'' he said. ''And I'm not in uniform. Shall we go and find some lunch?''

Takamura stubbed out his cigarette among the six or seven half-smoked butts in the ash-tray at his elbow and looked around Walker's modest living-room approvingly. To Walker it seemed nothing special. It had been good to get back to Ashiya and change his clothes, and nice to find everything in order, but that was yesterday. Now, after a rather euphoric day in the office, he found himself overcome by a flat feeling. Perhaps he had been slightly corrupted by even a brief experience of the opulent comforts of the Fujikawa house in Nagoya, and a long-drawn-out dinner with Takamura in the Prunier Room of the Osaka Royal Hotel.

''A really nice place,'' said Takamura contentedly. He noticed the expression on Walker's face and smiled. ''Don't look at me like that, Andy. You've been in Japanese homes. This is a family apartment, and the idea of a guy your age rolling around in it alone is just amazing. Reminds me of when I lived in the States.''

They were drinking brandy and Walker had finished his story. Takamura had listened attentively throughout dinner, but apart from occasional lifts of an eyebrow and a number of questions on points of detail, showed little reaction to the tale of Walker's experiences. Walker felt nettled by his calmness. It contrasted with the deeply satisfying effect he had created on walking into the Consulate General that morning, when Jill had grinned with spontaneous pleasure at his appearance, had got up from her chair and actually hugged him.

It had made up for a lot, as had Endsleigh's cry of "Andrew! I'm very glad to see you," when he arrived ten minutes later straight off the early train from Tokyo. This was a relief of a different kind to Walker, who felt guilty about not reporting his arrival back at least by telephone the previous afternoon. The sensation of being in free orbit after leaving Nagoya was so agreeable that he had crept back to Ashiya almost furtively and cocooned himself in privacy till now. With luck Endsleigh wouldn't notice the time-lag.

He hated drinking in the morning, but Endsleigh pressed a large glass of sherry into his hand and quizzed him for the next hour; a dry run, as Endsleigh put it, refilling Walker's glass, for the questioning he would undergo in Tokyo and in London. At the conclusion of it Walker told Endsleigh that he intended to repay his indebtedness to Takamura by telling him the story. "Just as well you didn't ask my permission, Andrew," the Consul General had said after taking a deep breath and rubbing his nose. "I should certainly have withheld it."

The least Takamura could do was show a little appreciation. "Well, Ken, what do you think? What about a Watergate style investigation, led by the *Kobe Shimbun* and fearless, hard-hitting Takamura?" Takamura put down his brandy glass carefully and looked for a long time at Walker. Outside, the dark hills of Ashiya were studded with lights in the warm summer night.

"It wouldn't work, Andy. And I don't know if I could even begin to explain why," he said at last.

Walker shifted in his chair. "Try," he said.

Takamura continued to stare at him almost unseeingly. He spoke quietly and unemphatically. "The Watergate investigation was a great achievement against heavy odds, but basically it succeeded because America is a puritan country. No matter how cynical people may think they are or claim to be, politics is thought of in moral terms. Also, government is very much a matter of us and them. The governors and the governed. Two elements in society. People may think they have no illusions about corruption in government in the West, but if the stink becomes strong enough and enough dirt is uncovered, governments can and do fall. It's different in Japan. Can you imagine any other country where they'd fire a Prime Minister over the Lockheed fuss and keep his government in office?''

Takamura picked up the brandy glass and sipped. "Ever noticed how often we talk about 'We Japanese'? Apart from China I don't believe there's such a totally integrated society as ours in the world. We're all part of the organism, and we all think and work in social terms. If society is corrupt, we're all part of the corruption. Okay, polling's the day after tomorrow. Supposing Otani does know who to pull in, and supposing he's holding back on the arrest till after the election, that's not particularly culpable. Nor is your pal Fujikawa necessarily doing the wrong thing in letting it ride. He's put an end to the murders by leaning on this Watanabe character, and that's the important thing.''

Walker was floundering. "What do you mean, who to pull in?''

Takamura explained patiently. "I mean the guy who actually *killed* Murrow. I would guess it's quite possible that Otani's informers will uncover that much. But then to connect it to the Minister—jeez, that's something else again, Andy. And Otani may not be *able* to do that, even if he wants to. He's an honest cop, but he's boxed in by the system.''

"So what happens now?'' Walker said, like a small boy being led by the hand.

"They'll make an arrest, sooner or later. And it doesn't really much matter when. You can bet your last cent that the guy will admit doing it, and just as certainly that he'll never say who hired him. He'll be sentenced, he'll get remission after a few years and he'll be well looked after by the gang.''

Walker experienced again the sensation of sinking into a quicksand under Takamura's level gaze. "But if all this is so, why was Murrow murdered in the first place? How can blackmail ever be effective if nobody cares about his reputation?'' He looked at Takamura almost plaintively as he gulped his own brandy.

"I didn't say that, Andy," said Takamura. "If the Minister were to be publicly accused, especially within a day or two of the election, the government would be seriously embarrassed. It would affect the voting, a bit. Fujikawa personally could affect it much more. But I don't believe even he could bring the government down. Nothing short of a revolution could do that, but the Minister would certainly be personally ruined. So, assuming Murrow really had threatened to expose him, he had plenty of motive."

Takamura got up with an impatient gesture and began to pace back and forth. "Now, although so many people know all this, it'll be hushed up. Do you seriously think that if I were to write up this story my editor would publish it? With Fujikawa capable of delivering or withholding a thousand votes for every one my paper could influence? You know, Andy, I don't think I'd have any more chance of selling the story to *Time* magazine or even the *Washington Post* itself. In the first place, Americans *expect* foreign politicians to be corrupt, and it wouldn't make much of a story. In the second place, the American government doesn't want to embarrass the Japanese any more than your own does. There's no morality about international relations."

Walker gave up. "I suppose you're right," he said unhappily. "I'm certainly learning a lot from all this." He brightened a little. "Tell me more about Fujikawa. He must obviously have connections I never dreamed about, but what about his daughter? What became of the mother?"

Takamura smiled. "I thought you'd ask about her, so I did some quick research. I told you his wife died in the same car smash when he lost his legs. The girl and her brother are the only children."

"Brother? What brother?" Walker asked.

Takamura looked surprised. "Why, Suzuki, of course," he said.

"How can he be called Suzuki, if he's Fujikawa's son?" Walker became furiously aware as Takamura replied that he was beginning to blush with confusion as the implications of what he said began to sink in.

"Suzuki," explained Takamura patiently, "was adopted

into his wife's family, so he took her name, of course. You must know about this practice, Andy. Surely everybody knows that Prime Minister Sato and Prime Minister Kishi were brothers? Why do you suppose they had different family names? The marriage was arranged, and linked Fujikawa with his only serious rival in western Japan. Sooner or later he'll marry the girl off and make *her* husband take the name of Fujikawa. That's if he can find someone he'd be willing to hand his interest over to eventually, and who wouldn't mind marrying a *buraku*." Walker was stunned. No wonder Mitsuko and Suzuki had seemed affectionate. But why couldn't she have explained? Why keep referring to him as "Suzuki-san", for God's sake? Could it be that she wanted to tease him?

Takamura looked at his watch. "I have to go, Andy. I have work to do tonight. Thanks for dinner. Have a good trip home whenever it is, and keep in touch." Walker saw him to the road and waited till a cruising taxi picked him up. Then he went back to the flat and sat down at his small desk. Taking a piece of paper he began a letter: "Dear Mitsuko . . ." Then he put the pen down and decided to wait till the next day. Andrew Fujikawa? It didn't bear thinking about.

Saturday

OTANI DECIDED TO GO SHOPPING WITH HANAE. IT WAS not something he much enjoyed, and he had originally intended to loaf about the house and try to occupy his mind with a new Nero Wolfe detective story he had bought in the bookshop at Sannomiya Station. At least things would work out neatly at the end, unlike any of the cases he had ever handled personally, and Archie Goodwin would have a large cheque to pay into the bank. He couldn't seem to get into it, though, and when Hanae got ready to go out he thought he might as well tag along. They went to Osaka rather than Kobe, and he took her to an eel restaurant for lunch, which was enjoyable. Strange that grilled eel with a thick soya sauce dressing could be cooling to eat in the worst days of summer, but it definitely was.

Kimura eyed Jill Braxon speculatively over the prawn cocktail to which she was addressing herself in the Texas Tavern in Kobe. He was at a loose end and there seemed little point in waiting till the following week to make good his promise to ask her for a date. The Texas Tavern had been his idea: he always enjoyed a little ostentatiously casual conversation with the American proprietor, and occasionally picked

205

up a new idiom from the hum of conversation among the foreign residents at neighbouring tables. The sensual way Jill attacked each mouthful was mildly encouraging, and the day was young. He thought they might take the ferry across to Awaji Island in the afternoon for a change of scene.

All over Japan loudspeaker cars garishly bedecked with banners and rosettes made the day hideous as they blared through towns and villages repeating over and over again the only message they were legally permitted to convey: "Good Day! My name is So-and-So, the candidate of the Something Party. Please show your favour to me! Good Day! My name is . . ."

It was noisy at the races, too, but in a different way, and Noguchi kept a lively eye on the runners and the odds as he talked quietly to another shabby and nondescript man. By contrast the small room at the back of the bar was both dark and quiet as Madame Yasuko, in a smart and fashionable linen suit, spoke with gentle insistence into a pink telephone.

Walker was sitting in one of the cane armchairs in the Endsleighs' garden, reflecting after his second large gin and tonic that he really must cut down on his drinking. There was something about being tipsy at lunchtime on a summer weekend which was at once more pleasantly relaxed and more alarming than being in the same condition in the evening. It really made one frightfully randy, for a start. There was Heather, practically old enough to be his mother, but he could quite see why James Murrow had felt driven to lay hands upon her. It would be a good thing to get out of this hothouse atmosphere in a week or two. He peered over towards Endsleigh, who was trimming the edges of a flower bed with long-handled shears. Nice of old Joe to suggest bringing his home leave dates forward.

* * *

The day wore on, the loudspeakers boomed and crackled, and Noguchi won just over eight thousand yen. He was also able to arrive at a satisfactory agreement with Konnosuke Yamamoto's personal representative.

Sunday

"I SEE. THANK YOU, NINJA," SAID OTANI, AND PUT THE phone down quietly. He made his way to the kitchen where Hanae was preparing their supper, and stood watching her as she sliced mushrooms and onions and arranged them on a flat basketwork platter woven from strips of bamboo. "Not the right weather for sukiyaki, surely?" he said, mildly intrigued.

Hanae brushed a wisp of damp hair back from her forehead and smiled at him rather timidly. He had been in a funny sort of mood ever since the first conversation with Noguchi-san in the middle of the morning, after which he had at once gone out without an explanation, returning equally taciturn in the early evening. It really was altogether too much to have telephone calls on official business from all and sundry in one's own home, especially on what was supposed to be Tetsuo's free day. But then one could hardly think of Ambassador Tsunematsu or Noguchi-san or even Kimura-san as "all and sundry". Especially Kimura-san, for whom she had a soft spot.

"It isn't for sukiyaki," she said. "They're to go with your steak, and I'm making a salad as well."

"Not the same steak you bought two weeks ago?" Otani asked, still in the same light, detached way.

Hanae pursed her lips and tried not to smile. "It's been in the freezer, darling," she said. "Still quite good. You'll see." Otani nodded absent-mindedly, but still hovered. "Is there something I can get you?" Hanae asked, tucking her kimono sleeves back and imprisoning them in her sash so as to bare her arms.

"What? Oh, yes. I was wondering what became of that bottle of Scotch whisky somebody gave us at New Year. I feel like having some while I watch the news. It'll be on Channel Five in ten minutes." Hanae darted a quick look of surprise at him before going to a cupboard and taking out the unopened bottle. He hardly ever touched anything except *sake*, and she had bought a fresh bottle of his favourite, Gekkeikan, just a few days earlier.

"You go and sit down," she said warily. "I'll bring it to you with some ice and . . . water, isn't it?"

He nodded. "I'd like it if you could come and have a drink with me, please, Ha-chan." He disappeared, and Hanae quickly put two glasses with the bottle on a tray, filled a small jug with water and tipped out a tray of ice cubes into a bowl. Her heart sank at the thought of drinking whisky, but she could hardly prepare *sake* just for herself, and there was definitely something odd about Tetsuo's manner.

She arrived just as the instant noodle commercial ended, and Otani poured them both drinks as the newsreader appeared on the screen. The national news was almost wholly concerned with the polls which had just closed, after what seemed to have been an average turn-out, much as expected. There followed short interviews with leading figures from each of the major parties, all confidently predicting victory.

Hanae sat and watched, more than a little bored, and wrinkling her small nose in distaste as she tried to drink the horrible liquid Tetsuo had taken it into his head to give her. Then he reached out a hand and took hold of hers as a photograph of a hangdog, thuggish young man appeared, and the newsreader identified him as Seiji Kitamura, 23, a day labourer arrested that afternoon in a cinema in Kobe and charged with the murder of the Englishman David Murrow.

Then to her astonishment there followed an interview with her own husband. She drank down the entire glass of whisky without noticing it as she kept glancing from the Tetsuo speaking with quiet dignity into the eye of the camera, to the rigidly tense man at her side. Superintendent Otani of Hyogo Prefectural Police acknowledged quietly the off-screen interviewer's satisfaction that the police enquiries had been pursued with such success as to lead them to the criminal within a very short time, and confirmed that the young man had already put his seal to a confession.

The newsreader gave the main headlines again, and Otani had actually reached out to switch off the set, his face still closed and impassive, when the even voice coming from the television set paused, then read a late item of news just received. "Death of a senior member of the ruling party. It has just been announced from Tokyo that shortly after the closing of the polls a member of the Cabinet was found dead in his office in the Diet Building. A handgun and a suicide note were found nearby. The security guard had been alerted by the sound of a shot. The dead man was . . ."

Otani turned the set off, and told Hanae the name himself. "I'm glad you liked your whisky," he said then. "I think I'll have another. You know, Ha-chan, if it had just been the arrest, I would still have told you about it, but it would just have been the beginning really, and I wouldn't have enjoyed my steak much." He gave her one of the huge smiles which transfigured his usually grim expression. "But this really does look like the end. In a way."

ABOUT THE AUTHOR

James Melville was born in London in 1931 and educated in North London. He read philosophy at Birkbeck College before being conscripted into the RAF, then took up schoolteaching and adult education. Most of his subsequent career has been spent overseas in cultural diplomacy and educational development, and it was in this capacity that he came to know, love, and write about Japan and the Japanese. He has two sons and is married to a singer-actress. He continues to write more mystery novels starring Superintendent Otani.

By the year 2000, 2 out of 3 Americans could be illiterate.

It's true.

Today, 75 million adults...about one American in three, can't read adequately. And by the year 2000, U.S. News & World Report envisions an America with a literacy rate of only 30%.

Before that America comes to be, you can stop it...by joining the fight against illiteracy today.

Call the Coalition for Literacy at toll-free **1-800-228-8813** and volunteer.

**Volunteer
Against Illiteracy.
The only degree you need
is a degree of caring.**

Ad Council Coalition for Literacy

LV-2